Pretty Amy

Pretty Amy

a novel by
Lisa Burstein

Entangled Publishing, LLC
2614 South Timberline Road
Suite 109
Fort Collins, CO 80525
Visit our website at www.entangledpublishing.com.

Edited by Stacy Abrams
Cover design by Liz Pelletier

Print ISBN   978-1-62061-119-7
Ebook ISBN   978-1-62061-120-3

Manufactured in the United States of America

First Edition May 2012

To my parents
(who are nothing like the ones who appear in this book)

One

Unfortunately, I am only myself. I am only Amy Fleishman.

I am one of the legions of middle-class white girls who search malls for jeans that make them look thinner, who search drugstores for makeup to wear as a second skin, who are as sexy and exotic as blueberry muffins.

I am a walking, talking *True Life* episode. Your high-school guidance counselor's wet dream, and one of the only girls I know to get arrested on prom night.

When my mother dropped me off at Lila's, rather than running like hell the way I usually did, I sat next to her in our minivan and waited for a speech. The speech mothers give to their only daughters on nights when those daughters are all dressed up and the mothers look all wistful and teary.

I assumed she was building up to it, was working through exactly what she was going to say so it would be perfect. I knew from TV that she must have practiced in the mirror, but maybe, faced with having to say all those things to me, she'd frozen up. I could understand that.

When I saw Lila peek out to see who was sitting in her driveway, and then felt my phone vibrate with a text that I knew must say, *WTF R U DOIN?*, I figured I had waited long enough.

"So this is it…," I said. My mother stared at Lila's small, birdshit-gray house and bit at what was left of her nails. After I'd started hanging out with Lila and Cassie, my mother gnawed at her nails the way a baby sucked her thumb. "…my senior prom," I continued.

Maybe she was overwhelmed. Her little girl was all grown up. Her ugly duckling had finally become a swan.

"I don't want to ruin this for you, so I'm choosing to hold my tongue."

My mother loved using old-time folksy sayings. *Hold your horses. The early bird catches the worm. The penis with two holes puts out the fire faster.*

All right, fine, I made up that last one.

She had been holding her tongue for a while now. When yelling at me about my "degenerate" friends hadn't helped, she went for the semisilent treatment.

Stupid me for trying to get her to talk.

"There's something very wrong with this, Amy," she said.

She meant that Lila's boyfriend, Brian, had arranged a date for me. My mother had never met this boy. *I* had never met this boy. It may have seemed wrong to her, but I was used to Lila bringing the boys. And, it was still my senior prom. It was still my night, and she couldn't even have a special, sappy moment with me.

"I want to tell you to have a good time, to enjoy every moment, to be safe, but I know you won't listen anyway. I know you'll do what *you* want to do."

She was talking to herself again.

My mother's favorite hobbies were talking to herself and bitching. Though I suppose those were hobbies for most mothers, my mother honed them like skills. If bitching were karate, my mother would be a black belt.

I looked down at my dress. It was strapless and light blue to bring out my eyes, which weren't blue, but raccoon gray, and picked up whatever color I put next to them. The bodice was tight and shiny, like what a superhero might wear, and the skirt flared out and fell just below my knees. When my mother had seen it hanging on the bathroom door earlier tonight, she'd said it looked trampy, which made me even happier that she hadn't been there when I picked it out.

She also hadn't been there when I got my shoes and clutch purse dyed to match. Sure, she had given me money, but she hadn't been there. Not like I would have asked her to be there, but she hadn't offered, either.

"Thanks for the memories," I said, opening the door.

Her only job tonight was to tell me I was beautiful, that I was her beautiful baby girl all grown up, but she couldn't even do that.

"I can't help the way I feel," she said, like some self-help-book junkie. Well, not *like* one—she *was* one. For Chanukah last year she had gotten me an itchy sweater and

Chicken Soup for the Daughter's Soul. The inscription had read, *FYI.*

Seriously.

. . .

I found Lila sitting at her vanity, playing with her hair. She was wearing a lilac dress and smelled of lilac perfume, like some flower-variety Strawberry Shortcake doll. Her vanity was really just an extra chair from the kitchen and a small desk with a mirror propped up on it, but nonetheless the effect was the same.

Lila saw me walk in but stayed seated. This was what she did; she liked to force you to watch her for a moment, to drink her in. And since I knew this, I hung in the doorway and waited while she put on mascara.

As lame is it sounds, Lila was the kind of person who danced through life on her tiptoes, a ballerina with woodland animals holding up the train of her dress. And, as much as I hated to admit it, I was one of those woodland animals.

"What were you doing out there?" she asked without turning around. This was another game she liked to play— she was busy and you were interrupting her.

"The usual. Ruining my life and ruining my mother's in the process."

She swept a blush brush over her cheeks. She hadn't dipped it in anything, so I wasn't sure if this was also part of her act or if it was some beauty secret I was unaware of.

"What do you think?" she asked, standing with her hands on the skirt of her dress, then twirling around slowly so I could see her from every possible angle.

"You look great."

Lila asked how she looked, in one way or another, at least every twenty minutes. Sometimes I was supposed to say *You look great*. Sometimes I was supposed to say *You don't look fat*, or *I love your jeans, your hair, your shirt, you smell soooo good*.

It was okay. I knew it was my payment for hanging out with her.

Besides, I can't really say anything about needing constant reassurance. Just because I don't get it from Lila doesn't mean I don't need it. I'd taught my parrot, AJ, to say *Pretty Amy*, among other things. And when I'd asked him how I looked that night, he'd obliged as usual.

"You really mean it?" Lila asked.

"I love your dress," I said, just like I was supposed to. I guess when it came to Lila I was just like AJ, repeating meaningless phrases.

"You need more eye shadow." She pushed me down into her seat. Once she got going it was hard to stop her, and before I knew it, she had redone my whole face.

Rather than the soft, natural effect I'd had when I arrived, after Lila was done I looked like I was ready to go up onstage. Not the way people onstage look when they're actually onstage, but the way they look when you see them close up before or afterward.

"Much better," she said, stepping back to appraise her work. I knew how I wanted to respond, but instead, I responded how I usually did when it came to something I didn't agree with. I said nothing.

I wondered if she had done this on purpose, like some bride/bridesmaid thing. Lila did act like a bride at a wedding that never ended. She always had to be the most beautiful, the most interesting, and in this case, the least likely to be mistaken for a blind prostitute.

Cassie threw open the bedroom door and entered the room looking like the photo on a slutty Halloween Devil costume, all fire-engine red and skin and cleavage.

"Wow," we both said. Well, really I said it, but I could see Lila's mouth open to make a word and stop in a perfect *O*. I'd never seen Cassie in anything other than an oversize flannel shirt and cargo pants. She usually dressed like a lumberjack—it might have been part of the reason Lila put up with her.

That night, it was obvious that Cassie was far too attractive to be as crabby as she was. Maybe that was why she always tried so hard to hide it.

She lit a cigarette. "I know, I know," she said, exhaling, "I look like the lead singer of a Vegas lounge act. My brother already told me."

"Not at all," Lila said, looking to me like a combination of shocked and jealous.

I nodded in agreement. I was shocked and jealous. At Brian's house later, two boys would have two girls to choose from. The way Cassie looked that night, she would be chosen first. I would be the one who was left, as usual, but that is the arithmetic that equals love in high school.

"Turn around," Lila said, walking toward her and reaching for her dress.

"Fuck off," Cassie said, pushing her away. "You can see

my ass on the way out."

Cassie pointed at me with the tip of her cigarette. "What the hell did you do to her face?"

"How do you know I did it?" Lila asked.

"Because Amy thinks light blue is daring."

I hated to hear it, even though she was right.

"Don't listen to her," Lila said, holding my face between her hands and squeezing like a proud grandmother. "She wouldn't know beauty if it crawled up her butt and pitched a tent."

"Well, I know what it looks like when something crawls out," Cassie said.

"Maybe it's a little too much," I said, looking over at Lila with eyes that begged for tissues, water, *turpentine*.

"It *is* too much," Cassie said.

Lila stood there with her hands on her hips, her nails painted shiny silver, waiting for me to disagree. With Cassie on my side, there was no way.

"Fine," Lila said, throwing me a box of those blessed tissues.

"At least now when we show up at Brian's, he won't try to be her pimp," Cassie said, putting out her cigarette and walking downstairs.

• • •

Cassie started her rusted gold Civic, took off her red heels, and threw them over her shoulder. One of them barely missed my face.

"Hey, be careful." I was sitting in the back, as usual. I picked up the shoes from where they had landed and placed them next to each other on the seat, so it looked like there had been someone standing there who had suddenly vanished.

"What do you want from me? I can't drive in those things," she said, lighting another cigarette.

Cassie, Lila, and I smoked a lot. We were proficient at leaning against things—walls and cars and fences—and we liked to lean against them and smoke. Like we'd seen James Dean doing in posters for movies we didn't know the names of. When we couldn't lean against things and smoke, we just smoked.

Lila lit her own cigarette and threw one to me in the back. "You can't drive, period," she said to Cassie, pulling the rearview mirror toward her so she could put on more lipstick.

Cassie glared at her and moved the mirror back.

"I'll tell you if there's anything coming up behind you," Lila said.

"If I believed you could actually take your eyes off yourself for two seconds, I'd feel a little safer."

"Then Amy can do it," Lila said.

I just smiled. There was no way I was going to ride turned around with my knees on the seat, clutching the back window like some panting dog. Well, at least not while I was wearing a dress.

"Isn't this great?" Lila said, watching her reflection in the window. "The three of us together for the most memorable night of our lives." It was as if she wanted to see herself saying it, and then compare it with the way other girls had said it on nights like this.

I knew exactly what she meant, though. There was some kind of magic that resulted from being dressed up and young and headed for a night you were supposed to remember forever. I was about to try to put that incredible feeling into words when Cassie said, "This song sucks. Shut the fuck up and put in a new CD."

Not quite what I would have said, but this was Cassie we were talking about.

"There's no way I'm getting my hands dirty searching around the floor for your CD case. Why don't you have an iPod like the rest of the world?" Lila asked.

"Why don't you have a car?" Cassie retorted.

"Amy," Lila demanded. And, since I knew I wouldn't be able to get away with saying no twice, I rooted around on the floor, using only the very tips of my finger and thumb to pick up what I found. I didn't find a CD case. I found a lot of sticky change, a glass pipe, and about twenty empty packs of cigarettes.

Cassie turned around. "It's not there. My fucking brother." That was the way Cassie referred to the members of her family. They were all her *fucking* something. Actually, that's the way Cassie referred to everybody.

"Who cares?" Lila said, rolling down her window. She was not about to let Cassie ruin any part of this night for her.

The car screeched as we turned off Lila's street, Macadamia Drive, a name that made it seem exotic somehow, but really it was just one of the streets named after nuts on the other side of Main.

Lila pulled her cigarette out of her mouth and checked

to make sure there was a ring of lipstick around the filter. Things like that made her happy.

"Don't worry," Cassie said, "they can see your lips from space."

• • •

We sat in Brian's driveway arguing. Well, Lila and Cassie were arguing about whether we should walk to the door together or Lila should go on her own.

"I'm not sitting in the car like someone's mother," Cassie said, turning to me and gesturing for her shoes.

"But they don't know you yet," Lila said. "It's probably better if I go alone and bring them out."

"I don't care either way," I said, but the truth was, I kind of liked the idea of waiting in the car. There was no point in giving my date the opportunity to back out by letting him have a look at me first.

"Good, then let's go." Cassie slammed the door behind her and clomped up the walk.

She rang the doorbell and we waited. Waited for Brian to swing open the door and smile at us like a game-show host, telling us we looked stunning and introducing Cassie and me to our bachelors for the evening.

But the door stayed closed.

"I'll do it," Lila said, pushing her way through, her reasoning for Brian's absence apparently the fact that Cassie didn't know how to ring a doorbell. "They're probably in the basement doing bong hits." She rang the bell over and over so it made the impatient sound of a car alarm.

"Where are they?" Cassie asked.

"They have to be here," Lila said, as much to herself as to us.

"Maybe we're on *Punk'd* or something," I said.

"That show is only for famous people, stupid," Cassie said.

"Well, maybe we're on a new show that we don't know about yet," I tried.

Cassie smirked. "Did you tell them the right night?"

Brian did attend a rival high school. It was possible he had been misinformed of the date of our prom. Even though I knew it was a crock, I attempted to hold onto this like a drowning person grabbing for an outstretched hand, because I was drowning.

I was.

Lila ignored Cassie and stuck her face to the sidelight window. She banged on the door like she was locked on the inside of it.

"There's obviously no one home," Cassie said, in a tone that suggested she was talking as much about Lila's behavior as she was about Brian's empty house.

I couldn't breathe. I felt like I had been punched in the throat. This was supposed to be the night where my date would realize that he couldn't live without me, that he would love me forever. But that date didn't exist.

"I'm going to look around back," Lila said, walking away in what appeared to be an attempt to shut Cassie up; this rarely worked.

"She's so fucking clueless," Cassie said, plopping down on the grass. She pulled out a handful of blades and burned them with her lighter. "Maybe he'll come home if I burn his house down."

I nodded. Not that I wanted her to burn his house down, but a small grass fire might attract some attention.

"This is so typical," she said, lighting a cigarette. "I didn't even want to go. Fucking Lila."

"We don't know they're not coming," I said. I wasn't ready to let myself believe that this was going to be my memory of prom night for the rest of my life.

"Well, maybe *we* don't," she said, taking a long drag, "but I do."

I stared at my nails. I had painted them in the same light blue as my dress. I thought about how the nail polish was still sitting on my nightstand, how when I got home I would scrub my nails raw and throw it away.

We looked up, startled by a crash that came from the back of the house.

Cassie shook her head. "You should never climb a trellis in heels."

"You think Lila's breaking in?"

She grabbed another handful of grass and lit it up. "You know what would be classic?" she asked, smiling like she was trying to keep a bird from flying out from behind her teeth. "She finds him in there with some other girl." She watched me for a moment, gauging my reaction. "Don't tell me that wouldn't make you happy."

It would have, so I didn't.

Lila came around the side of the house. "No one's there," she said, as if that were news. "I did find this, though." She threw a gallon Ziploc bag of pot on the ground in front of us.

"Holy shit," Cassie said. "This is better than a stupid dance any day." She held it up.

I knew Brian was a dealer, but I guess I didn't know what that really meant. *This* was what that really meant.

"I've been stood up for my prom, in case you haven't noticed," Lila said.

"You're the one who took it," Cassie said, opening the bag and smelling it.

"Not for us; to piss off Brian. How can this be happening to me?"

"It's happening to all of us." I wasn't about to let Lila take all the pain for herself, even though this was probably the first time she had ever experienced what I had felt so many times before—the pinprick pop and subsequent deflation of rejection.

"But he was my boyfriend," Lila said.

I had to give her that. At least I hadn't had sex with the boy who was dumping me. Though it did concern me that my date was rejecting me even with the knowledge that I might have.

"What are we supposed to do now?" Lila asked in a voice that seemed like someone yelling to the heavens after hitting her last straw.

"I have an idea," Cassie said, shaking the bag.

I didn't care what we did as long as it didn't involve going home to my mother.

"How pathetic. My best prospects for dates are you two," Lila said, a tear running down the side of her face, shiny and fat like a worm. "I can't believe Brian would do this to me." Lila looked like a wilted flower in the center of the lawn.

"Shut the fuck up about Brian; it's over," Cassie said. "Let's go party."

"I'm too upset," Lila said, not moving.

I shrugged. Cassie could try, but I doubted we were going anywhere without Lila.

Cassie harrumphed and walked over to the front stoop. She pulled her dress up and her underpants down.

"What the hell are you doing?" Lila asked.

"Leaving him a present," Cassie said as she peed all over the evening edition of the *Collinsville News*. "*Now* we can go have some fun."

Two

Maybe Cassie meant to drive by our school, but maybe she just couldn't avoid it. Collinsville is dissected by four major streets. Collinsville South High was positioned at the intersection of two of the major-est.

"Duck," Cassie said as we drove by. The pot smoke was thick in the car. I didn't think anyone could see us—not that anyone was looking, anyway.

Even though I was supposed to be ducking, I couldn't help watching the limos lined up like a trail of ants marching from the street to the school driveway. Kids from our class were streaming out in cake-frosting-colored dresses and black tuxes; girls were hugging, boys were fist-bumping, and everyone was taking pictures with their phones.

I was hiding in a car smoking pot.

I wasn't nearly as excited about having it as Cassie was,

but I kept smoking. I'd only had pot a few times. Usually at parties, when other people were around to see me. I'd have just a small hit or two to look like I belonged there.

But that night, I inhaled and coughed, inhaled and coughed, until my lungs burned. I probably should have been scared to smoke that much, but I needed to be annihilated. I had to forget tomorrow, when I would wake up in one of the three hotel rooms we'd rented, alone in that big bed, my dress crumpled up on the floor like a discarded attempt at a love letter.

"Maybe Brian is there already," Lila said. It seemed unlikely, but no less unlikely than being stood up for prom, no less unlikely than driving by our school in Cassie's car pretending we didn't want to be there.

"He's not," Cassie said.

"He could be," Lila said. "Let me text him again."

Maybe our dates were already inside. I let myself believe it. Let stupid hope take over.

"We're wasted. I'm not going in there," Cassie said.

Lila looked at me in the side mirror. I'd seen that look before. It was time for me to observe and obey.

"Then drop us off," she said, still looking at me.

"Yeah, drop us off," I said, feeling stupid as I said it, knowing I was reciting just like AJ.

Cassie huffed. "Ten minutes," she said. "And you owe me." She met my eye in the rearview mirror. "Both of you."

I knew that look, too.

We parked a few blocks away and went in the back entrance of the school—the door we'd sneak into after we'd ditch out during lunch. We couldn't arrive, just the three of us, in front of everyone. It would be as bad as walking up all alone.

It was strange being there after hours; the hallways empty, overhead lights on, music coming from the gym. It smelled different, like dust and ammonia. The things you couldn't smell when the halls were filled with people. I was so messed up that the gray lockers lining the hallway made me think of intestines, so messed up that the fact made more sense than it ever had. Like intestines, the hallways at school could dissolve you into a nameless, faceless drone. Unless you made yourself different.

We walked past the cafeteria, the nurse's office, the janitor's closet, and the boys' bathroom, our heels slapping the floor like horses' hooves.

"Let's have a smoke first," Cassie said, pushing open the girls' bathroom door.

"What if they *are* waiting inside for us?" Lila asked.

"They made us wait," Cassie said. "Now they can wait."

"Amy?" Lila asked.

"I could have a smoke." I shrugged.

Smoking with my girls was something I was used to. I was not used to being stood up. I was not used to entering my prom through the back door of my high school, so no one else would know that I had been stood up.

If having a smoke for five minutes allowed me to stop thinking about that, then yes, I wanted a smoke.

"Fine," Lila said as we followed Cassie inside.

Smoking at school was definitely against the rules, but I guess I felt like what had happened to me was, too. Some cardinal prom law had been broken. That had to balance out anything I needed to do to pretend otherwise, even getting so high that my head felt like one of the shiny balloons that probably covered the gymnasium ceiling like bubble wrap.

Our shoes echoed as we walked into the bathroom and all the way back to the last stall. We stood around the toilet as Cassie took a cigarette from her small red purse and lit it.

"I'm so fucked up," Cassie said. She wobbled in her heels and started to laugh. Her laughter bounced off the sea-green tile walls.

"Just try to keep it together till we get inside," Lila said, grabbing the cigarette from her, taking a drag, and then passing it to me.

I started to laugh, too. It was funny crowding into a bathroom stall in our fancy shoes and fancy dresses and fancy hairstyles; like sophisticated city women at a cocktail party—with a toilet.

"Great, now you got Amy going." Lila snickered.

"Shh," I said, trying to keep the giggles from escaping. They were starting to simmer up, like my lips were the hole in a volcano model that was ready to blow. I put my hand over my mouth. Just because we were breaking the rules so deliberately didn't mean I wanted to get caught.

Getting in trouble—in our fancy shoes and fancy dresses and fancy hairstyles—seemed like another cardinal prom law that wasn't supposed to be broken.

"I think if they're not here yet," Cassie said, taking a quick drag, "we should stay. We should stay and we should dance. This buzz is too good to waste in my car."

"*You* want to dance?" Lila laughed.

"Sure, why not?" Cassie said.

I couldn't keep the giggles in anymore. Cassie dancing? I pictured her as Frankenstein—big and green, lurching to techno in her slutty red dress.

"What?" Cassie said.

"I didn't know you liked dancing," Lila said, looking at me like she knew exactly what I was picturing, trying so hard to keep her mouth from curling up into a smile.

I let loose one of those laughs that come out when you're trying not to and it sounds like you're spitting all over yourself.

"Shut up," Cassie said, pushing me, but not in a mean way or the way she sometimes did to remind you that she could kill you if she wanted to, but you were lucky because she liked you.

"Okay," Lila said, calming her giggles. "Okay, we'll stay and we'll dance."

Cassie threw the cigarette in the toilet and lit another one.

"I thought you wanted to *dance*," I teased, realizing that I was starting to have fun. It was like I hadn't exhaled since I'd begun getting ready that afternoon. I had been waiting for my date to take my hand, but laughing with Lila and Cassie would do for now.

"In a minute," Cassie said.

"Can't wait," Lila said, smiling at me again.

"You do realize we all have our cell phones," I said.

"You upload anything to YouTube and I'll be uploading my own video," Cassie said, inhaling sharply. "It'll be worse than my dancing, believe me."

"I'm not sure what could be," Lila said, laughing again.

"Shut up," Cassie said, giving Lila a light shove.

Cassie's dancing felt like a big joke. But her wanting to delay it made sense. Locked in the stall, it was only us. Boys made things complicated.

Our dates might have been inside waiting for us, or they might not have, but standing in a circle around the toilet, we didn't have to worry about that—*yet*. We could smoke and laugh and pretend this was just like any other time we were together, when the smoke was hovering above us like insects and we were laughing and whispering about nothing.

When nothing felt like everything.

"They are here; I know it," Lila said as we left the bathroom. We turned the corner past the trophy case and walked toward the welcome table in front of the gym.

Joe Wright and Leslie Preston sat there, she in a purple dress, he in a tux with matching tie. He was sweating and his usually spiky blond hair was matted down, as though he had just come off the dance floor.

"We're in hell," Cassie muttered.

"Tickets, please," Leslie said, looking at us the way everyone looked at us—like we were flies that were bothering her.

I didn't really know Leslie, but I knew Joe, or had known him. He lived across the street from me. We'd played together when we were younger, like kids on the same street do. We'd shared a bus stop until last year, when I stopped taking the bus; we'd been friends until three years ago, when I started hanging out with Cassie and Lila.

Were Leslie and Joe dating? It didn't seem possible. Of course, she dated anyone there was to date, was on any committee there was to join, and was friends with anyone there was to be friends with. Well, except for losers and dorks, or rebels like Cassie, Lila, and me.

"Our dates have them. I think they're inside," Lila said.

"Names," Leslie said, looking at a clipboard.

"You know our names," Cassie said.

"Their names." She squinted. I'd never said anything to her before tonight, but from the way she was acting, my guess was Cassie had, and that it involved swear words.

"Brian Reynolds and Kevin and Aaron," Lila listed, ticking them off on her fingers.

"Kevin and Aaron?" Leslie asked.

Lila shrugged.

She didn't even know their last names. I wasn't sure if that, or the fact that we were now begging to get into our own prom, was worse.

"Not here," Leslie said, looking at her list.

The gym door opened—three girls from our class leaving to go to the bathroom. Three girls dressed just like Cassie, Lila, and me, having a totally different night. The music was loud, bass thumping. I saw kids from our class jumping up and down in circles in the middle of the dance floor in their stockinged feet. I saw a glimpse of blue and white balloons and sparkly lights as the door slammed shut.

We should have stayed in the bathroom.

"Can't we just look?" Lila asked.

"Not without tickets," Leslie said. "This prom took a lot of work and cost a lot of money, not that you would know."

"We bought tickets," Lila said.

"Then where are they?" she asked.

"Probably scalped for weed," Cassie said under her breath.

I looked at Joe. He looked down. I couldn't remember who'd stopped talking first. Who'd started glancing away when we saw each other on the sidewalk, in the hallway. I guess it didn't matter. We'd fallen into that rhythm as easily as we had fallen out of our old one.

The gym door opened again. A slow song seeped out as school gossip-monger Ruthie Jensen entered the hall. She stood there in her pale pink dress, acting as though she wasn't listening.

It was like she had a sixth sense for when your life was sucking.

"Come on, you know us," I whispered.

"Sure," Joe said, looking through me, "but you still need a ticket."

"We go to this school. Why would we not buy tickets?" I was this close. There was no way I wasn't getting inside, with or without a date.

"School policy," he said, shrugging.

Leslie smiled and snuggled into him.

I shouldn't have been surprised. He had no reason to be nice to me. We never liked seeing each other. It was always uncomfortable. I hated that he knew who I had been before I was me.

"You don't have your tickets?" Ruthie asked, trying to gather more information. She pulled her pale pink wrap tightly around her. She was telling *everyone* about this.

"Let's go," Cassie said, turning toward the door. "Thanks a lot, assholes."

I didn't bother asking if she still wanted to stay and dance. It didn't even seem funny anymore.

I looked at Joe, giving him one last chance. He didn't take it.

• • •

We drove around aimlessly, smoking cigarettes.

"Well, that totally sucked," Lila said.

"You suck," Cassie said.

I took a drag and watched the ash fall like snowflakes as I tapped it on the open window. "Which one was supposed to be my date?" I asked.

"Aaron, I guess," Lila said.

"Who cares?" Cassie said.

"What does he look like?" I closed my eyes. Maybe I was out of it enough to create a fake memory.

"I don't know," Lila said.

"Like I said, who cares?" Cassie said.

I opened my eyes. Why *did* I care? He had stood me up. He obviously didn't care.

"Brian's friends with him on Facebook, if you want to look him up," Lila said, trying to give me her phone.

I held up my hand like a crossing guard, my light blue nails still mocking me. I dropped it in a fist on my lap and shook my head. There was no way I could handle the possibility of seeing what Aaron was *really* doing right now.

"This is so boring. Isn't there anywhere else we can go?" Lila asked.

"Everyone we know is at the stupid prom or hiding from us," I said.

"Brian isn't hiding from us."

"Okay, whatever," Cassie said, looking at me in the rearview mirror.

"He forgot," Lila said, having convinced herself. "He does a lot of drugs. He only has a select number of brain cells left."

"That explains why he likes you, I guess," Cassie said.

I snorted. I couldn't help it.

"Shut up, Amy."

I covered my mouth.

"This is just like some sort of fucked-up fairy tale," Cassie said. I could see her smiling to herself in the rearview mirror. "Like Cinderella, except all twisted up and without Cinderella."

"So, what does that make us?" Lila asked. "The ugly stepsisters? Thanks a lot."

"You're welcome," Cassie said, lighting another cigarette and swerving onto the shoulder. "Fucking car," she said as she righted us.

"I am not ugly," Lila said, crossing her arms and screwing up her face like a kid having a temper tantrum.

"We know," Cassie said, rolling her eyes.

"All dressed up and no place to go," Lila wailed, like a cringeworthy audition from that one girl in drama club, the one who never gets the part.

Her prayers were answered by the lights and sirens of a police car coming up behind us.

"Fucking police," Cassie said as they pulled us over.

I looked at the enormous bag of Brian's marijuana on the seat next to me. *Crap.*

We *definitely* should have stayed in the bathroom.

Three

Lila smiled out of habit when the flash went off for her mug shot. She held a number just below her chest, facing forward and then turning to the right and the left. Her features all seemed to belong on a stuffed animal—perfect, pearly black teddy-bear eyes, a pink embroidery-thread stitch of a mouth and nose.

Cassie gave them the finger as she held her number, gripping the board so both her middle fingers pointed straight up at the sky, her shoulders forming a perfect line, all her edges as sharp as a pocketknife.

I looked like one of those crazy movie-star mug shots on TV: shocked and scared and stoned out of my mind.

The cops took it upon themselves to call our parents and give them the news, which was probably the only thing that went my way that night. At least I didn't have to deal with my mother screaming into the phone for the five minutes I would have been allotted for my call.

The policemen also let us know that instead of paying bail, each set of parents would have to sign a piece of paper that stated they guaranteed we'd come back when we were called to our first court appearance.

I didn't think that would be hard to enforce. I doubted that, after this, any of us would be allowed out of our parents' sights ever again.

Cassie was zigzagging the holding cell, *click, click, click*ing her way from one end to the other, pacing with the force of a hamster on a wheel. Lila and I sat on opposite benches watching her, Lila with her knees up under her dress, making a tent the way I used to do with my nightgown when I was little. She was crying softly, like in one of those gauze-covered scenes where a forlorn girl looks out a rain-soaked window, the tears on her face mirroring the rain on the glass.

I probably would have been crying, too, if Lila hadn't started first and if I hadn't been so high that my eyes felt like Ping-Pong balls. My plan to try and forget everything had brought me here.

There was no way I was forgetting *this*.

By that point we weren't talking. Cassie and Lila had already fought about whose fault it was the whole ride over and all through booking. They never figured that out, but each did come to the conclusion that the other was a stupid bitch.

"This is fucking bullshit," Cassie said, *click*ing back over to the bars and kicking them. Kicking them so hard that her heel broke. It hung from her shoe like a just-ripe banana; she ripped it off and flung it through the bars.

The parents all seemed to arrive at the same time. We could see each of them—Cassie's parents, Lila's mom, my dad—come into the station looking confused and teary-eyed as they entered, like they had all been hit in the head with a rock right before they walked in.

When Cassie saw her parents she said, "Fuck," and put her head down. They may have been the only people in the world who Cassie was truly afraid of. Her father had that father look to him, the one that says this is the life he has chosen and he will stick with it no matter what, a sort of smile hiding a scream. Her mom smoked Salems and was smoking one when she walked into the station. She was exactly like Cassie, twenty years later.

I was glad it was my father who picked me up that night, his hair an assemblage of small brown cowlicks, so that it resembled frosting on a cupcake. He wore his long tan raincoat and unlike on TV or in the movies, it did not cover pajamas and there were no slippers on his feet. He had taken the time to get dressed.

"Who the hell are you?" Cassie's mother asked.

"Jerry Fleishman, DDS," he said, like he was reading the sign on the front of his office.

I looked down and covered my face with my hands.

"Who?" she asked again.

"Amy's dad," he said, trying to make his voice sound proud despite the circumstances.

"Congratulations," she said, walking past him and up to the desk.

"That one's mine," Lila's mom said, pointing at her like

she was a dog in the pound. "Lila Van Drake," she continued, maybe because she didn't want anyone to mistake Cassie for her daughter. Maybe because she didn't want anyone to mistake me for her daughter.

Lila's mom was a woman who, after losing her first love and raising his two children, had married the first guy who came along, which made her act like she was always open to meeting someone new.

"So that's the famous Lila," my father said.

I'd forgotten that he'd never met her. My mother had forbidden Lila and Cassie to enter our house and it's not like my father had driven me anywhere before Cassie got her license.

"Amy talks about her all the time." I pretended I hadn't heard him, and luckily, that night I was too preoccupied to be embarrassed.

"I know," Lila's mom said, and I realized I wasn't too preoccupied to be mortified.

· · ·

As we made our way outside, I walked behind my father, staring at the dirt that had somehow gotten all over my shoes.

"Your mother says she can't even look at you," he said, not turning around.

I nodded. I wanted to say thank you—for picking me up, for being able to look at me—but I just couldn't say the words. I could never say the words.

"So here I am." He held his arms at his sides like he was acting out an enthusiastic *ta-da*. In one hand were his car keys, in the other a clear plastic bag with everything that had been confiscated upon our arrest: my wallet, my cigarettes, my phone, the pearl earrings he had bought me for my Bat Mitzvah. He sounded tired, very tired, but not from lack of sleep—from this, from me. "You look very nice, by the way."

I wanted to hug him, but his compliment was too late. He hadn't been there to see me off; he'd had a pediatric dental emergency, a child who needed him more than I did.

He opened my door and put his palm on my back. His hands were always cold, as if that truly were a requirement for dental school.

He started the car and turned to look at me—I knew to make sure I had my seat belt on, a habit of his for as long as I could remember. He listened for the *click* and drove out of the parking lot.

I thought about saying I was sorry, but I wasn't even sure what I had done wrong, other than turning into the kind of girl my mother had warned me I would be.

We rode in silence the whole way home, driving down the quiet, empty streets of my neighborhood, streets that wound and wound like ribbon candy, the hood of the car slicing through the sweet, warm air like the hull of a boat slicing water.

My father stayed silent as we waited for the garage door's routine rise. He stared straight ahead, watching the headlights bore two holes into the back wall of the garage, where our bikes hung. He turned off the car and looked at me. I needed him to tell me it would be okay. I needed him to hug me, to just be my dad.

"What's going to happen?" I asked, finally starting to cry.

"We'll talk about it tomorrow," he said, touching my shoulder and then leaving me sitting in the car, crying.

I guess I couldn't blame him, but it felt like I was always waiting for tomorrow.

Four

That night I didn't sleep. I didn't even take off my prom dress. I sat with AJ, putting him on my finger and then on my shoulder.

Pretty Amy, pretty Amy, he repeated as I cried into his yellow feathers. *I love you*, he squawked as he rubbed up against my wet cheek.

I knew he was just saying the things I had taught him to say, but that night I really needed to hear them. It made me wonder if my mother had actually had some forethought in getting me AJ instead of the puppy I had begged her for. I had begged for a puppy, but I had really wanted a sister. I had really wanted a friend.

I got a bird.

She had said that birds were better than puppies because they could talk, and I couldn't deny that for this one long night at least, she had been right.

I stared out my bedroom window at Joe's house across the street, into the dark windows and its two shining porch-light eyes. His mom was probably sleeping inside. Joe was probably somewhere with Leslie *not* sleeping and I had my nose up to the glass, praying that the night would never end. Not in the way girls usually wish their prom night will last forever; I prayed for time to stop. I wasn't ready for whatever was waiting for me the next day.

Eventually daylight came, not all at once but slowly, like the sky was set on a dimmer switch. The moon and stars finally snuffed out.

Good morning, AJ squawked as we heard my mother wake up. Heard her bedroom door open and close. Heard her walk down the stairs. Heard her breakfast noises in the kitchen. I guess she wanted to be able to have her coffee and hear the *thwack* of the morning paper against the screen door before she could deal with the fact that her daughter was a criminal.

The choices of what to do at that moment floated in front of my tired eyes like mirages. I could either stay in my room all day in this dress, or I could go downstairs and get the initial yelling over with. I knew there would be yelling, probably a lot of it, and probably crying, too. Crying and questions: *Was I not a good mother to you? Did I not give you everything you could have wanted? What did we do to make you turn out this way?*

I wished I had taught AJ to say, *I don't know.*

I put AJ back in his cage and finally decided to go downstairs because of the coffee. It was like some kind of warped Folgers commercial: me sniffing the air and thinking that there really is nothing better the morning after getting arrested than drinking a steaming-hot cup of java with my mom.

I found her sitting at the kitchen table in her bathrobe, which was odd, since she tended to change upon waking into her sweat suit. The kind that is shiny and puffy and has no real purpose for athletes, but that makes suburban moms feel like they're up and at 'em and ready to go.

She didn't look up from the newspaper when she heard me, forcing me to stare at the back of it. I saw letters from grocery advertisements swimming around, forming words like spoonfuls of alphabet soup: FAILURE. DISAPPOINTMENT. FELON. FOSTER CARE.

"Is there more?" I asked, pointing to the empty coffee maker. I figured it was the most civilized thing I could say at that moment and I really did want some coffee.

She poked her head out from behind the paper. Her eyes were rimmed with red. "Do you think this is funny?"

I shook my head. It seemed safer than anything that might come out of my mouth.

"Then why are you still wearing *that*?" She spat out the word. The dress was an illusion. The dress was a joke. "Just sit down and don't say another word."

"I'm sorry," I said, trying to preempt a fight, getting right to what she wanted to hear, even if I wasn't sure what I was sorry for yet.

"Don't be sorry to me," she said.

I didn't know what I was supposed to say next. Usually *sorry* was enough, even if I said it just like AJ would have if I'd taught him to.

"You're in serious trouble, Amy," she said, as if I needed a reminder.

"Then help me," I said. It hadn't worked with my dad. I don't know why I thought it would work with her.

She shrugged. "This is yours to handle."

"What does that mean?" I felt like I was a helium balloon and she had just let go.

"Your father is calling his friend Dick Simon to represent you. Now that you can't make your money selling illegal drugs to neighborhood kids, you'll have to get a real job so you can pay for him."

"I'm sorry," I said again, but even as I said it, I knew it didn't matter.

"How could you do this, Amy?" she screamed, slamming her hands so hard on the table that her coffee cup shook.

"I don't know," I said, my way of filling up space while she yelled.

I'm sorry and *I don't know* were probably the first words I'd taught myself—to make my mother leave me the hell alone.

She shouldn't have been surprised I was messed up. Anyone forced to wear a pink tutu and a Miss America ribbon that read *Novocain Princess* while holding a rolling-pin-sized syringe and touting her father's dental practice on basic cable was bound to end up with some problems. Not unexpectedly, drug related.

"Amy, answer me!" she yelled.

I thought of AJ in his cage upstairs, the way he would squawk as loudly as my mother would scream—when she still bothered to scream at me—like he was trying to drown her out, make me not have to hear her angry words.

"We didn't—" I began.

"We," my mother interrupted. "What about *you*, Amy? You can't hide behind your friends anymore."

"I—I'm not," I stammered.

Her eyes were wide, waiting.

"We…" I paused. "I…" The words came out in trickles. "It wasn't our fault…"

"Really." My mother chuckled angrily. "Whose fault was it?" She cocked her head to the side, waiting for my answer.

Whatever thought I had of telling her the truth was squashed down—driven into the back of my throat by her cruel laugh. She didn't want to hear what had really happened.

She never wanted to.

"I don't know," I said again.

"Well, the police don't agree," she said, going at her nails like they were corn on the cob.

"The police are idiots," I mumbled.

"And what does that make you?" She squinted.

I had no answer. I hated to admit it, but she was right. As much as I'd whined about my life before, it was about to *really* suck now.

"I'm sorry," I said, yet again. I think it was the most I'd ever said it. Maybe I was going for the Guinness World Record.

"This is the worst thing you've ever done." She started to cry. "You can deny it as much as you want, but it doesn't change the fact that you have been arrested." When she said *arrested* she started crying even harder, as if the words *you* and *arrested* coming out of her mouth in the same sentence made it all the more real to her.

It made it all the more real to me. I couldn't deny it anymore. The sun was up and I was still arrested. Nothing had changed—which meant everything had changed.

"We're through paying for your mistakes," she said.

Apparently overnight my mother had become versed in the tough-love theory of child rearing. I could picture her under the covers with a flashlight, my dad sleeping next to her, reading those pamphlets she had gotten when they first suspected, and then kept in her nightstand drawer: *Teen Drug Use: 50 Warning Signs—Suggestions for Parents of Difficult Teens.* I saw her reading and rereading and, knowing her, using a highlighter to figure out what they were supposed to do with me. Reading through the prescribed lists: *Signs of drug use. Signs of rebellion. Signs that your teen is the Antichrist.*

"You'd better start applying for a job today," she said.

I had been hoping to lock myself in my room and crawl into bed, AJ on my pillow.

"I mean it, Amy," she said, like she knew what I was thinking.

"Where am I supposed to find a job?"

"I honestly don't care," she said, walking out of the kitchen, the bottom of her robe trailing behind her. "Just make sure it's legal this time."

I guess that was all the help I was getting.

Five

My mother gave me back my wallet but kept my phone.

"Now I know what you really needed this for," she said as she put it in the cabinet on a high shelf above the desk in the kitchen, like I was a little girl and having something up that high would keep it out of my reach.

I was grounded from my phone, from Cassie and Lila, and from breathing without asking first. I had to bring her my dress. She said she was going to take it back to the store, that she wouldn't tolerate paying for something I hadn't even used.

As I walked toward Main Street, I couldn't help but smirk when I thought about how she was going to explain to the cashier how this dress that had never been worn had fingerprint ink all over it.

I stopped in at Gas-N-Go to buy cigarettes and filled out an application, one of those that come in a pack of fifty, white, light blue, and red, that asks when your earliest possible start date is. Then it asks you to list your job experience, your references, and your special skills. For that one I wrote, *You tell me*. Like Cassie would have.

My mother always called Cassie a hopeless delinquent. I guess that's what I was now.

After I filled it out, I followed a sign that said INTERVIEWS into the break room.

It was a cardboard box sort of room, with a vending machine that hummed and gurgled like an old refrigerator and a long cafeteria table ringed by orange plastic chairs.

A man I couldn't help thinking looked like one of the cops who had arrested us sat in one of the chairs. He gestured for me to sit.

I was so tired that for a moment, I thought I was back in the police station. Until I looked down and saw the job application in my hand, my name at the top.

He was insanely sweaty and had to wipe his hand on his pants before he took mine, which he shook in a way that reminded me of an empty sock.

"Name's Mancini. You get hired, you'll be required to call me Mr. Mancini." His hands were cut up and ruddy like he treated them every night to a massage with a meat grinder.

It made me look at my own hands. The fingernails were still painted the same light blue as my dress. I sat on them.

"Job experience?" he asked.

"I've done some babysitting," I said.

He looked at me skeptically. We both knew that babysitting had given me experience in little more than eating other people's food.

"Up to four kids at once," I said, even though it was a lie.

I decided to leave out that I spent most of my time raiding the mother's bathroom cabinet for makeup. I'd take her lipstick, daring pinks like Fuchsia Frenzy or Hot Salmon, and picture her getting ready for a night out, searching in every cabinet and drawer and then forcing her doting husband to go to the grocery store to buy more.

I liked picturing someone having a doting husband.

"You ever work a cash register?"

"Sure," I said. I hadn't, but how hard could it be?

"Why should I hire you?" he asked, in the same kind of voice my mom used when she didn't believe something I told her. The voice she used all the time.

I thought about it. He probably shouldn't. Considering what had happened last night, the place would probably burn down just because I was in it. I shook the thoughts out of my head. I wasn't about to start crying in front of this guy.

"Do you not want the job?" he asked.

I didn't want it. I needed it; a much worse position to be in. "I can start right away," I said, forcing myself to smile so hard that my face hurt.

He seemed like he should be chewing on a cigar, but instead he chewed his pen, and then rapped it against his capped molars as he waited. "Good enough for me. I had this guy come in today wearing only one shoe, and he was the best person I'd seen up until you." He looked back at my application. "Don't know why I interviewed him. I wouldn't even let a customer walk in like that, but in this business that's the caliber of people you come to expect."

I guess that meant I was now in that caliber of people. After having worked for four years to claw my way to the middle of the high school social-status pyramid, one night had kicked me all the way back down to the bottom.

"Never thought I'd be doing this myself, but life gives you shit, you make a sandwich. You know what I'm saying?"

I nodded. With the shit I'd been given last night, I should have been able to make a forty-eight-inch party sub.

"Honestly, I don't care why you want this job. I don't care what you do when you're not here. I don't even care if you like me. All I care about is that you get here on time. You work when you're supposed to. You stay awake behind that counter, and you don't steal from me. You can do whatever you want, as long as you don't cost me a dime other than your salary."

I wanted to laugh at him calling the measly $7.25 an hour I would be making a salary, but the fact that I actually needed it kind of dampened the humor.

"And if you ever do think about stealing from me, I have twenty-seven cousins named Salvador who I won't hesitate to sic on you in a dark alley."

I guess that was his way of telling me I got the job.

I walked out of the store, lit a cigarette, and headed quickly toward home, hoping to avoid seeing anyone I knew. Then I remembered that prom had been the night before and that anyone I knew would probably be sleeping, in a hotel room or on their best friend's floor, the music still buzzing in their heads, hung over and happy.

That was where I wanted to be. That was where I wanted to be with Aaron. Twenty-four hours ago, I had been in a bubble bath shaving my legs and daydreaming about slow dancing under sparkly lights. Now I just wished I could go back there, live in that before for a little while longer.

I was a block away from my house when I saw Joe walking toward me. I threw my cigarette in the gutter. His suit jacket was off, his purple tie around his head like a headband. His cummerbund was missing. Maybe Leslie had kept it as a souvenir.

I looked down and walked faster.

"Where's your dress?" he asked. I could tell he was still drunk, which was probably the only reason he even bothered to stop. It was the most he had said to me in three years—well, not counting last night.

"Where's yours?" I asked, channeling Cassie. Afraid that if I let my guard down, he would be able to tell what had happened, would be able to break me right in two.

"You used to be nice," he said, putting his hands in his pockets. He did that when they started to shake. That was why he loved playing volleyball. I wished he'd never told me that.

"Go away, Joe," I said.

"Exactly," he said. His pupils were big; big black moons in his hazel eyes. He shook his head. "You used to be *you*."

He was definitely drunk, but not too drunk for me to know what he meant. "What do you want?"

"You ever find your date?" he asked, slurring.

Things had gotten *so* past finding my date. At least he didn't know that yet. At least he was still living in the before.

I looked at him with the eyes I used anytime I walked past him on my way to Gas-N-Go to buy cigarettes, or saw him in the hall at school, or stood across from him in gym class, waiting to be picked for a team. Eyes that said, *I can't see you.*

He wobbled forward. He took his hands out of his pockets to steady himself, but they were still shaking. It had started after his dad left. I wished he'd never told me that, too.

I wished I'd never told him any of the things I told him, either.

"Happy prom, Amy," he said, walking past me, starting to whistle.

He had a day of sleep ahead of him—that beautiful, warm, liquid sleep that comes from a night without any— then waking up to his mom making him fresh waffles and asking him all about his special, perfect night.

I had no idea what I had ahead of me.

Six

Dick Simon's secretary led us into his office and told us to take a seat.

"Water, juice, coffee?" she asked in her rehearsed secretary voice.

The way things had been going, I wanted vodka, straight, but I figured that was out of the question.

We waited for Dick on a caramel leather couch with gold buttons like bullets at the center of our backs. It felt strange sitting with my parents like that. We never sat that close to each other unless we were at the movies together, and it had been years since we'd done that.

I tried not to think about how much I used to love those times, and how horribly different this was.

He walked into the office like he was making a stage entrance, palms out at his sides waiting for applause. He took my father's hand and shook it, along with his whole body. He gave my mother a kiss on the cheek. She accepted, and then he came to me.

"Amy? Gosh, is this Amy?" he asked, grabbing both of my hands and pulling me up. "I haven't seen you since you were ten years old. Look how big you are."

I didn't remember meeting him when I was ten years old, but there was no doubt I would remember him now. His face was pockmarked and craggy and he smiled too much—smiled and licked his lips so it looked like he was ready to get down and eat something.

Dick guided me back to my seat, then sat down himself behind a desk the size of a dining-room table.

He looked at his computer and laughed. "This is a good one. My buddy Warren sent me this," he said, looking directly at my father. "You know why women play with their hair at traffic lights?"

My mother glanced at her watch. I knew this was grownup code for *I have other things to do and other places to go. You are only the first of the many annoying appointments I have today.*

"Because they don't have any bleeps to scratch," he said, laughing again. "You can fill in the blank yourself. I realize there are women and children present." He winked at me.

This was the guy who was going to rescue me.

He stood and smoothed out his pants. "You all look like someone's died or something." He came around the front of the desk and leaned on it.

"Dick, we're not here for jokes," my mother said, as if he had forgotten.

"I know, I know, I'm just trying to lighten the mood," he said, smiling his stupid laugh-at-me smile.

"Dick," my father said. Considering the way this guy was acting, he could have been saying it for more reasons than just because it was his name.

"All right, fine, back to work," Dick said. He held a manila folder above his head. "This is your folder." He shook it for emphasis. "What we need to do is fill this up with stuff that proves your innocence. So far, as you can see, we have nothing."

This was my parents' solution? I was going to be working my ass off to pay for this guy and so far he had nothing?

"I'm not going to ask you if you're guilty, because I don't care," he said, sitting on the edge of his desk in that way people sit on the edge of their desks that is supposed to let you know they are being serious.

I was glad. There was probably a lot I was guilty of. Being in the wrong place at the wrong time: check. Being a horrible disappointment as a daughter: check. At least I didn't have to admit to any of it out loud.

My mother gnawed on her cuticle like it was a dog bone. "She's also been suspended for the last week of school for being intoxicated while coming from a school function."

She and my father had received the call from Mr. Morgan the night before, once he had been alerted to our arrest and the fact that we had been stoned out of our gourds on the way from the prom. The police had asked Cassie where we were coming from and she'd told them, trying her best to pretend she was sober.

Obviously, it hadn't worked.

My parents were horrified, but I was glad for the reprieve. If I'd thought people whispered about me before, there was no way I was prepared for what they might say now. Besides, the last week of school wasn't really "school" for me. As a fourth-semester senior, I was done with my finals, so classes were redundant. I'd had a week ahead of me of locker cleaning-outing and yearbook signing and senior pranking and study halls with nothing left to study for.

There wasn't anything in my locker I wanted anyway.

"How are your grades?" Dick asked.

"Fine," I said.

"Honor roll," my father said.

"They got her into State," my mother said. "She'll still be going, right?"

I wasn't surprised she asked about that. She had been orchestrating my college career since the day I was born. What she didn't know was that I was planning on deferring my acceptance for a year and traveling around the country with Lila and Cassie. We were going to work at owner-operated truck stops and stay at seedy motels. We were going to be free of stupid Collinsville, New York, and have hot wind blow on our faces as we drove from town to town. Of course, I wasn't planning on telling her that until I absolutely had to.

Besides, I wanted to prolong college for as long as possible. Even I knew that the way things really were was the exact opposite of what my parents had told me. Hard work and a college degree no longer meant anything other than moving right back in with the parents who had lied to you about it in the first place.

"We'll do everything we can," Dick Simon said.

Would I even have the choice to not go to college, or would it be made for me?

I felt sick.

"The Assistant District Attorney is a very old friend of mine, something your compatriots don't have," Dick said, clasping his hands together, then pretending to pull them apart and being unable to.

Lucky me. Dick Simon had jerked off with the Assistant DA when he was thirteen.

"Who cares about her compatriots?" My mother laughed. The first real laugh Dick Simon got out of any of us.

When she said that, I realized I hadn't been thinking about them at all. I wondered if they were thinking about me. I wondered if they were in rooms just like this one with their own lawyers, trying not to think they were in rooms just like this one, the way I was.

"What is she being charged with, specifically?" my father asked.

"Oh, you know, the big PISS," Dick said, waving the folder around. "Possession, Intent to Sell, Sale." He paused and looked down at a paper on his desk. "Your little friend Cassandra's got a DUI on top of that."

"I bet you're happy now I didn't let you borrow the car," my mother said, sounding satisfied.

I couldn't help rolling my eyes.

"The good news is I got my buddy to issue a continuance on your arraignment. Give us some time to get our ducks in a row." He paused. "The bad news is I tried to get you charged as a juvenile, so we could keep you out of *jail*-jail if it ever got to that point, but you're seventeen." He shrugged. "He wants to try you as an adult."

"I'm going to jail?" I asked, my voice hesitating, afraid to say it out loud.

Jail. The word felt like I'd swallowed a bug—I wanted it out of my mouth. I'd been wishing my whole teen life to be treated as an adult. This was not what I'd meant.

"Dick?" my mother shrieked. "Jerry," she shrieked again, looking at my father.

"Dick?" my father repeated, reaching over me and putting his hand on my mother's knee. I fought the urge to grab his hand.

"Don't worry," Dick replied. "The law says you could end up with a year inside, but we can probably get you off with probation if you cooperate. At least that's the feeling I'm getting from my buddy." He paused and pointed at me. "He's going to need to see a real commitment before he's willing to give you any deal."

"But we weren't even doing anything. We didn't sell anything or intend to sell anything," I said, using the words he had given me for what I was supposed to be sorry for doing, even though I hadn't done it. "It wasn't even ours," I added.

"Whose was it?" he asked.

My mother looked at me from one side, my father from the other. I looked down.

"Welcome to the twisty web of drug law," Dick said. "It wasn't what you were doing with it, or even that it wasn't yours, but the amount you had when they picked you up."

I found myself wishing that we had been pulled over later, after we'd had a chance to smoke more. Though I'm guessing the amount we would have had to smoke would have taken six months or killed us in a week.

"She'll cooperate," my mother said, looking at my father. I knew she was picturing the scandal, the whispers and shaking heads.

"Just tell her what she needs to do," my father said, finally taking my hand and squeezing. I squeezed back harder, involuntarily, a game we used to play when I was little, going back and forth until our hands ached. But he wasn't paying attention.

"You need to be just like corn. All ears," Dick Simon said, looking at me and pointing to his head.

His secretary walked in and handed a piece of paper to my mother. She looked at it and handed it directly to me.

It was my first bill. My mother was really going to make me pay him. As he listed everything I would have to do to keep myself out of jail, I stared at it. The amount listed made me consider surrendering. The time I would need to spend working to pay him for just the first hour of his services—not to mention everything else he was telling me I would have to do—made being locked up seem like an easier option.

I knew I had to pay him. Just like I knew I had to do everything else he told me to. I could barely survive standing in line at Starbucks. There was no way I could last any amount of time waiting for freedom, when I couldn't last five minutes waiting for a latte.

Seven

For my mother, finding the therapist Dick Simon insisted I start seeing was as important as finding my future husband. We even sat at the dining room table, which we never did unless it was a special occasion. Evidently I was supposed to believe this was.

She walked into the kitchen to grab the phone book, and for the first time that week I thought about my cell phone—still turned off, still up on that high shelf.

I found myself craving it at first. I wanted to talk to Lila. I wanted to talk to Cassie. I wanted to talk to anyone my own age.

Then I realized that everything waiting for me on it would probably be in response to the arrest. Unending unanswered texts and e-mails asking *WTF happened?* and I was suddenly thankful it was locked away, jealous that I didn't have an off button, too.

"Why am I even here for this?" I said as she sat down. The question was not just one I was asking that day, but about the whole process. The world would still be making plans for me, whether I was present or not.

She ignored me and dialed the first number. As the phone rang, her face looked like she was waiting at a starting gate. I noticed her eyes contract as someone on the other end answered. She took a deep breath and began. The voice that came out was one I heard only rarely. It was her first-impression voice. All enthusiasm and inquiry, all *How do you do* and *Gosh, you're sweet.* It was enough to make you puke.

She talked with one pencil behind her ear, another quickly jotting on a stationery pad next to her. As she wrote she looked at me, as if seeing how well I would match up with the therapist she was considering at the moment.

Down the line she went, crossing out names in the phone book for those who were not accepting new patients or for therapists she knew were seeing her friends or her friends' children. There was no way she was taking the chance that my arrest and her subsequent shame would leak out.

I couldn't help wondering whether, if this therapist she finally found wasn't the first or second or third choice of any of her friends, that meant he probably wasn't all that good.

But then I wondered if it mattered, anyway. I wasn't going to a therapist because I wanted to, but because I had to. It didn't really matter if he helped me, as long as it looked like he did.

. . .

My mother and I sat next to each other in the waiting room. Magazines formed glossy Chinese fans on the end tables around us. The walls were decorated with the sort of monochromatic fuzzy pictures you find in hotels. A red barn and pinkish-hued pond, sunset-induced. A brown, thatched-roof cottage in a field of wheat.

The man who would be my therapist came to greet us with his hands clasped behind his back like a waiting butler. He was short and had glasses with thick black frames that sat so close to his eyes they made him look like a raccoon. He had a long brown ponytail and wore a tie-dyed shirt that looked like a tornado had collided with a rainbow.

"Amy, it's very nice to meet you," he said, his hands still behind his back.

I liked that he chose to ignore my mother and only introduce himself to me. But as the three of us walked down the hall to his office, I wondered if he was just acting like doctors or dentists act when you're a little kid and they're meeting you for the first time, pretending to treat you like an adult but treating you like a child in the process.

My mother looked behind her. I could tell she was questioning her decision, realizing that she had sent her daughter, who was up on drug charges, into the care of a hippie. But I guess that's what can happen when you try to cure your kid by playing Eenie, Meenie, Miney, Moe in the phone book.

"Have a seat," he said as he closed the door behind us. This was not as easy as it sounded. The room was filled with chairs and couches—a leather love seat, a woven beanbag chair that looked like a huge Hacky Sack, a recliner, a rocking chair, a few metal folding chairs, and one that seemed like it had come from his dining-room set.

My mother looked confused. Maybe this was our first test. Maybe the chair we chose told him something about us. I took the rocker. My mother sat in the one from the dining-room set. He sat in the beanbag chair, which I had assumed was his, anyway.

I waited for someone to start talking. I'm not sure what my mother was doing because I was looking down, watching my feet push me back and forth in the rocking chair. Filling the room with a noise that could have been heard from the hallway, and which might have sounded like two people going at it really heavily on the couch.

My mother glared at me to get me to stop, which just made me rock harder. I couldn't help it. It felt good to be doing something so simple.

She shifted in her seat. It was just like her to choose the chair that would make her the least comfortable.

"There's nothing to be ashamed of," he said. "Plenty of people need help at one time or another in their life." I could feel him looking at me.

I stopped rocking. I guess he was waiting for me to say, *I'm one of those people; I need help; it's my time.* But there was no way I was saying that in front of my mother. I'd asked for her help and gotten Dick Simon.

"Oh, I'm not afraid or anything." My mother laughed her meant-to-be-charming laugh. "All of this has just been a lot to take."

"It is stressful when a family member is facing incarceration. Amy, what are your feelings about all of this?" he asked, coaxing me with his grin.

"She feels nothing. Her life is careering into a ditch and all she can do is sit and stare. That's all she does," my mom said, wrapping her purse strap around her hand like a tourniquet.

"You don't even ask me what I'm feeling," I said, the words coming out before I even had a chance to think about them.

"I shouldn't have to ask; I'm your mother."

"Tell us then, Amy," he said, leaning forward. The beanbag chair he was sitting on made a hissing noise.

I couldn't. I didn't want to say it out loud—it was embarrassing. I felt like my life was over. Like overnight I had changed into someone I would feel bad for. Like I had taken my stupid, boring life for granted and now it was all gone.

"See," my mother said, when I didn't answer.

"Do you find it hard to talk about yourself?" he asked, looking at me.

My mother snorted.

"Thanks a lot, Mom," I said.

"What did I do?" she asked.

He wrote something down on his pad. I hoped it was that my mother was acting like a bitch, because that's what I would have written.

"Maybe Amy and I should talk alone," he said, and gestured toward the door.

"She'll get you into a conversation and twist it all around.

That's what she always does," my mother said.

"Even so," he said, standing.

My mother *humph*ed her she's-all-yours *humph* as she closed the door behind her.

Maybe he did actually know what he was doing. In five minutes he'd done what I couldn't in seventeen years—shut my mother up.

"She just cares about you." He watched me for a moment. "Why do you think you ended up here?"

"Because I was arrested," I said.

"Nothing beyond that?" He paused. "Once you know why you did certain things, it will be easier for you to undo them."

I thought about the macramé bracelets I used to make in middle school, the ones that started out in the shape of something like a sailboat—two colors of string, one for the mast and another for the sail—and then once they were woven together, showed no signs of their modest beginnings.

It made me think about how I had made one for Joe, navy with flecks of yellow. I hated that just talking to him put him back in my head. That in addition to everything else that was crashing around in there, I had to deal with Joe again, too.

"How can I undo this?" I asked. I could feel my voice cracking. Crying in front of my father hadn't gotten me anywhere, and I doubted crying in front of this guy would, either.

"You can start by talking to me," he said.

I waited, trying to decide if I could trust him.

"No?" he asked.

I kept my mouth closed tightly, like I was afraid of something he was trying to put into it. Besides, what was I supposed to say? How had I ended up here? Why did it matter, considering I was already here?

"Fine, I'll have to fill in the blanks myself," he said. "It won't be that hard. You think I haven't heard your story before. I've heard it. Maybe there are different characters, a different setting, a different plot, but you," he said, pointing, "you are always the same."

He was kind of a jerk for a hippie. I looked down. I knew he was just trying to get me to talk, but I still couldn't believe I wasn't even getting sympathy from the one guy who was being paid to give it to me.

"Dick Simon tells me you have a few accomplices. Want to tell me about them?"

Not like I would have, but he gave me no time to answer him, apparently too determined to prove his point.

"Okay, I'll guess, then. You needed some friends and they took you in. Before you knew it, you were using drugs. That was fine with you because you sort of wanted to try drugs, but also because you wanted to keep these girls as your friends. It's hard for you to make friends."

I started rocking in the chair again, trying to drown out his words.

He watched me. "I get paid to talk whether you listen or not."

"So talk," I said, still rocking.

He shrugged, talking over the creaking chair. "So you're using, and that gets heavier and heavier, and you all decide, hey, it might be fun to sell drugs; let's give it a go. But before you know it you're in over your head and before you know *that*, you've been arrested. Do I have it about right?"

"We never sold drugs," I said, slamming my feet to a stop.

"Who's going to believe you?" he asked, his eyes squinting. He had a small silver hoop in his left ear. With that and his ponytail and his tie-dye, he reminded me of an older version of one of the druggie boys at school. The same boys I smoked pot with at parties to look like I belonged with them. Maybe this was what they turned into when it was time to grow up and be boring.

"It wasn't like that." He didn't know anything. He just said all of those things because it was easy. Easy to judge me quickly and put me into the category he deemed fit.

"That's the way you're presenting yourself. Silent, sullen, misunderstood. Without words, you are every rebellious teenage girl in the world."

"You're wrong," I said. He was. He had to be. Before I was friends with Lila and Cassie, I had been every teenage girl in the world. Being rebellious made me special—at least, that's what I had thought.

That equals special, when it's as close as you're ever going to get.

Of course there had been others before me. Kids just like me who stared out from the pages of my shiny yearbook and said, *Be like me and become yourself.*

Probably a kid just like he had been. Maybe that was why he thought he knew all about me.

"Okay, then what is it that should make any judge care about you or not? What makes you matter?"

I said nothing. I had no answer. I had been searching for that all through high school. The thing was, I had never been called on it before.

I wondered if he had ever sat in a room like this one while a therapist of his own forced him to defend the person *he* was. Maybe that was why he'd become a therapist, because he had no defense.

"That is what we're looking for. That will get you probation," he said, grabbing a date book off his desk. "Are you ready to let me help you?"

"How can you help me?" I asked.

"Keep coming here, start talking, start realizing that I am not the enemy," he said.

"I don't think you're the enemy," I said, even though I kind of did. Adults were the enemy, that's what Cassie always said. Especially adults who wanted to open up your head and play around in there.

"Good," he said. "That's the first step. Just think of all we can accomplish." He leaned toward me. I could see my reflection growing larger in his glasses. Two little Amys levitating above his eyes.

Even though I heard AJ's voice in my head repeating *Screw you, screw you, screw you* like an uncontrollable mantra, I held out my hand for the appointment card.

"It's settled, then. By the way," he said, holding the door open for me, "if you'd like to start referring to me as something other than *you*, my name is Daniel."

Eight

Hungry Amy, hungry Amy, hungry Amy, AJ tweeted as I closed my bedroom door behind me. I pulled him out of his cage and put him on my shoulder, feeding him seeds from my hand as I snuggled into feathers that smelled like home.

I perched him on my finger and launched him, his yellow and green wings spreading as he flew around the room. Watching AJ always made me feel better. It reminded me of when I was little and would watch at the kitchen window as the robins flew in our yard to catch worms. So little that I believed I could be one of them when I grew up, like my father was a dentist and my mother was a mother.

Something I wish I had never admitted to Joe. Something I would never admit to Daniel.

What no one understood was that AJ was the only one who really knew *me*. He was the only one who knew the whole story, the only one I had let see me cry in the safety of my room during my freshman year of high school. Even if my mother said she shouldn't have had to ask how I was feeling, it's not like she ever did.

In high school you are not given a choice as to who you become, you are signed up long before that based on looks, smarts, and talent, and then corralled into your group. The problem was, I didn't like my group. Girls who were not popular but not dorks, either, who were not pretty but not totally disgusting. Girls who floated somewhere in between, somewhere boring; who didn't get asked on dates, who never had to stay out past curfew, who never had to lie to their parents.

Joe had still been my friend outside of school, but in school he had been rounded up, too. He'd become friends with the boys on the volleyball team, and from what I could tell, he liked it.

In my room during those nights, with AJ repeating how pretty I was and me struggling to believe it, I would lie on the floor in my pajamas and look at my yearbook that told me differently. I looked at the pictures of the chosen girls, attempting to rebuild myself with their features. Ordering their noses and eyes and chins and mouths like the yearbook was a menu. Closing my eyes and seeing the girl I could be if I only had a choice in the matter.

I would tell myself that tomorrow would be better. And then when tomorrow wasn't better, say, *Well then, next week will be better, next month, next year.*

Someday.

Back then, I still believed my life would improve if only I were patient. Obviously, I was an idiot.

But I would fool myself. It was the only way I was able to survive.

Like that day in freshman year when I decided for some insane reason to wear orange jeans. I must have looked like a traffic cone.

I was in the bathroom with one of the girls in my group. She was the one I was closest to, but we weren't really close at all. We gave nothing to each other because we wanted so much to be liked by other people.

I had yet to meet the kind of girlfriends I had heard you could have in high school: the ones who know your every thought and can finish your sentences like you're connected at the brain stem, the girls who you cross canyons of maturity with, equally dirty and out of breath when you reach the other side hand in hand.

Friends like Lila and Cassie.

We were both pretending to wash our hands. The girl from my group looked up at me, then at herself, then back at me, but she did it in a way that I was not supposed to notice.

I knew what she was doing, because I was doing the same thing, my brain working very much like one of those old room-size computers, calculating, then comparing within a decimal point each feature, each freckle: her blond hair was shorter than mine, she was paler, her eyes were brown and smaller than mine, she had a flat chest.

Using some perfect example that had been saved on my brain's hard drive, I continued to compare our features and then, based on those findings, I started complaining about how ugly I looked.

I said something like: *God, I look so horrible today.*

To which the ever-trusty girl beside me retorted: *No, I look horrible today*, just like she should.

Then it was my turn: *But look at my nose.*

Her turn: *Look at that zit with its own parking garage on my chin.*

Me: *Well, I'm fat.*

Her: *No, I'm fat.*

Me: *My hair is totally wrong.*

Her: *Are you kidding? I love it! I wish my hair looked like that.*

Me: *I'll never have a boyfriend. I'm so ugly. I should probably just get it over with and kill myself.*

Her: *Then I should kill my whole family for creating something as disgusting as I am.*

And on and on, layering on the complaints and then the compliments until the warning bell rang for our next class.

She never even mentioned my orange jeans. That was how much we could lie to each other. That was how little we cared.

That year, I could only wake up every morning because I knew there was someone worse off than I was, or at least someone who would tell me that repeatedly until I believed her.

But that was all before I was friends with Cassie and Lila, and now that I wasn't allowed to be friends with them anymore, I was right back where I started. I'd have to learn how to do everything all over again, all by myself.

No wonder I was so *sullen*, Daniel.

Putting AJ back in his cage, I couldn't help but wonder where the hell I was going to find someone who was worse off than I was now.

. . .

After my parents fell asleep that night, I went into the computer room, determined to look up Aaron online. Lila and Cassie were out of my life, but maybe he wasn't. Maybe I could find him. He had agreed to go to the prom with me, for whatever reason; he had liked me enough to say yes, even if he hadn't gone through with it.

I turned on the computer. My parents had stupid AOL, so when the computer logged on, it told them they had mail. They had mail and I had nothing.

I opened Facebook, went to Brian's profile, and there he was, Aaron Chambers: terracotta hair in a ponytail; loose, worn jeans with holes in both knees; a smile with one crooked tooth. Activities and Interests: skateboarding, horror movies, music. Relationship Status: single.

My life would have been so different if only Aaron had shown up for our date. I wouldn't be working at stupid Gas-N-Go. I wouldn't be doing whatever Dick Simon told me to do. I wouldn't be trying to keep Daniel and Joe out of my head. Lila and Cassie would still be my friends. Most likely we wouldn't even have been arrested.

Looking at Aaron's profile in the dark computer room, the monitor the only light, I could try to pretend that things hadn't gone so wrong. I could try to forget everything that had happened.

I could write our conversation in my head. Could make him say the things he was supposed to say, just like the girl in the bathroom. Hear him tell me the things I wanted to hear: *He was so happy he found me, he was sorry, prom night hadn't been his fault.*

I could try and believe it. I could try and fool myself.

Nine

Gas-N-Go was probably a place you wouldn't choose to spend more than five minutes in, and for that night at least, I had six hours to go.

"This kid," Mr. Mancini said, slapping the back of my manager, Connor, "knows everything. You have a question, you go ask him. He's got his own way of doing things and I don't want to step on his feet. Tell you the truth," he said, leaning in like he was telling me a secret, "he knows more than I do."

I wasn't sure how much of a compliment that was. I would have ventured to say that the expired milk I had been instructed to *scratch at with those girly nails of yours so the date won't show* knew more than Mr. Mancini did.

Connor would have been described as a big boy, even at twenty-two. His hair was brown and as dry and fake-looking as doll hair, and as far as I could tell, it covered every part of his body. It tufted through the neck of his Gas-N-Go polo like a baby bird reaching for food. It clothed his bare arms. I could only dream about the rest.

I smiled and nodded in that silly way you do when you're in a new place and you're not really listening at all, just nodding and saying *absolutely, great, super*, since you know that once you're on your own you're going to do what you want anyway.

"You'll have her clean the bathrooms, right?" Mancini asked.

There was no way I was cleaning the bathrooms. I had to hang on to some dignity.

"Remember that you don't want to let just anybody in there," Mr. Mancini said, looking around to see if anyone was listening. In reality, there was no one in the store. "You have to be careful who you give the key to. Someone comes in all twitchy or something, you say, 'Out of order.'"

Connor nodded and crossed his arms.

I stared at the obligatory aisle of car accessories—air fresheners in the shape of pine trees and rainbows smelling like Christmas and new cars. Windshield wiper fluid the color of blue Kool-Aid. Assorted cans of oil stacked up like soda.

"And if anything gets a little dicey, there's a baseball bat behind the counter for emergencies." Mr. Mancini sniffed and looked around. "So, you got everything?"

Everything was a red Gas-N-Go signature polo that came down to my knees and a hair net I had to wear while working in the deli that I vowed to continually lose.

As he left the store, he winked, like Connor and I were

being left alone on a couch by some perverted father who was hoping to live through his son's sexual exploits. I might have looked desperate, but there was no way I was that desperate.

We watched his truck—which was teal with pink detail so that it looked like someone had swallowed a can of paint and then puked it all over the sides of the cab—as it roared away.

"Let's start with the cash register," Connor said, indicating I should follow him behind the counter. He walked in that way you do when you've done something thousands of times before. A walk that said there were no surprises. A walk of resignation.

"How long have you been working here?" I asked, eyeing the chip and candy aisle. Things were stocked in terms of their taste-bud quotient: the remarkably salty, the obscenely sweet, the mind-numbingly sour, the throat-hackingly bitter.

"Does it matter?" He continued before I could answer. "You have to do this all manually." He turned a key on the side of the register so it was in nonrecording mode. "Why don't you try ringing up a pack of gum?"

I tried, but it didn't quite work out. I rang it up for $99 instead of $0.99.

He came around my side and voided it. "All right, now watch this time."

I didn't watch. I thought about how I had come into so many places like this without giving the people behind the counter a second thought. Now I realized they all had some reason to be there. There was no way you chose this without a metaphorical gun at your back.

"Are you listening?"

"Yes," I said, but I think he could tell I was lying.

"I know it's not rocket science, but it pays the bills. It keeps my kid in diapers," he said, shrugging.

"You have a kid?" I covered my mouth, trying to hide the shock in my voice, but luckily he didn't seem to notice.

"Two. Here," he said, reaching into his back pocket for his wallet.

I hadn't asked to see a picture, but I accepted it when he gave it to me, like you are supposed to do when someone gives you a picture of his children. "Cute," I said, like you are supposed to say when someone shows you a picture of his children.

It was one of those holiday pictures. The kids sitting on a bed of cotton meant to be snow, wearing red and green and bells and bows and holding fake wrapped presents in their hands. The cotton made them look like they were pieces of strange jewelry sitting in a box.

He smiled, like parents do when they are presenting pictures of their kids. "Do you have any?" he asked, like he was hoping this was something we could bond over.

"No," I said, so quickly I think he could tell I was offended by the question. "I'm only seventeen."

"I had my first when I was your age," he said.

I tried to picture it—me, with a *baby*. It was obvious I could barely take care of myself, but I guess I couldn't talk. What if I were still working at Gas-N-Go five years from now and training someone else? Would I tell her that I had been her age when I was arrested for the first time?

The first time. I shook my head.

"Listen, I get it. You think you're too good for this place," he said.

I had *thought* I was too good for it, but I was realizing that what I thought had little to do with reality.

"You think I want to be here?" he asked, his voice rising. "You do a poll and I would say most people would choose to be somewhere else, doing something else, and if they really had the option, being someone else."

He was right, and I hated thinking that even before all this, I was *most people.*

"But, here we are," he said. "You can choose to stay and make the best of it, or you can leave."

Make the best of it. That was something I had heard my whole life. Most of the time I could, because I wanted to believe something was waiting for me at the end of the tunnel I was perpetually looking through. But now, what was the point?

He tapped his foot. "You just take all the time you need. It's not like we're on the clock or anything."

I looked at the cash register. I looked at him. I shrugged.

"Why don't you just get going on those bathrooms? I find the bathroom to be a place of serenity, especially the ones here. They'll give you a lot of time to work things out."

"You find cleaning up after other people's crap to be some kind of meditative experience?"

"Only when I'm not the one doing it," he said, handing me a mop and bucket.

• • •

After work, I walked home. The town was so quiet that it looked like a movie set—building façades darkened, houses with porch lights on, gaslights lining the street every twenty feet like Johnny Appleseed had planted them that way.

On nights like this, Cassie, Lila, and I would hang out in the oceans of cemetery that surrounded our town. We would stumble, drunk, down the rows next to all those grocery-store flowers, still in their plastic, still with the price tags on. Maroon bows holding the stems together, sitting in their stands, petals fluttering and ribbons blowing like wind socks in the breeze. We would dance past the high obelisk stones set up like a giant chess game, past stones flat to the ground like fallen dominoes, past stones popping out of the soil like vegetables in a garden. I always wondered, if we could be there like that, could death really mean anything? Could life?

Homework-doing and dishwasher-emptying and everyday-ness and who the hell we were meant to be became noiseless whispers when we were faced with the death that bordered our town, squeezed at it like a clutching fist.

It would never be that way again.

A few blocks from my house, I heard Joe's bike coming up behind me. I'd ridden around with him enough after dinner in middle school to recognize the sound. It was so distinct that I used to know from the dinner table that he was coming up my driveway, in the summer when the windows were open. The bell was broken so it jingled when he rode it. You would have thought he would have just taken the bell off, but then you would have thought a lot of things about Joe.

"I heard what happened," he said, pedaling up next to me. He was wearing his varsity volleyball jacket. A big white ball on the right shoulder, his name embroidered on the left.

I knew someone would confront me about the arrest eventually. I guess I'd just hoped it would be someone else.

"Nothing happened," I said. I looked up. The stars were faint, like they all needed their bulbs changed.

"Okay," he said, walking his bike next to me. The tires clicked like a prize wheel. "I won't say *I told you so*."

"You never told me anything," I said, lighting a cigarette. But that wasn't true. He had told me to stay away from Cassie and Lila. Not that he knew what he was talking about.

"No," he said. "You just didn't listen." Then he made a big deal about coughing and waving the smoke out of his face.

I tipped my head back and exhaled, the smoke shooting up like water from a whale's blowhole. "I'm not in the mood, Joe."

"I'm not judging. I'm just talking to you."

"It's the same thing," I said. Maybe he thought that because he was on his bike, that bike, he could talk to me this way. But he couldn't.

He looked at me. The silence made me anxious. I tried not to think about what he'd said the last time I saw him. Maybe I used to be nice, but nice was boring. Nice hadn't gotten me anywhere. I was still figuring out where mean was going to get me.

"So, that's it, then?" He gripped his handlebars tighter,

another trick he used to keep his hands still.

"I guess." I was glad we were done. I was afraid that if we kept talking, I might break down and start crying right there on the street. It would have been easy to talk to him like I had when we were who we used to be. When we would hide under his porch with peanut butter and strawberry jelly sandwiches and grape-juice boxes. But I didn't know him anymore. He was a stranger. Like Daniel, like anyone else who was trying to pretend they gave a crap.

Joe had wanted to keep the old Amy in a little box that he could take out after school and on weekends to be her friend when he was bored. And when that wasn't good enough for me, I became not good enough for him.

I stopped and stomped out my cigarette.

"You should have stayed at the prom." He shrugged.

I guess we *weren't* done. I guess he was going to try to present his simple Boy Scouts solution to a far more complicated situation. Like he always did.

"You didn't let me in, remember? You and your *girlfriend*." I wasn't sure why my voice had such an edge to it. Maybe because I didn't want to believe the words.

"Leslie's not my girlfriend."

"Whatever," I said. I didn't care if Leslie was his girlfriend. I didn't care about any of this. I started walking faster. It was stupid. It wasn't like I could outwalk his bike, but I wanted to get away from him. From everything he made me think about and not want to think about.

"You still should have stayed," he said.

I wondered whether, if he'd known how things would

turn out that night, he would have let us stay, even without our sacred tickets. He probably would have, but he didn't, and he hadn't, and it was too late now.

"My mom is even more naggy than usual, so…," I said, making the international sign for *Hurry up*.

"I'm on my way out, anyway," he said, hopping back on his bike. He took his right hand off the handlebar and shakily saluted me. What he used to do when we were little and he thought I was being bossy.

I stood there. I didn't know how to react. If I had been the old me I would have laughed. I would have laughed and he would have laughed. But I was the new me, so I stood there. The street was dark and quiet.

He pedaled away, the bell on his bike becoming fainter and fainter as his back reflector light got smaller and smaller, like a lens closing, as he made his way down the street.

• • •

I found my mother lying on the couch, waiting up to make sure I came home. Not only because this was what she always did, but because Dick Simon had told her that I couldn't get in any more trouble, which just gave her another excuse to be a total pain in my ass.

She was watching David Letterman with one eye open and one eye flat and closed against the pillow. She wore her flannel nightgown even though it was summer. I guess she wanted to look the part for her newly instated nightly vigil. Like some sailor's wife on a widow's walk, a lit candle held in her praying hands.

"How was it?" she asked, sitting up and looking at me. The TV covered her pale pink nightgown and exposed skin with fluorescent blue.

Freshman year, that used to be a question I could answer, when I went to dances and football games and came home at a decent hour. When I could say *Fine* and that was all I ever had to say, even if it wasn't true. It was better than going back over whatever trauma I had suffered. It was easier than saying the real words.

Not this time.

"It sucked. I feel like I'm losing ten brain cells for every minute I'm standing behind that counter."

"Don't take this out on me." She squinted. "Besides, that's probably less than you were losing when you were spending all your time smoking those doobies."

"Great, Mom, perfect. For your information, no one has 'smoked a doobie' since 1979."

I saw a light flick on behind her eyes, like she'd remembered our appointment with Daniel and she was determined to prove that she really was trying. "I care about you, Amy," she said in her practiced *I am a good parent and I'm doing the best I can* voice.

I turned away from her, practically running for the refuge of my room, which that night felt like no refuge at all. As I walked up the blue-carpeted stairs I had walked on every day since I was five, I realized that my room was not mine. I hadn't chosen to live in it, just like I hadn't chosen to live in this house, or live on this street, or be born into this family.

I hated my room and everything in it. I hated the pink

Lisa Burstein

carpet. I hated the sheets on my bed. I'd liked them when I received them for my thirteenth birthday, to replace my cartoon-character ones. But that night, I realized sheets were a pretty crappy birthday gift.

I lit a cigarette and smoked out the window, but it felt like Joe's house was staring at me. I stubbed it out and yanked down the shade. I even hated my view.

I hadn't gotten any of the things in this room because I'd really wanted them. I had gotten them because they were what my mother thought I was supposed to have. She had bought me all of these things because she was trying desperately to turn me into the daughter she wanted me to be.

There was no chance of that anymore.

I grabbed a sleeping bag from my closet, and AJ's cage, and made my way back downstairs.

My mother was still lying on the couch. "There's dinner in the fridge," she said.

I ignored her and unlocked the basement door.

"What are you doing?"

"This is my new room." I rolled the sleeping bag down the basement stairs and hugged AJ's cage tightly.

"You've got to be kidding."

I walked down the stairs before she could say anything else.

She followed me, ducking her head so she didn't hit the ceiling. "There's no reason to get dramatic."

"I'm moving out. I can't live here anymore."

"Living in the basement is not moving out."

"It's as close to it as I can get." I set my sleeping bag on the small green carpet and hung AJ's cage from one of the rafters on the ceiling.

"This is insane. Where's your father?"

I got into the sleeping bag and turned away from her, watching AJ's cage swing back and forth, back and forth.

"Amy, please, it's disgusting down here," she said.

Usually the wavering in her voice would have been enough to make me turn and look at her, but everything was different now.

"Fine," she said, walking up the stairs, "do what you want. Live down here all alone; see if I care. I'm going to bed." She slammed the door behind her.

It *was* dirty; I had to give her that. It was also uncomfortable, and I hadn't had enough arms to carry both AJ and a pillow, so my head lay right on that terrible green burlap carpet that looked like puked-up spinach. It was itchy and with my only other option being sleeping on concrete, I made a covert mission back up the stairs to get my mattress and pillow.

While I was in my room gathering supplies, I called Lila's cell. My mother hadn't thought to take the cordless phone out of my room.

Before the arrest, Lila, Cassie, and I were together all the time. It was hard to believe that it had been almost a week since I had spoken to either of them. It made my stomach feel like I was going down the first huge hill of a roller coaster when I thought about it.

"Amy, oh my God, how are you?" Lila whispered as she picked up the phone.

"Horrible," I said. It felt so good not to lie. I was horrible. I was worse than horrible.

"Aren't you on twenty-four-hour watch or something?" Lila whispered.

"You still have your phone?" I asked. It was a dumb question. I mean, I had called her, but I was surprised.

"The police said I should keep it in case Brian tries to call me."

She was talking to the police. Why wasn't I talking to the police?

I could hear her climb out the window to her balcony and light a cigarette.

"Have you talked to Cassie?" I asked, mostly out of selfishness. I didn't want them to become inseparable in my absence.

"Forget Cassie." She took a drag. "Have you?"

"No," I said.

"Good," she said.

At least one nice thing was coming out of this—I was the favorite now.

I heard her dog, Barnaby, bark as he settled down in his customary position next to her. She adored him, even though he was the most disgusting thing I had ever seen. He was sheared, with a terrier's head and long spindly legs like a goat. Sometimes I felt like the human version of Barnaby.

I listened to the air on the line. I could hear cars going by and the smoke exhaling out of her lungs like a sigh.

I wanted to say I missed her, that I didn't blame her. But I was too scared, because I knew if I did she would have to reciprocate. "Are you okay?" I asked.

"I'm bored," she said. "And horrible." She laughed.

"I know," I said.

"My fingers are still black from that ink," she said.

I looked at my hands, still painted with that light blue polish. They were chipping.

"Mine are okay," I said. What were we even talking about?

"This sucks," she said.

"I know," I said.

We sat there, quiet, listening to each other breathe, until she said she heard her mom coming and had to go. As much as I hated to realize it, we had nothing else to say anyway. This was my life now. Without Cassie and Lila it was like I was on a seesaw minus one kid, lonely and powerless.

After I hung up I went to the bathroom. I poured nail-polish remover onto a cotton ball and breathed in, filling my nostrils with the horrible smell. I scrubbed my nails clean, until they were pink and raw. Then I took the bottle of polish off my nightstand and threw it in the trash.

Ten

The next morning I woke up facedown and open-mouthed on the basement floor. I looked with bleary eyes around my new home.

I was surrounded by boxes filled with old winter clothes, shoes that had lost their mates, and clothes I had grown out of—hand-me-downs waiting to be handed down to someone who never came. They were filled with my parents' old notebooks from college, photo albums from before they knew me, and wedding presents they'd never used. Things my parents no longer wanted to look at but couldn't bear to part with.

There were shelves stacked with the books I'd loved as a child. All the girls I'd wanted to be like. A pile of yellow hardback Nancy Drew books, shiny paperback Ramona books, a pale purple copy of *Margaret*. Ramona didn't care; she told the world to piss off with her short hair and freckles. Margaret, with her hair like spun gold, cared too much. Nancy, the fiery redhead, was too smart to worry about anything.

When I was young, I'd wished for their strength and wit and intelligence and compassion. Their words were my words, but then one day they were gone.

As I got older, I had to live in images. Started living with an outlined face and body layered upon me by a huge overhead projector lit by the sun. Staying with me constantly, reminding me and everyone else of what I was not.

I went upstairs and found my father sitting at the kitchen table, eating his morning bagel and staring. I grabbed some coffee and settled into the seat I always sat in. My mother and father had a seat they always fought over, the one at the head of the table, and my father sat in it that morning, as he would when my mother wasn't around. Even before the arrest, I lived a life of fascination and intrigue.

"How's life down under?" my father asked, waking from his trance to look at me.

I shrugged. I knew he had asked in an attempt to make me laugh, had probably been working on that line since my mother had told him about my decision, but I wasn't in the mood.

"Have you seen this yet?" He held up the *Collinsville News* and shook it for emphasis.

"What now?" I asked.

He tossed it over to me. It was open to the Police Blotter. I read the following: *Three local girls arrested in connection with area-wide drug-distribution ring, caught en route from the Collinsville South High Prom.*

"Your mother thinks we'll have news crews camped out on our lawn," he said.

I was less concerned about that and more concerned that it was now forever in black and white that we had been dateless for the prom.

"It doesn't even use our names."

"She still thinks people will know," he said.

I guess that was how Joe had found out.

But my mother wasn't worried about Joe; she was worried about her supposed friends and acquaintances, who from what I could tell would corner her at the grocery store, their carts boxing her in at right angles, wedding rings tapping like timers on the hot-dog-colored hand-grips while they demanded information. Apparently the food she purchased to make dinner, perfect triangles of green, white, and brown on my plate, was supposed to be a pie chart illustrating her skill as a mother.

This news would, as my mother would say, blow that out of the water.

"You don't have to stay down there," he said, taking the paper from me.

I shook my head. Moving back into my room would be as good as telling my mother she was right, not just about sleeping in the basement, but about all of it. I grabbed the other half of his bagel and took a huge bite.

"Watch your right maxillary tooth," he said.

I closed my mouth and put my hand in front of it. I was at my father's office every couple of months for a filling.

It was lucky that he was a dentist, or my parents would be broke. It was like my teeth were made of talc. They were cavity prone, sensitive, and, before braces, had looked like fence posts put in by a blind man.

"Where is she?" I asked, trying to gauge how much longer I had to drink my coffee before slipping back downstairs and locking the door.

"She's getting ready for your big shopping trip," he said, grabbing the other half of his bagel.

Were we going to buy my supplies for jail, like we had every year when I went to summer camp? Going down the list Camp Eagle Lake provided and buying a flashlight and bug spray and a rain poncho?

My father must have sensed my confusion because he said, "I don't know, for your arraignment. I get a new tie. Don't let her buy anything with yellow. She's been trying to convince me all morning that yellow is calming." He shook his head. "Well, not to me."

I got up and looked at the calendar that sat on the desk next to the kitchen phone. Sure enough, *Amy's Arraignment* was written in my mother's script in the square two days from now. It was written no differently than *Marilyn's Birthday*, which was three days after my arraignment and *Amy's Graduation*, which was written two Sundays after that.

Who the hell was Marilyn?

"You'd better get ready," he said. I knew he couldn't care less if I wore a burlap sack, but if I wasn't ready and my mom came down, she would blame him for not making me get dressed.

"Great, this is just what I want to do today," I said, slamming down the calendar.

"You had other plans?" he asked, giving me a cream-cheesy kiss on the cheek as he made his way upstairs.

I guess he had a point.

. . .

My mother spun around, trying to get her bearings. This was how she always looked when she entered a department store. Like she was playing Pin the Tail on the Donkey and someone had just put the blindfold on her and spun her around, dizzying her beyond all hope of rational thought. That was what clothes did to her.

I looked through the store, searching for a red ponytail. Maybe Aaron was there. I knew it was about as likely as Lila or Cassie showing up, but it didn't hurt to daydream.

I hadn't had the nerve to send him a friend request, so I wasn't sure what I would do if I actually ever did see him in person. Probably nothing. Especially that day, considering I was at the mall with my mother buying a freaking suit.

"How about Smart Separates? Or, no, Working Woman," she said, snapping her fingers. My mother believed in the power of shopping and therefore she believed in the vocabulary of it. If there were an area of the store called *Amazing Arraignment,* we would definitely be looking there.

"These are perfect," she said, handing me a stack of suits, which she slung over my arm like a huge, unwieldy coat.

"Yuck," I said.

"Stop complaining. Debra Lippitz and her daughter go shopping together all the time," she said.

"Debra Lippitz's daughter has crabs," I said. I wasn't trying to be snarky—she really did.

"Go try those, and I'll find some more," she said, ignoring me and darting off into the racks.

I ran toward the solitude of the dressing room. Of course, the full-length mirror inside would have its own disappoint-ments, but I would take dealing with a fat ass over dealing with my mother any day. At least you can do something about a fat ass, in theory.

I came out in the first suit, a navy-blue pinstripe, to find my mother sitting on one of the chairs provided for waiting mothers, her ankles crossed, rubbing at some dirt on her pants.

"That is just darling," she said, standing and fussing with the collar. And I could see in her eyes the hope that I would wear this to a job interview someday. I decided not to remind her that the only place I would be wearing this suit was to court. That afterward it would sit in my closet gathering dust, just like all the other lame clothes she bought me.

An elderly saleswoman with white-blond hair like cotton candy poked her head in. "So, what's the occasion?"

"Possession with intent to sell," I said under my breath.

My mother glared at me. "No occasion," she said. "It never hurts to have a good suit in your wardrobe."

"Absolutely," the saleswoman said, nodding. "How can I help?"

"Maybe something a little brighter. It is almost summer,

after all," my mother said.

"Do you have anything that screams, 'I'm innocent'?" I asked.

"You know, to match her age," my mother said, glaring at me again.

"I think we have something in peach. I'll just go get it," the woman said, shuffling out onto the sales floor, her hair leading the way.

"Peach? What am I, a cruise director?"

"You'll try on what she brings because it's polite. Trying something on doesn't hurt anyone," she said, crunching on her index finger.

I decided not to respond. There was really no rational way to discuss the color peach.

"And stop talking about your problem," she whispered.

My problem, like it was an oozing growth or a sexually transmitted disease. Truthfully, either one would have been preferable to what was awaiting me.

"What do you think of this?" she asked, pulling at the sleeves.

"I hate it," I said.

"I suppose, dear, you'd rather wear something lying on your floor right now, maybe your jeans with the hole in the crotch? That will really make a good impression." *Dear* was not a term of endearment for my mother. She used it the way a fairy-tale witch would.

The saleswoman came back and handed me a pile of peach fabric and pearl buttons. "We also have one in sea-foam green, which I thought would be just beautiful with your eyes," she said, handing me another pile that was the color of Comet.

To think that after all those years of searching, the perfect thing to accentuate my beauty was right under our sink.

I wanted to say something, but I couldn't figure out what, so instead I went back into the dressing room and sat on the floor, my knees up to my chest, my arms crossed over them. It was as much energy as I could expend on a tantrum.

"Get up," my mother hissed through the curtain.

"No," I said, not because I didn't want to get up, but because I didn't want to do anything she told me to at that moment. I didn't want to do anything anyone told me to at that moment. I was tired of this, and it was only just beginning.

"Please, Amy, not now, okay? Just one more," she said, poking her head through the curtain, trying to sound like she was offering me a compromise.

How had it come to *this*? To my mother begging me to try on suits for my first appearance in court? I felt nauseous.

"Fine," she said, walking into the room, "get up. We'll just buy this one."

"Does that mean we can go home now?" I said, looking forward to spending the afternoon smoking cigarettes in my new room with AJ.

She looked at me in disbelief. "Shoes," she said. "Of course, navy is a hard color to match and with a navy suit, you really need navy pumps. Finding the right color could take some time."

I suppose I shouldn't have been surprised that the

first and only suit I tried on basically shackled me to my mother for the rest of the day. I hoped the shoe store had a smoking section.

Eleven

I guess you could say I met Lila and Cassie because of a cigarette. And I'd rather say that, because then I don't have to admit I was hiding.

It was the first football game of my sophomore year and I'd done what I thought I was supposed to. I'd helped put streamers on the float and had painted my face half blue, but my school spirit was low. I was tired of acting like I was friends with all the people around me, and I was tired of them acting like it, too; at least the ones who were desperate enough to bother.

When our float rode onto the field pulled by an old pickup truck, we were supposed to scream *Sophomores!* over and over until our throats burned, but I couldn't do it. I couldn't pretend anymore.

I just wanted to get *away*. The faces around me were half blue like mine, but their mouths were open and I could tell they were feeling something I wasn't—like they belonged. Something I didn't know if I would ever feel.

Instead of watching the game in a line of half-blue faces like I was supposed to, I ducked under the bleachers on the visitors' side of the field. I walked to the far corner, the game noise and lights far away as I sat on the cold ground against a metal beam. I rubbed at the blue side of my face with my sweater while I tried to figure out how long I had to wait before it would seem normal for me to go home and be with AJ.

I saw a lighter spark at the other end of the bleachers. Two girls stood there, one tall, one short, neither with their faces painted half blue like mine.

I scooted up against the metal beam and tried not to breathe.

"We see you," the tall girl said. I knew her name was Cassie, but I didn't really know her. She scared me. I think she scared everyone.

I didn't respond. Just sat there hoping that if I didn't talk or move, they would go away. Ignore me like everyone else did so I could sit there until the game was over, and then go home and act like I was supposed to act again, so at least my parents would think I was normal.

"Hello?" Cassie said with an exaggerated wave. "Maybe she's deaf." I heard her laugh.

I still didn't answer. I was invisible to everyone else, so why not to them?

"Hello?" she said again.

"Leave her alone," the short girl said. I knew her name was Lila, but I didn't really know her, either. She was in my

English class and all the boys liked her a lot, even though she acted like she didn't care.

"No," Cassie said, "she's weirding me out sitting over there all alone. Yoo-hoo, Earth to freak girl sitting in the dark."

"What?" I said, not moving. I *was* a freak girl sitting in the dark, but I guess I didn't want her to think that I was.

"What the hell are you doing over there?" Cassie asked.

"Sitting," I said. "Waiting, hating," I mumbled.

"You want one?" Lila said, showing me her cigarette.

"You look like you need one, Smurfette," Cassie said.

"No thanks," I said, touching my face. My fingers came away blue. I'd never smoked before. I didn't want to look like an idiot. Well, like more of an idiot.

"Hey, aren't you in my English class?" Lila asked.

"Yeah," I said, feeling weirdly happy that she'd realized it, too.

"Mr. Rudolph is such a skeeve," she said.

She wasn't just saying that; it was true. We were reading *Romeo and Juliet* and he always read the part of Romeo, but he was no Romeo. He was a gross old man. He said the boys in class were too immature to understand the complexity of tone in Shakespeare, but it seemed to me and anyone else with eyes that it was because he was a total perv.

"He's sick," I agreed.

"There's probably, like, a whole course English teachers take on how to flirt with their students without getting sued," Lila said.

"Yeah," I said. "It's called *Adolescent Ass-Chasing 101*." It wasn't my line; it was Joe's. We'd had this conversation before. He had Mr. Rudolph fourth period.

Lila laughed. "You're funny," she said.

"Um, hello, I'm *not* in your English class," Cassie said. "So either come over here and smoke with us, or shut the fuck up."

"Cassie, jeez." Lila giggled.

"What? She keeps yelling like that, someone is going to come down here and bust us."

"Sorry," I said, walking over.

"Why did you do that shit to your face?" Cassie asked, handing me a cigarette. I held it, not ready to put it in my mouth yet.

"School spirit," I said. I knew I sounded like a total dork, but it was better than the real answer. Because I was a minion, because I did what I thought I was supposed to do to fit in. It was obvious these girls did not.

"You shouldn't let them do that to you," Lila said, as if she could read my mind.

"I did it," I said. I had put it on in my bathroom. Wiping the blue makeup on my sad face, like a disillusioned clown.

"That's not what I meant," Lila said. She sucked on her cigarette.

It was easy for her to say—the way she looked, no one could make her do anything. But she didn't have to say it to me, either.

"You look dumb," Cassie said.

"I know." I felt my stomach braid up like pretzel dough.

"She just looks like the rest of them," Lila said. It made me hate that I had ever wanted to.

"Yeah," Cassie said. "Dumb."

"You going to light that?" Lila asked, passing me a lighter.

I lit it and immediately started coughing like something had gone down the wrong tube.

"Not so much," Lila said, rubbing my back. She was so pretty. "Don't inhale at first."

"Thanks," I said. I could feel my eyes watering, probably making trails down the blue side of my face. I heard the crowd erupt into cheers. Our team had scored.

"So, you got any cute older brothers?" Lila asked.

"No," I said, "just me."

"Figures," Cassie said. "That's a minus one for you." She pointed at me with her cigarette. "How much money do you have?"

"On me?"

"No, stupid, like your parents," she said.

"Cassie, seriously?" Lila laughed.

"What? I'm just trying to figure out what we're dealing with."

"I'm not really sure," I said. I mean, I knew we *had* money. Enough for a house and a yard and a bird and anything else I wanted, but no one my age had ever asked me about it before.

"On a scale of one to ten," Cassie said.

"I don't know," I said.

"If you don't know, then you have money," Cassie said. "We need to start hanging out at her house." Cassie looked at Lila.

Lila shrugged.

"So, can we stay at your place tonight?" Cassie asked.

"Me?" I asked, feeling stupid.

"No," Cassie said, "the other girl whose face has blue balls."

I thought of my pink room. I thought of AJ. I thought of my mother. If I was actually going to be friends with these girls, there was no way they could see *any* of that.

"Another night?" I said, hoping I hadn't just ruined everything.

The crowd was heavy with boos, a bad call for our team.

"Listen to the cows," Cassie said.

"More like sheep," Lila retorted.

I just listened, leaning against the back of the bleachers like they were, the cigarette still smoking in my hand. I took another drag, not inhaling this time. It went down smoother. I exhaled the smoke back out, the way I used to pretend to when I was little and the cold turned my breath to steam.

"We can stay at my house tonight," Lila said.

I looked down. I didn't want to appear too eager. I had been burned by my eagerness before.

"Okay." Cassie shrugged. "At least I don't have to go home."

"Cool," Lila said. "Let's go."

I stood there, unsure of what to do. I put out the cigarette, my boot squishing it like a bug.

"You coming, Smurfette?" Cassie asked.

I looked at Lila. I guess I needed reassurance.

"I have an extra sleeping bag," she said, smiling her Lila smile that no one could say no to.

"She has soap, too," Cassie said.

I rubbed at my face. That stupid blue paint.

"It's still there." Lila laughed.

"Come on already," Cassie said. "My pubic hair is turning gray."

I followed them out from under the bleachers and away from the game. Even though I was nervous, I didn't feel like I was doing it because I *had* to. Even though I barely knew them, it felt like they were the ones I should have been screaming *Sophomores!* with.

Maybe it was because they were saying all the things I thought but was too afraid to say. Maybe it was because they were actually talking to me, instead of talking to me while they were looking around for someone more popular to talk to. Of course, it's not like the popular kids hung out under the bleachers.

That night, we wandered the streets of Lila's neighborhood, singing at the tops of our lungs. Ringing her neighbors' doorbells at 2:00 a.m. and running into the bushes before they shuffled down the stairs to answer. We lay on Lila's driveway counting stars, cigarettes in our mouths like smokestacks. That night I was finally able to tell the world who I really was; who I really wanted to be.

Lila and Cassie were going to help me get there.

Twelve

To find the perfect place for me to make it look like I gave a crap, I went to see some female social worker that Daniel recommended. The minute I saw her I knew why she was there. It wasn't so much out of the goodness of her heart, but because nobody else would have her. She had warts all over her face and was balding. In fact, she had more hair on her warts than she did on her head. I guess charity work not only made people feel good inside, it also gave ugly people somewhere to go.

I felt bad thinking it, especially when I realized I was standing there, too.

I was about to turn and run, when a sickly sweet whisper came out from between her lips, a combination of a life spent whispering under one's breath and a new life in a position of questionable authority.

She asked me personality-based questions about which

colors and shapes I preferred and how I dealt with certain improbable situations and feelings. The sum of my answers, which it seemed to me had about as much scientific significance as a quiz from a magazine, told her I would do my best work with a roadside cleanup crew. Forget children, the homeless, and the elderly—my calling was trash.

I was sent to volunteer with an organization devoted to taking girls like me and turning them into girls who were not like me. It was volunteer work combined with a weird sort of rehabilitation therapy. I'm not sure about rehabilitation, but it definitely crossed garbage man off my list of possible career choices.

At 6:00 a.m. on the morning following my test, my mother dropped me off at the designated rest stop on the highway.

"Where are they?" I asked, finding the expected white van, but seeing no one in or around it.

"Just go; you'll be late," my mother said, already hitting reverse.

I didn't move, hoping I'd been left behind. Hoping I could go home and go back to bed.

She slammed the car into park. "Do you want me to come…?"

I opened the door and jumped out of the car before she could even finish. The answer to that was *no, no, no.*

I had learned my lesson from past instances when I had allowed her to act as my ambassador. The worst of these times was when she took me to the doctor because I wasn't getting my period.

She talked about it like it was Punxsutawney Phil, the

Lisa Burstein

famous groundhog who had to see his shadow in order for there to be a shorter winter. To her, the question the onset of my period answered was whether I was a freak or not. And every month it didn't appear, my body was saying, *It's just as you suspected.*

As birthdays thirteen and fourteen and fifteen passed and nothing came, my mother would look at me over the breakfast table every one of those mornings for all those years with the same question in her eyes. Since I couldn't provide her with the answer she wanted, she would ask my father about it and he would say what he always said when she asked him about anything medical.

"Beverly, I'm a dentist."

And she would say, "Well, in your professional opinion?"

And he would say, looking at me and smiling his sappy dad smile, "From what I can see, she's just holding onto being my little girl for as long as possible."

In my embarrassment, I would pray for the gods of puberty to bring my period on like a torrent, so it would flood the house and kill them both.

At sixteen, I was booked an appointment with my mother's gynecologist, my great-uncle Saul. It was very messed up that my mother saw my father's uncle as her gynecologist, but it was even more messed up that at every family holiday I had to sit at that long table and watch him eat with the same hands he would have all over my uterus.

When we got to the office, my mother went up to the receptionist's window while I sat in one of the chairs ringing the waiting area. There were three other women and all of them had that curly, old-woman hair that was set weekly. I doubted any of them had menstruated in the past thirty years. If I had to start a conversation with one of these women, at least we would have this in common.

"Is that Amy?" I heard someone ask, and I looked up to see the squat, frog-faced receptionist stand. "Get over here, girl," she said, clapping her hands like she was calling a dog. "There's no reason to be shy."

I didn't move. I was trying to pretend that I was fully enthralled in the pamphlet I was reading—*Genital Warts and You*—and that I hadn't heard her.

"Amy," my mother hissed, "come here and meet Margie."

Genital warts would have to wait. I huffed and walked to the window.

"I have just heard so much about you," she said, with a smile that looked like someone had slit her face from cheekbone to cheekbone.

"Thank you." I had never heard a thing about her.

"I know all about your problem," she whispered.

I glared at my mother. Apparently she'd heard *everything* about me.

"Amy, it's fine," my mother said, "Margie's a medical professional."

Somehow that was little consolation, considering I was moments away from basically getting to third base with my great-uncle.

"I wouldn't worry about it one bit," she said. "Some girls are just slaves to the pituitary. I myself started when I was in sixth grade. Came like it had been coming for years, but I had a cousin didn't get a little ketchup with her steak till she was in college."

Gross.

Waiting in the examination room wasn't much better. The fact that we were family didn't give us any special privileges. I still had to wear one of those surgical-green patient gowns. I still had to sit up on the table with the butcher paper. I still had to have my mom smoothing out the gown, saying, "Gosh, is this thing wrinkled," and putting her hands to work like makeshift irons.

"I don't understand what he's checking for. I mean, if nothing's happening, what is he going to be able to see?"

"Just be quiet; you're lucky we have someone to go to about this sort of thing."

The luck o' the Jewish: there was always some doctor in your family you could go to with your most humiliating problems.

There was a knock at the door, and then it opened to reveal my great-uncle Saul. "Hey, hey, hello," he said, looking at his clipboard, I'm sure as much out of habit as anything else. He took a seat on the wheel-around stool that later would enable him to be at eye-level with my crotch. "So I understand you haven't started menstruating yet?"

I felt my cheeks burn. I couldn't believe a man was asking me that question, especially one who used to make quarters magically emerge from my ears.

"Yes," my mother said, "just like I told you on the phone. There's something wrong."

And, for some reason, this hit me hard. Not only did she think I was a freak, she wasn't afraid to tell countless other people that, too.

"Well, as I said, there's probably nothing to worry about, but better safe than sorry, right? In reality," he said, lowering his voice and cupping a hand at the side of his mouth, "your mother told me that if I didn't check you out, she would stop bringing her famous Jell-O mold to Shabbat dinner. I couldn't risk it."

My mother smiled like some schoolgirl. Compliment her about anything, even a Jell-O mold—which she only needed to boil water in order to make—and she turned to, well, Jell-O.

"What was it you said about her breasts?" she asked, looking serious again.

This was too much.

"Menses onset usually occurs with the growth of breasts and the appearance of pubic hair."

"Well," she said, pointing at me, "she's obviously way past onset."

I pulled the paper robe tighter around me. I had to escape. I looked around, wondering if an anatomically correct model of fallopian tubes could be used as a deadly weapon.

"She's sixteen already. She's late, right?"

"It could be her diet. Do you drink enough milk?"

"Milk is for babies."

"We'll stop at the store on the way home," my mom said, smiling at Uncle Saul.

"Whole milk." He nodded. "None of that watery junk."

Great. When I finally became a woman, I would be totally fat.

"Okay," he said, putting on a pair of latex gloves with a *snap*. "Let's take a look."

I got my period two months later, which my mother insisted must have been because of her whole-milk campaign. My guess was that it was really my body exploding with repulsion at the prospect of another visit to Uncle Saul.

· · ·

I finally saw a woman yelling through a megaphone. She looked like a lifeguard, or at least she was dressed like one. She wore a white tank top and khaki cargo shorts, with a whistle around her neck. On her head was a hat complete with plastic shark teeth.

"I guess you think you can show up whenever you want."

Next to her stood five girls about my age, each wearing an orange vest.

She threw one on the ground in front of me. "That's yours. Let's go." She turned to the girls. "What do we say to people who think they get to live by their own rules?"

"No siree, Bob," they said in unenthusiastic unison.

"That's right," she said, putting the megaphone to her lips again as if she had just remembered she still had it. "You get here on time all the time, or you walk." She pointed to the highway. "At your own risk."

When we got to our designated mile marker, she lined us up and rode back and forth in front of us in an old-person scooter, like some paralyzed drill sergeant. "First thing you need to do," she said, screaming through the megaphone, "is to be able to admit to yourselves why you are here. You all have your reasons and I don't need to know what they are. Only *you* need to know that."

Not like we could have told her, anyway. We weren't allowed to talk to each other, or to her unless she talked to us first, which seemed like a hurdle to the whole therapy thing. Apparently I was supposed to have some sort of psychic connection with the girls around me, but I tried saying, *OMG, WTF, This f-ing sucks!* telepathically, like I might send a text, but I received no response.

"You each have your refuse sticks and bags," she said. "You will be required to pick up at least two pounds of trash, and we will stay here until every last one of you picks up your two pounds," she yelled, standing in the seat. "This is to teach you accountability to your community. You need to learn that the things you do affect those around you."

I didn't think you were supposed to spell out things like that. I thought you were supposed to allow the patient to make her own connections. Evidently she didn't have time for that.

She also didn't have time for introductions. I didn't find out her name, which was Ginny, until she passed around a time sheet. On the top was her name and below that six others that I tried to match up with the girls around me. I wondered if they were doing the same thing and if I had been mistaken for anyone else. I hoped it was the waif-thin girl with the Barbie-doll blond hair or the pretty brunette with full, red-grape-colored lips. It would have been nice to have someone see me that way for once.

We went to work, hobbling like hobos on the side of the road, scattering like little bugs on the shoulder of the highway. Ginny yelled through her megaphone as we worked, telling us to view the trash we picked up as a gathering of all the souls we affected with our drug use. To see each piece as one more person who forgave us.

I picked up an empty box of adult diapers and wondered who that was supposed to be.

"Hey," whispered the waif-thin girl with the Barbie-doll blond hair. "What'd you do?"

I looked over at Ginny. She was busy shining her megaphone. "Pot," I whispered back. "I got pulled over with my two best friends on the way from prom."

"That was you?" she said, her eyes getting wide. "Cool."

I got respect for being bad—that's something Daniel and my parents would never understand. Something Joe would never understand.

"Yeah," I said. I couldn't help basking in her admiration.

"Cocaine," she said. "Well, I got caught shoplifting, but I had cocaine on me."

"Crap," I said.

"Yup," she said. "I'm pretty much screwed."

"Me, too," I said.

"Not as much as me," she said.

"It was a lot of pot," I said.

"It was *cocaine*," she said.

"No talking," Ginny yelled from her newly shined megaphone.

Without Lila and Cassie, was this the way the rest of my life was going to be? Empty conversations with girls I barely knew and would probably never *know*, where we talked about whose life sucked more?

Like before.

We went back to work. The side of the highway is where average trash goes to die. I picked up used condoms splayed out like squashed earthworms after a rainstorm and plastic bags of unidentified brown, yellow, and green stuff. I grabbed greasy wet paper bags with any number of surprises inside: maggot-infested, half-eaten hamburgers; the contents of someone's car ashtray; fruit like rotted-out teeth. The list of shit went on and on, while Ginny yelled through her megaphone, "Remember why you are doing this. Remember that you can make a difference. That your life has consequences, that your actions have repercussions."

I tried to do what Ginny asked, but it's hard to heal when you're supposed to find significance in picking up a used tampon.

Besides, wasn't I the only person who had been affected by my drug use?

I was the one who had been arrested. I was the one who would have to answer for it and who had to go through all this crap. I was the one who had to try to figure out what to do next.

Thirteen

When my parents and I arrived for my arraignment, we found all of the lawyers schmoozing and shaking hands like they were at a cocktail party, asking about one another and one another's families in small oscillating circles around the courtroom. This was like their prom, coming together from all their small towns to the big, important courtroom in the city.

The plaintiffs and their families looked like they were waiting in line at the DMV: rows and rows of torsos and heads that sat like marble busts until their number was called. Of course, we sat all the way in the back.

My mother probably hoped that there would be less likelihood of being seen, and as for my father, he always wanted to sit in the back so he would be close to the bathroom. That day, I was thankful for his embarrassing habit, because I had been throwing up steadily all morning.

Of course, I knew I wouldn't be able to leave once the arraignment started, but I'd brought a white-and-tan Liz Claiborne purse that my mother had bought me back when she still thought she could change me.

When she saw me carrying it, she said, "At least you're finally getting some use out of that. It was a good choice with the navy suit."

I didn't tell her I planned to use it as a barf bag.

The white headband she'd made me wear dug into my scalp. I looked around the room trying to find Cassie and Lila, but I didn't see them. My mother liked to be early and so we found ourselves like this all the time—sitting in a line, my mother, my father, and me, waiting longer than other people waited for whatever we were waiting for.

The bench felt and looked like the wooden pews that filled our temple, and for a moment I found myself wondering if there was some supply store that only churches, temples, and courtrooms used.

I saw Dick Simon come in and heard him walk over to one of the groups of lawyers and give them a hearty hello. He was carrying a stack of binders, balancing them with his chin, as he made the rounds shaking everyone's hands.

"It's as cold as my wife's side of the bed in here," he said, laughing. "There's my girl." He pointed at me and walked toward us.

"How are we all doing today?" he asked, sitting next to me.

How did he think we were doing? I hate it when people say things because they're used to saying them in other situations, without any thought that they are saying them in a completely inappropriate situation now.

We all looked at him, but none of us answered. He took my hand between both of his, making it look like our hand sandwich had the meat on the outside and that the meat was moldy olive loaf.

I pulled my hand away—just because this guy was my lawyer didn't give him any right to touch me.

"Don't be nervous," he said, and I could smell ketchup on his breath, ketchup and root beer. He certainly wasn't nervous. He was gorging himself at every drive-thru in town, while I couldn't even keep down a piece of toast.

"This will be over before you know it," he said. The thing people say before you get a shot. Before something painful and horrible is about to happen.

I looked around. Cassie and Lila still weren't here. Had they gotten out of this somehow?

"Hey," he said, smiling at me, "why did the strawberry get a lawyer?"

I gagged and opened my purse.

"Because it got itself into a jam," he said, slapping his knee. Then he burped, loud and long.

My father laughed. He couldn't help himself. If I had been without an audience I might have laughed, too. Laughed and then cried.

"I always know when I'm going to win a case because I'm gassy. Don't worry, I should be able to recreate the same conditions on your trial date, if it gets that far."

Why was he talking about a trial date? I'm sure my face looked green.

"It won't get that far," he said.

"How long until Amy's case?" my mother asked, sticking her whole hand in her mouth, so she could get at all her nails at once.

"Not sure," Dick Simon said, looking around and sniffing in that way people do when they know more about something than you do. "Depends on the docket. Could be fifteen minutes, could be more."

Just like that, my destiny had been whittled down into the estimated time it took for an album to download.

Finally, Lila walked in, her mother two paces behind her and her lawyer two paces behind that. I felt myself rise involuntarily to greet her, and then felt my mother tug at the back of my jacket as she hissed, "Don't you dare."

I saw Lila look over at me. She seemed tired, had big blue bags under her eyes, a reflection of the eye shadow above them. Even from where I was sitting, I could see that her eyes looked glazed and bloodshot. I wondered if it was because she wasn't sleeping or because she had been spewing the contents of her stomach all morning like I had.

Cassie walked in with her father. Her mother walked behind them, and Cassie's lawyer walked behind all of them, like some weird wedding procession. As Cassie sat, she put her head down, not even bothering to look and see where Lila and I were sitting.

"Not to worry; those two are rookies," Dick Simon said, tipping his head toward Lila's and Cassie's lawyers. "Court appointed."

I couldn't care less about their lawyers; Lila and Cassie were not wearing suits. They weren't even wearing skirts, and they definitely weren't wearing headbands. I glared at my mother, adding yet another line to the seemingly never-ending list of all the ways she didn't get it.

At some point the judge came in, a man so tall and skinny that his robe hung like his shoulders and neck were a clothes hanger. He was younger than my father and Dick Simon and his hair was shiny with gel. I heard someone say, "All rise," and then some other stuff I couldn't bear to listen to, and before I knew it we were waiting for Case Number 276, our case, *The State of New York v. Lila, Cassie, and Amy*. We waited through real criminals: guys who were charged with possession of illegal firearms, women charged with prostitution, dirty-looking people scrubbed clean and put into orange jumpsuits to face the judge. Men charged with assault wearing shackles around their ankles and cuffs that pulled their arms behind their backs.

As I saw each one, I knew with more and more certainty that we did not belong here. We were nothing like these people. These people were real criminals. Our only crime was being stupid.

It felt like my stomach was an elevator and as I waited, it traveled down one floor for each number called until 276. At which point someone would snip the cable and it would go sailing fast to land at my feet.

There was a digital clock at the front of the courtroom below the judge's bench; it was the size and shape of a license plate, with big red numbers like a bomb timer. As I stared at it, counting down the seconds until the end of my life, it became blurry, and then the room around it became blurry, and when I looked down at my hands that had been gripping the bench in front of me, they were also blurry.

Then I heard someone call our case and say my name and everything I had been charged with, and it was like my whole head was underwater. The court reporter's voice sounded distant and muffled, in the same way it feels when you're dreaming and you try to scream, and nothing but a moan comes out.

Count one: Possession. Count two: Possession with intent to sell. Count three: Sale. Your standard PISS, as Dick Simon had put it so eloquently.

I felt Dick pull me up and take me to the front of the courtroom. We stood behind the table with the pitcher of water that no one drank from, clear plastic glasses stacked together neatly at its side.

The judge asked me the questions he had asked every plaintiff before me.

"Are you correctly named in the indictment?"

I answered "Yes," and then Dick Simon nudged me and I said, "Yes, Your Honor."

"Are you selecting Richard Simon to represent you in this case?"

And I said, "Yes, Your Honor," even though I wanted to say, *Are you kidding me?*

"Do you understand the charges brought against you?"

This I didn't answer right away, because I didn't. I didn't understand why this was happening to me. I didn't understand how I ended up in this room with a judge staring down at me, with these criminals who were nothing like me, with these people who should never have crossed paths with mine. I wanted to say that I didn't understand and I didn't agree. I wanted to yell, *I object, I object, I object.*

But instead I said, "Yes, sir," my mouth almost touching my chest because my head was down so far.

"How do you plead to the counts against you?"

Dick Simon said we were deferring our plea, and then proceeded to point out everything he'd made me do to repent for the plea we were deferring: the job, the shrink, the volunteer work. But, to his credit, he made it look like I had pursued this on my own, to help me work through whatever demons were inside me that had caused me to act out in such an antisocial and morally reprehensible way.

I could feel Cassie's eyes rolling. I could feel Lila wondering why I hadn't told her about any of this. I could feel my mother looking around, hoping no one recognized her, and my father seeing me up there on the wrong side of the courtroom and having something catch in his throat.

The judge released me until my trial. I would have that time to formulate a case, to come to some tough decisions. And, hopefully, to gain enough maturity to understand the "full impact" of what I'd done.

After my portion of the case was completed, Dick Simon rushed us out. Shielding us with his body, balancing his binders like pizza boxes, he pushed us from the courtroom like we were taking part in a fire drill. He closed the door behind him just as Lila's name was called.

"You need to detach yourself now," he said, out of breath and red in the face from hurrying us those ten feet. He leaned against the wall, wheezing. "You need to show up front that you are no longer associated with those girls in any way. That you have so separated yourself from them and from what you've done that you don't care what happens to them."

My mother and father nodded, engrossed in his every word. This was territory unfamiliar to them. They would take any advice Dick Simon gave.

But I wanted to see how Lila would react, what Cassie would say. I wanted to see if either of them would cry, or scream, or do any of the things I was too afraid to do.

I wanted to know if they were as scared as I was, and trying just as desperately to hide it.

Fourteen

"So, what are we in the mood for?" my father asked as he started the car.

What was I in the mood for? A gun with one bullet in it. A bottle of strong liquor. A rewind button. Certainly not lunch with Jerry and Beverly.

I didn't know what other families did after their daughter had been arraigned on drug charges, but my family strapped on a feed bag.

"Whatever," I said, which I had said on many other occasions when I had been asked for my opinion, but I had never truly meant it before. I hoped they didn't see it in a crying-wolf kind of way and saw it in the way it was intended—as one more sign that I had given up.

My mother glanced at my father, a look that even in profile I knew said, *Why did we have this child if she can't answer a simple question?*

I saw her turn and face the window and go through a Rolodex of restaurants in her mind, side-referencing articles she had read in magazines giving you tips for every situation. Every situation, it seemed, but what to eat after your daughter has been officially charged for selling drugs that weren't even hers.

We ended up going to one of those restaurants where the waiters and waitresses dressed up in costumes, like it was Halloween every day. It was exactly what I didn't need—loud, boisterous, terrifying.

The person who came to seat us wore a penguin suit; as he waddled us over to our table I wondered how much worse it could get. Not only was I a suspected felon, I was at this place with my parents, in a *suit.* I had been so upset about the arraignment, I hadn't even insisted that they let me go home and change first.

"I'm not hungry," I said.

"Well, you have to eat something," my mother said.

I pushed my chair away from the table and crossed my arms. I guess I was just supposed to deal with the fact that instead of actually talking about what had happened and what could happen, my parents were doing what they always did—ignoring my feelings and covering them up. On that day, it was by eating at a place they should have taken me for my birthday when I turned six.

"You can't just sit there taking up space," she said from behind her menu. "Just order something to pick at." I could hear in her voice that to her, this conversation was over.

It wasn't.

When the waitress arrived dressed as a sexy nurse, I

ordered six entrees, soup, salad, and jalapeno poppers.

"Obviously someone needs a little more time. She can't make up her mind; everything looks so good." My mother laughed. Then smiled her *Please bear with my crazy family* smile.

The waitress smiled back her *The customer is always right* smile and said she'd put their orders in.

"We know what's going on. You don't need to be difficult. This is hard on all of us," my mother said with a quiver in her voice.

"Then why are we here?" I asked. If it was so hard on all of us, why was she expecting us to stuff our faces like we were preparing to hibernate for the winter?

"Amy, listen to your mother," my father said, which was his way of saying that he wasn't, but at least one of us should be.

"So we can have one moment of peace in this horrible day." She put her menu down on the table in front of her and turned full around in her chair. "This was a great choice, wasn't it, Jerry?"

I wanted to give her the finger. Everything in my body was telling me to, but I couldn't do it. I played with the ice in my water glass.

My father was cleaning his glasses with a napkin. He used the time we fought to clean and primp up various things—his nails, his wallet, his pockets.

"I just don't understand why you can't be cheerful like her," she said, pointing with her chin to the waitress. "At least while we're out."

My father nodded, even though I was pretty sure he still

wasn't listening.

"Your grandmother was a nurse, you know," she said, as if this solidified the point she was trying to make.

"She's not a nurse, Mom, she's a waitress. It's her job to be *cheerful.*" There was an edge to my voice that I couldn't control. Why were we talking about our waitress? Why weren't we talking about me?

"Do you hear this?" She looked at my father.

He was elbow-deep in the French onion soup that had just arrived, and appeared to be more interested in the cheese that had melted over the sides of the bowl than in my mother. I couldn't blame him; French onion soup cheese probably *was* more interesting than my mother.

"Amy, stop fighting," he said, twirling the melted strands around his spoon.

"How am I supposed to react?"

"All I said was that you could at least try to enjoy yourself. She has to deal with customers all day and she's still smiling."

"Mom, she looks like a hooker."

"Well, she might look like one, but at least she hasn't been arrested for it."

"So," my father said, forever the subject changer, "Brenda's getting married."

Brenda was my father's newest and youngest hygienist. I'd only met her once, and though it was while my father was filling several cavities for me, the only thing I could remember about her was a dried-out perm and dye job. She kept trying to hold my hand and I kept pulling it away and shoving it under myself like a fussy toddler. Her insistence on intimacy bothered me more than her hair, and her hair was pretty freaking bad.

"That's wonderful. How lovely," my mother said, her voice trilling. It didn't matter who was getting married. It could be a twelve-time convicted rapist and a pit bull and it would still be *lovely*. "When's the date?" she asked, not because she really cared, but because that was what you asked when someone was getting married.

My father said he didn't know, and it forced me to think about where I would be on whatever date had been chosen. Maybe instead of going resentfully with my parents to Brenda's wedding, I wouldn't even have the option.

That day it was never more real that I could actually be locked up, and, instead of dealing with it, my parents wanted to talk about weddings and slutty waitresses.

I needed a cigarette. So I said what people say in movies when they need a cigarette. I said I needed some air.

As I walked out of the restaurant, all I could see in front of me was beautiful billowy smoke and the feel of it tugging at my lungs. Like a cartoon pie cooling on a windowsill with a beckoning finger of cinnamon steam.

The only place to smoke was right in front of the restaurant, next to one of those ashtrays that are really just trash cans filled with sand. I found the sexy nurse out there smoking with some guy dressed as a pirate and considered whether or not to tell my mother about it.

I took a cigarette out of my pocket and realized my lighter was at the table in my Liz Claiborne barf bag.

Crap.

Asking for a light from people you don't know isn't

as easy as it sounds, especially when you're dressed like a young Republican and are out with your parents. So I stood there with the unlit cigarette in my mouth, hoping one of them would notice. I must have looked like one of those guys who are about to get it from a firing squad, minus the blindfold.

After being ignored for what felt like days, I finally broke down and asked the pirate. There was no way I was asking the nurse.

He sighed and made a face like I had just asked him to help me move my grand piano across the street.

During the whole process he didn't look at me once. Which was fine, because I didn't want to look at him, either. The outer parts of his cheekbones were covered by big red zits with white pustules in the middle that looked like he had balls of butter-cream frosting stuck to his face.

The nurse did look at me. I knew she couldn't help it—being a girl, she had to make sure that she was the best-looking one in a ten-foot radius and if she wasn't, she needed to prepare herself for it.

She must have recognized me as the girl who had ordered enough food for six people and then insanely decided she wasn't hungry at all, because she started laughing. At least, I hope that was why she started laughing.

Her laugh was the last, last straw during a time filled with last straws.

"Problem?" I asked, thinking that's what Cassie would have said if she were standing next to me. Lila wouldn't have had to say anything, because people didn't laugh at Lila.

"What?"

I considered ignoring her, saying nothing and smoking my cigarette. But something in my empty stomach gave me courage. "I said, do you have a problem?"

She started laughing harder, then the pirate started laughing, which meant that anybody looking at this scene from far away would see these two and assume they were laughing at me, which they were.

I wasn't scary without Cassie. I wasn't cool without Lila.

I was just me. Wearing a suit.

Apparently the world didn't care who I wanted to be. I couldn't change who I was. And now, I didn't have Lila and Cassie to hide behind anymore, either.

I walked around the corner and sat on the curb next to a Dumpster. I could still hear them laughing, the kind of uncontainable laughter that I hadn't laughed since I'd been arrested. The kind of uncontainable laughter I would probably never laugh again.

I would definitely tell my mother I'd caught the waitress smoking.

I was just about to put out my cigarette and go back inside when I heard a skateboard coming down the street. It sounded like waves, like a conch shell against your ear. That full, empty sound.

Maybe it was Aaron. I conjured up my stupid daydream, the one I used to fill my head when I couldn't deal with any of the other stuff in there—that he would find me, that he would apologize, that he would tell me that prom night hadn't been his fault. I went through what he would say, what I would say. The same lines I had written and played over and over again.

The difference this time was that when I looked toward the sound, he really was there.

It was *him.*

Aaron.

He was skateboarding down the sidewalk like it was made of water, his red hair pulled back, wearing the same loose, worn jeans with holes in both knees from his Facebook picture. He carried a backpack, like he might have been coming from the library, but I doubted he ever went to the library.

I ducked and hid around the side of the Dumpster.

It didn't seem possible. I was full-on hallucinating. The arraignment had pushed me over the edge.

I peeked out to find him walking toward me, carrying his skateboard under his arm. He was real, but what was he doing here? Had he followed me?

I lit another cigarette with the end of my last one; any excuse to stay put, anything other than looking like I was waiting for him. Then I remembered I was wearing a suit.

"You got another one of those?" he asked. His eyes were blue. I hadn't noticed that in his picture.

My hands shook as I gave him a cigarette. I thought about Joe putting his hands in his pockets. I concentrated on trying to make them stop.

He brought a silver-and-black Zippo to his mouth, flipped it open with one hand, lit his cigarette, and slapped it shut. The whole thing took seconds, but it felt like he was doing it in slow motion. "Thanks," he said.

Maybe he had just stopped to get a cigarette. Maybe it had nothing to do with me.

It probably had nothing to do with me.

I tried to make myself say something, but I hated talking to boys. Unlike AJ, they couldn't be controlled as to what they were going to say next. I took another drag.

"I know you," he said.

I coughed and tried to pretend that what he'd said was not the reason.

He laughed. "Where do I know you from?"

I couldn't tell him. Telling him that he'd stood me up for my own prom would have been way too embarrassing. It would tell him that I still cared enough to remember.

"I'm friends with Lila and Cassie," I said, wishing I could have been wearing my favorite jeans and tight black T-shirt, wishing that my hair wasn't pulled back in a headband like I was a nun.

"What are you all dressed up for?" he asked.

Of course he hadn't followed me. If he had, he would have known that I had just come from court and that I was trying to do everything I could to forget it.

"I work here," I said, thinking fast. "I'm supposed to be a librarian."

"You don't have to lie," he said.

I shrugged. Maybe Brian had told him what happened.

"I'm Aaron," he said. He might have known about the arrest, but at least he didn't know that I'd been stalking him on Facebook. That I knew his first name, last name, *and* middle name.

"Amy," I said, waving hello with the cigarette in my hand.

He smiled. His crooked tooth looked sharp, like a shark's.

"Though you do make a cute librarian."

I tried to keep myself from coughing again. "This suit sucks," I said. It seemed cooler than saying *thank you*. It seemed cooler than getting all squishy over what he said, even though that was how I felt. "I'm only wearing it because I was just at the courthouse," I said, trying to counteract the nerdiness of the suit with some badass-ness.

He nodded. "We all have them," he said. "We're all forced to wear our stupid monkey suits for the stupid monkey man when we do something wrong."

I felt my cheeks get warm. "What did you do?" I asked.

He put a finger to his mouth and shushed.

"Wow, that bad?" I asked.

"That good," he said, flicking the ash off his cigarette.

I tried to decide if anything that had happened so far was good. There was this. This was good. Maybe this wouldn't have happened if everything else hadn't.

"What did you do?" he asked. I considered telling him, but maybe he would be able to put the pieces together. Realize that he was supposed to have been my prom date.

I shrugged.

"I'm not supposed to talk about what I did, either," he said.

I looked at his skateboard.

"You wanna try it out?" he asked.

"I'm wearing dress shoes," I said, then regretted it. Why had I reminded him I was dressed like a loser?

"So?" he said, holding the skateboard out to me upside-down, the way you might hand someone a rifle butt-first. The deck had a mural of blue sky and white-capped mountains hand-painted on it. The wheels were covered with stop-motion birds, so that when they spun it must have looked like the birds were flying.

There was more to this boy. More that I wanted to know.

"I guess I could," I said, but then I remembered my mother, sitting at the table inside eating her Cobb salad. She would come looking for me soon.

I shook my head. "I should go."

"You got a cell phone?" he asked.

"Not that I'm allowed to use anymore."

"Parents," he said. He pulled a sketchbook from his backpack. Maybe he had painted that beautiful mural. He ripped out a piece of paper, wrote something down, and handed it to me.

It was his phone number.

I tried not to act surprised, tried to act like boys gave me their numbers all the time, especially when I hadn't asked for them.

"I had to use the pay phone up the street from my house the last time they took mine away," he said. "You know who uses a pay phone? No one. It smelled like homeless ass."

I looked at him. With his number in my hand I was afraid to do anything else, to say anything else. I was afraid he would take it back, especially if my mother came out looking for me.

"I should go," I said again.

"You got another smoke?" he asked.

I gave it to him. My hand was still shaking. He put it behind his ear.

"See you around, Amy," he said. He dropped the skateboard next to him. It landed perfectly on its wheels like a cat would on its legs.

As he skated away, I looked at his number; the paper was as soft as fabric. I folded it smaller and smaller and hid it in my bra. Maybe he hadn't said what I wanted him to say, but he had found me.

He had found me.

Fifteen

I was supposed to hang up my suit so it wouldn't get wrinkled, which was why the next morning it was crumpled next to me on the basement floor, under AJ's cage.

I'd spent the night before feeding him peanut butter from my finger, which he loved but which always made him a little bit sick. He pooped all over the pants and when I showed them to my mother triumphantly, as in, *Look, I can't wear these*, she reminded me of the matching skirt just as triumphantly.

I was stuck. There was no way she was going to believe that AJ had pooped all over the skirt, too.

I had to meet my high school principal and after that I had another therapy appointment with Daniel. My mother informed me that I would have just enough time after that to eat dinner before I had to go to work. She could have told me I was supposed to go up in the space shuttle and I would have had to believe her.

I'd slept with Aaron's number in my pillowcase. I guess I wouldn't be calling him anytime soon.

My life had turned into a series of appointments, each one more unbearable than the last. Being arrested turned me into the type of person who had to look at her calendar. Of course the people I was seeing and the things I was doing totally sucked, but I guess if someone saw it without bothering to read it, I would look like a really popular person.

I tried not to think how sad even having that thought was.

"Get ready; we're going to be late," she said.

When I asked my mother what loophole had been discovered that allowed me back on school grounds since my suspension, she answered that when a parental guardian accompanies you, you can go anywhere.

Yeah, anywhere that sucks.

I could only assume I was being called back to the hallowed halls of Collinsville South High for another one of Mr. Morgan's life lessons. The stories he had told me every time I was called into his office. They all had the same gist to them. Good kid—in my case, good girl turns bad—ends up poor, pregnant, or dead. The means by which she got to each of these ends was always different, depending on what I had been caught doing. I think I knew how the story was going to go that day.

Collinsville South had the traditional look of a brick colonial house, complete with ivory white columns and thick window trim, like the frosting on a gingerbread house. I couldn't even hack it in a building that looked like Rydell

High on steroids.

There had to be something seriously wrong with me.

We parked on the street in front of the school. Toilet paper hung from the branches of the huge oak trees on the lawn. Red streamers vined up the columns at the entrance of the building so that they looked like huge candy canes.

My classmates' lame attempt at a senior prank.

"What a mess," my mother said, *tsk-tsk*ing.

"They do it every year on the last day of school," I said quickly, before I felt the punch in the gut of realizing what that meant.

It was the last day of school.

It was the last day of school and I was here with my mom, in a *suit*.

Our appointment was at noon, my usual lunch period. Had Cassie, Lila, and I been in school that day, we most certainly would have been doing something to celebrate the fact that school was over and that we had plenty of days of celebration yet to come that summer. Probably smoking cigarettes in the parking lot and drinking stolen parental alcohol from a flask, chased by juice boxes from our lunches.

Laughing and making fun of everyone else we went to school with for not having the sense to get buzzed like we had.

But instead, I walked through the front doors of my school and prayed that I could go back to being as invisible as I had felt during my freshman year. If anybody saw me, my loosely held label as *bad girl* was over. I had to get in and out before the bell rang for next period.

Mr. Morgan stayed seated in his chair when we were brought in. I looked at his desk, trying to find any clue as to why the hell we were there. In the past, all that Mr. Morgan had held against me were canary-yellow disciplinary slips. I had no idea what he held against me that day.

One thing I did know was that my offense could not be written away with the word *tampon*. Skipping classes to get a tampon, or being late to get a tampon, or not being able to swim during gym class because I forgot a tampon, were not going to work that day. There was no way Mr. Morgan was going to believe that the police had mistaken a box of tampons for a huge bag of weed.

"It's a pleasure to finally meet you, Mr. Morgan," my mother said, fake as ever, as we sat in the empty seats set up for us on the other side of his desk.

"Yes, well," he said, "I wish it were under better circumstances."

Then they both looked at me, in case anyone had forgotten what those circumstances were.

"I know this is a disappointment to your family, Mrs. Fleishman."

She nodded and looked down.

"It is a disappointment to the family of our school as well," he said, leaning forward in that way people do to punctuate what they are going to say next. He went on to tell us that in addition to being suspended from school, which would be on my permanent record—*big deal, I have a more perilous permanent record to contend with now*—I was also not allowed to attend the senior carnival or graduation. When he said it, he looked at me with those eyes of his that were more eyelid than eyeball, and waited for my response.

Perhaps he thought that after everything that had been taken from me, this would affect me the most. But I just wanted to get out of there. Besides, if you've ever had a fat woman deputy stick her hand up your prom dress looking for drugs, not much else can faze you.

My mother, apparently, did not agree. "You can't do this," she said. "It has to be against the law."

"Actually, it is the law. School-board law. Any student caught using drugs or alcohol on his or her way to or from the prom can be barred from graduation. It's meant as a deterrent. And though we don't know for sure that Amy used drugs, I think it's pretty safe to assume..." When he said this, he looked at me with his smug *I know things about you that you don't know about yourself* look that all high school principals have. Though I was pretty sure Mr. Morgan didn't know the difference between his wife and a train tunnel.

"I didn't even go to the prom," I said.

My mother looked at me. I guess I hadn't told her that part.

"That may be true, but you were on school grounds; we know that," he said.

They knew that. I thought about Ruthie. I thought about Leslie. I thought about Joe.

"What is it supposed to deter her from now?"

"Now it's a deterrent for other students. It's our newly amended zero-tolerance policy. Considering what she's done, I'd say we're being generous."

"I'll still get a diploma, right?" There was no way I was going through the last four years of high school again.

"Of course," he said.

"In the mail, like some GED, like some mail-order education? No, thank you," my mother said. Her ring finger went to her mouth and she started to chew.

"It will be the same diploma everyone else gets, Mrs. Fleishman."

"Well, if she's getting the same diploma, why shouldn't she be able to accept it like everyone else? Isn't she going through enough right now?"

"That is our decision," he said, folding his hands together on the desk in that way you fold your hands together when your side of a discussion is over.

"Well, am I still allowed to attend?" my mother asked. Her question was like asking the groom if you could still come to the wedding, even though he decided not to marry your daughter.

Mr. Morgan looked at her with a look I had given her myself numerous times; it was a look that asked, *What the hell is wrong with you?*

"We'll be broadcasting the ceremony via webcast for the first time this year for out-of-town relatives, people with large families," he said, sounding really proud of himself. "You're welcome to watch it."

"You can't stop me from going. I've already purchased my tickets," she said, standing and grabbing me from my seat, trying to get us out of the room before he could tell her no.

I was actually glad. The bell was going to ring in seven

minutes. Being told I was not going to graduation would be eclipsed as the worst thing that had happened that day if I got caught in the hallway with my mom, looking like this, while classes were changing.

"You can do whatever you like, as long as Amy isn't there," he said, looking at her with a *You flipped out and I suppose I understand why with a daughter like that* look.

"If the general public can go, then I should be allowed to go, too. It's discriminatory to let some people attend and not others, and I haven't done anything wrong." I could see tears forming in her eyes.

Since the arrest, much like me, she had gained the ability to cry at will. But unlike me, she didn't hide it. All of a sudden her eyes were filled with tears, like there was a valve she'd turned on.

"Good luck to you, Amy," he said.

I didn't bother saying thank you like I was supposed to. His luck would do me no good now.

"Come on, Mom," I said, pulling her out of the office. I had to put my arms around her to hold her up as I brought her into the hallway. Three more minutes and *everyone* would see me in this suit, with my mom, with my arms around my mom, who was crying, *in this suit*. I rushed her out of the hall and through the front doors of the school.

"When do I get to be proud of you?" she asked.

I knew it was a rhetorical question, but it didn't make hearing it any easier.

We got in the car and drove. I could hear the bell ringing in the distance as we turned out of the parking lot. Safe. I was safe.

My mother was breathing like she had just run a marathon.

"After you are finished at Daniel's," she said, not looking at me, "you are going to put on your cap and gown and we are going to take our graduation photos." She grabbed my wrist, hard, as if she would fall down into the seat of the car like it was quicksand.

And because it hurt, I said okay. At least she didn't want to take pictures of me in this stupid suit.

Maybe Mr. Morgan didn't understand why my mother wanted to go to graduation without me, but I did. There were aunts and uncles and canasta group members to consider. There were pictures to be taken for those people to see.

I guess my mother just needed some normalcy. If she went to graduation she would at least be able to get a program with my name in it—surely they wouldn't have had enough time to remove my name and reprint it. And she could take a long shot of the graduating seniors, just the backs of their heads, which would all look the same. She could point to any one of them and say, "That's my Amy."

I suddenly felt bad for her. I suddenly felt bad for me.

"When we're finished with the pictures, you are going to return that cap and gown and get a refund. There's no reason to pay good money for something you're not even going to use." I could see her starting to tear up again.

I turned and stared out the window so I didn't have to look at her.

Maybe she would let me put it toward my Dick Simon fund. Of course, it only paid for about half a minute of his services. There's a real glimpse into what a high school diploma is worth. Four years of hardship, toil, boredom, and memorization; of each day feeling the happiest you think you could possibly feel and then sadder than you ever imagined, equaling the length of time it took for Dick Simon to constitute a really good burp.

Sixteen

Before Daniel could sit down, I ran for his beanbag chair. It was hard sitting in it wearing a skirt, but I didn't care.

He was wearing another tie-dye—blue blobs covered the *V* cut into his chest by the bright green Guatemalan poncho he had over it. It was the first time I'd actually seen someone wearing one of those in real life. Well, someone who wasn't Guatemalan.

"Why are you sitting there?" he asked, reaching over me to get his notepad. He kept looking at me, and I guess that meant my answer had better please him.

So I took my time and crafted a response that would make any cold-blooded psychologist proud. "I just wanted you to feel as uncomfortable in here as I do," I said, even though it was obvious I was the one who was uncomfortable. The beanbag chair sounded like someone sanding a piece of wood as I shifted awkwardly.

"Uh huh," he said, sitting in the recliner.

I pulled my skirt down and readjusted myself. At least my mother had let me leave my jacket with her in the car.

"You seem to be taking things well," he said in a voice I knew meant he thought just the opposite.

I looked at him. If I opened my mouth I was afraid I would start crying and be unable to stop.

"You might want to try talking to me," he said. "I may be called as a character witness for the case."

"You've met me twice."

"Perhaps your mother would be more suitable, or maybe you have someone else in mind?"

I wanted him to think I was ignoring his question rather than the truth of the matter: there really was no one else. Well, I guess there was Joe, but considering what he thought about me, he would more likely be called for the prosecution.

Sitting in the beanbag chair, I was eye level with a small wooden table that had a framed picture of a girl in a softball uniform on it. "You have a daughter?" I asked.

He looked at the picture. "Yes, and a wife and a father and a mother, too," he said.

"Is she as messed up as I am?"

"How was the arraignment?" he asked.

I guess that was his way of changing the subject. How come he was allowed to do that and I wasn't?

"Amy," he said.

I didn't want to talk about it. Not with him.

I had wanted to talk about it with my parents, instead of going out for lunch to stuff our mouths so we *couldn't* talk about it. I had wanted to talk about it with my father, while he squeezed my hand tight, tight, tight like he used to during the game we played when I was little. But they were paying this guy to talk to me instead.

Daniel looked at me like he was trying to shake the last bit of salad dressing out of a bottle.

"It was fine," I said. So he knew I was upset, big deal.

He sighed. "You're just masking your fear and low self-esteem." He turned the page of his pad. "You can choose to share what you're feeling verbally or attempt unsuccessfully to hide it."

"I choose neither," I said.

I thought I was hiding it pretty well. I struggled off the beanbag chair and looked out the window. I saw my mother sitting in the car talking to herself—and *I* was the one in therapy.

"You are a textbook case," Daniel said.

I could feel my filter waver. I wanted him to continue. Maybe he really did know something. Maybe he'd learned it from dealing with his own daughter. I turned to look at him.

"You were craving someone, anyone to notice you," he said.

I could feel Aaron's phone number in my bra. The paper made my skin itch, but having it there made it impossible not to think about him and I wanted to think about him. He had noticed me.

"If negative attention was all you could get, you would take it," he continued.

I shook my head—though I couldn't deny I had spent

more time with my mother in the last couple of weeks than during all of high school. But that couldn't have been the attention I wanted.

I wanted Aaron's attention and I had gotten it by being the girl everyone was telling me not to be. None of them understood.

Daniel put his pen to his lips and stared at me. "You need to look inside yourself and think about whatever feelings you may have about all of this. It's the only thing that will help you."

I didn't want to do that. I was afraid if I started searching around in my *feelings*, I might never come back.

He took a deep breath, made a big fuss about it, like breathing was the hardest thing he'd ever done. "Your mother says you moved into the basement. Why did you choose to do that?"

I stared at his poncho. It was as green as a traffic light. Its symbolism was probably supposed to make me want to *go*, but all I felt was just the opposite. "She's out in the car, if you want to ask her," I said.

Daniel should have considered himself lucky. I wasn't the kind of person who went on and on about Momma and how weak and under Poppa's thumb she was, her small mind and big dreams, too big for our shed-size house with a child-drawn curl of smoke coming from the chimney.

Of course that wasn't my story. My story was a lot more complicated. I had two parents who loved me as best they could. Who gave me everything I asked for and yet it still wasn't enough. So, what did that say about me?

Maybe it wasn't about them. I wasn't totally sure what

it *was* about yet, but I didn't think my parents were my real problem. I didn't even know if I *had* a real problem.

"I think you see it as some kind of symbolic hiding. As a physical way of keeping out the greater world."

"I'm not alone. AJ's down there with me."

"Who's AJ?" he asked, like I might be talking about an imaginary friend, like he had hit the mental-illness jackpot.

"My bird," I said.

"Exactly my point. You let your bird in, but you won't talk to a person."

"I like my bird." Maybe Daniel couldn't understand why I liked AJ better than most people, but he should have. If he knew as much about me as he claimed he did, he should have.

He shook his head. His ponytail fell over his right shoulder. His hair was so long, longer than Aaron's, longer than mine. He had to have been growing it for years, through who knows how many messed-up kids sitting across from him trying to deny they were messed up. I wondered how many of them he had actually helped. I wondered how many of them made him wish he'd never had a daughter.

"You need to look at the people and things you choose to populate your life with, otherwise you'll never understand why you do the things you do."

What was there to understand? Lila and Cassie were my friends. They were the only people in this world who understood me and now they were gone. They were gone and my life was gone. I didn't need Daniel to help me figure that out.

I held out my hand for the appointment card. The small,

ivory, 1" by 2" rectangle that would tell me when I would have to come and see him next.

"Do you even want to keep coming here?" he asked.

"I don't have a choice," I said.

"You have a choice to talk," he said.

"You're only listening because my parents are paying you," I said, glancing at my mother in the car. I could see her ripping at each nail on her right hand from pinkie to thumb. Then back again like a typewriter.

"Maybe," he said, "but I am listening."

• • •

I sat on the front stoop and smoked a cigarette while my mom went inside to iron my cap and gown. I would have to put them on and smile when the flash went off. I would have to pretend that it was my graduation day, that I knew what that day felt like, even though I never would.

My mother hated when I smoked in front of the house, but we were beyond her saying anything about it. We were beyond me caring, even if she did.

I pulled my skirt up high on my thighs, trying to tan my very white legs. They were suffering from my annoying schedule, too.

I heard a bike bell jingling down the street. Joe, probably on his way home from school. This was getting ridiculous. I hated being in my house far too much to have to risk seeing Joe every time I was outside of it.

All I wanted to do was talk to Aaron. All I wanted to do was talk to Lila. All I wanted to do was talk to Cassie. I guess I was going to talk to Joe. At least it wasn't Daniel or my mom.

I heard him getting closer, the bike bell like a jack-in-the-box being cranked, that scary, exciting sound. I took a drag. I wouldn't get caught off-guard this time. I would be ready.

Maybe he would ask me why I hadn't been in school that day. Maybe he would ask me why I looked so annoyed. Maybe he would ask me why I was in a suit. I considered how much I would tell him. How much I would let him in this time, if at all.

Maybe I would ask him if he had been the one who'd ratted me out to Mr. Morgan—him or his girlfriend.

I looked down at my legs, pretending to ignore him; the sun was already starting to turn them pink. I heard him ride up his driveway, heard his garage door open, heard him drop his bike on the ground and go into his house.

I guess we were back to avoiding each other. Back to that day early in sophomore year, when it was still warm enough to fool us into thinking it was summer—one of those days during fall when the leaves were just as yellow as the sun. When guys wore shorts and girls wore tank tops, and everyone hoped that a foot of snow wasn't just around the corner, even though it always was.

Joe and I walked home most days when it was nice enough, as long as he didn't have volleyball practice. Our walk took about fifteen minutes, longer than riding the bus, but on a nice day it was totally worth it to avoid those disgusting green seats and dungeon smells and intestinal sounds. We'd walk through the soccer field at the back of the school, which became a field of wild grasses and then undergrowth and woods before finally coming out at the mouth of our neighborhood—where the pavement and green street signs began.

We were quiet as we walked the length of the soccer field. Even though we had known each other forever, the older we got, the harder it was to find things to say. Maybe it was because we had known each other forever.

"Homework." Joe sighed, indicating his stuffed backpack. "English." He smiled.

"You'd think with as much as you talk, you'd be good at it by now," I said, falling into our lighthearted routine.

It had started in seventh grade when Joe realized I was better at English than he was, and I realized Joe was better at math than I was. We'd joke that if we were one person, we might actually get into Harvard.

He laughed. "You going to help me or not, Fleishman?"

"Sorry," I said, shaking my head. "No geometry tonight."

"You will have geometry homework again," he said, his voice going robotic. "It is statistically definite."

"Maybe if you give Spud a treat, he'll help you." I shrugged. I always acquiesced, but never right away.

The ground below us turned from perfectly manicured green to hay-field yellow as we left the school grounds.

"If I'd taught my dog to speak English, I wouldn't still be going to high school," Joe said.

"If you'd taught your dog to speak English, you wouldn't need help with your English homework."

We ducked into the woods. Branches broke under our feet as we walked. The sun speckled our skin with light through the leaves above. I guess that was why we still walked together—for this familiar talk and feeling and sound. It wasn't something that could happen while we were at school, while we were inside the walls that pushed us into being the people we were supposed to be.

"Maybe AJ can help me," he joked. "Is he busy tonight?"

"Fine." I sighed. "Come over after dinner."

"Success," Joe said, punching his fist into the air.

I pulled out a cigarette and leaned against a tree, stopping to light it. I had only just started hanging out with Lila and Cassie and smoking was a part of that, whether they were around or not.

"What are you doing?" Joe exclaimed, stopping to look at me.

I shrugged and exhaled smoke into the smell of fresh pine, trying to seem casual, even though my stomach felt like it housed a flea circus.

"Seriously?" Joe asked. "You're smoking now?"

It was the first time I'd had the nerve to smoke in front of him, to bring the new me into our old ritual. I wasn't sure what I'd been expecting.

Probably this.

"Don't worry. I won't start a fire," I said, still not admitting anything. I looked at the rough trail below. It was covered in fallen leaves—red, brown, and yellow. I could have started a fire easily. I held the discarded ashes in my hand.

"When did you start?" he asked.

"A while ago." I shrugged, but the fleas in my stomach were doing a trampoline act. It had really only been a few weeks, but for some reason I didn't want him to know that.

"*Why* did you start?" His eyes were squinting from the smoke.

"I like it," I said. It was true. Not the smoking itself, the way it burned my lungs and made my heart race, but the way I felt holding a cigarette. Like a completely different person.

"They make you smell," he said, waving at the air in front of him.

"Since when do you care what I smell like?" I pushed him playfully.

He didn't push me back.

"What?" I asked.

"You're different," he said, turning away from me and starting to walk away.

"So are you," I said, following after him.

He was. Maybe I was flaunting mine, but he was different, too. We could pretend as much as we wanted on these walks, but that didn't change anything that happened between bells ringing.

"You're really different," he said, staring straight ahead.

"Is that why you ignore me in school?" I guess these were the things that were hard to say, that caused our long silences, but if he was going there, I was, too.

"You ignore *me*," he said.

I didn't answer, just took a drag of my cigarette, letting him understand that we were talking about the same thing.

"Why do you even like those girls?" he asked. He heaved his backpack up, and I couldn't help looking at his hands. I saw the familiar twitch, even as he grabbed the shoulder strap tightly.

"They're nice," I said. "They're nice to me."

"Everyone says they're sluts."

"Who's everyone?"

He had no answer to that.

We walked out of the woods, the trail below us turning to pavement that was glittery in the sunlight. I stomped the cigarette out. Once, twice, three times. Though I had wanted Joe to know I'd started smoking, I wasn't ready for my parents to know it.

"Besides, don't guys like sluts?" I joked.

"Are they making you do it?" he asked, still not looking at me.

"No," I said. They weren't. They were letting me in.

"I'm not going to walk home with you anymore if you're going to smoke," he said.

"Is that a threat?" I tried to keep joking with him, but I knew it wasn't working. He was serious. He was telling me that I needed to pick—him or them.

That choice should have been easy. Our walks home were really the only time we saw each other during the school day. It wasn't like he met me at my locker between classes or sat with me at lunch. Lila and Cassie *did*.

"I bet AJ wouldn't like it," he said.

"Are you kidding me?"

He stared straight ahead. His soft, amiable profile looked angry.

"You'd better not tell my parents," I said.

"I bet that kid at camp wouldn't have kissed you if you smelled like an old ashtray," he said.

"Joe, shut up." I couldn't believe he was talking about that. I don't even know why I'd told him about it. Maybe because at the time I didn't have anyone else to tell.

It wasn't like the kiss had been that good, or at least not as good as I'd thought it was supposed to be. The kid kissed like a plunger with a snake's tongue. By the time we'd finished making out, the skin around my mouth was tender and pink, like I had fallen asleep in the sun with a ski mask on.

I'd never told Joe about that part.

"Not to mention, they're horrible for you," he said, his voice escalating.

I knew cigarettes were horrible for me. Who didn't know that? It wasn't what smoking was about, but I knew I wouldn't be able to explain that to Joe. He wasn't a girl. He wasn't me.

"Why are you so mad?" I asked.

"I'm not," he said. "Do whatever you want."

We turned down our street. Joe was walking so fast it was hard to keep up with him. "Slow down," I said.

He was a whole house length in front of me, his legs pumping like he was on his bike. I would have had to run to keep up. He didn't want me to keep up.

I trailed him all the way to his house. I watched as he unlocked, then slammed his front door, without turning around to say good-bye.

He was supposed to come over after dinner that night. We were supposed to sit on the floor of my bedroom while he tried to teach AJ swear words and I tried to teach him vocabulary words. But he never did.

He never came over again.

Seventeen

There was no gas at Gas-N-Go. There had been a time when they did sell gas, but it was long before me and long before Connor. What I think probably happened was that the place had gas when Mancini bought it and when it ran out, he was too cheap to buy more.

Mancini never got rid of the pumps because, according to him, even though there was no gas, he still wanted people to think there was. So a customer would drive up and try to get gas, realize there wasn't any, and stop in to the store to buy something, since they'd bothered to take the time to stop anyway. He was a marketing genius.

Every time the doorbell rang that night to announce someone's arrival, I hoped it would be Lila and Cassie, coming in to buy cigarettes and a chaser for whatever bottle of liquor they had taken from their parents, the way we used to. But it never was. Everything was different now.

I couldn't expect the things I used to expect, especially when it came to Lila and Cassie.

It was always just one of the typical Gas-N-Go customers; they all said the same thing. It was like they were talking dolls on a conveyor belt and when they got to the counter, I pulled their string. If it was cold out, they usually said something about how cold it was. If it was hot out, ditto. Basically any weather system was contrasted in relation to some apex of that system. It was captivating.

Men liked to drum their hands on the counter as they waited for their change and women liked to keep their hands on their purses like I was going to steal them. Kids my age tended to lean on the counter and play with the custom lone penny in the Take-a-Penny, Leave-a-Penny tray, sliding it back and forth like a rake in a baby Zen sand garden.

Connor stayed close to the cash register. Apparently when he'd balanced it out after my last shift, it had come up fifteen dollars short. If I had known more about the stupid thing, I could have used that to my advantage and actually taken some money.

"Do you need to stand so close to me?" I asked. Not only did he stay close to the cash register, he also stayed right on my ass.

"Mancini told me I had to watch you."

I tried to move away from him. "You smell like old diapers," I said, because he really did.

"Not all of us have the free time you do to devote to bathing," he said.

"Gross," I said, inching away.

"It's a lot of work raising two kids, working, making ends meet."

As busy as I was, I still found time to shower. I guess Connor was one of those people who had to let everyone else know how horrible he thought his life was. It was enough to make a person in my position sick with envy.

I heard the bell above the door and was relieved that someone was coming in, if only so it would end Connor's pity party. That is, until I saw who it was.

Leslie Preston walked down the aisles like she had been in to shop a thousand times before. Her honey-colored hair shone in the lights. Her teeth and eyes practically sparkled. It could only be my luck that I'd gotten a job where she bought her binge food.

In addition to being Joe's whatever, she had also been Homecoming Queen. In all likelihood she had been Prom Queen, too, not that I had been there to confirm it. So much had changed since prom. Since the night she and Joe had kept us out of the gym. I felt sick. At least Joe wasn't with her.

"Oh, crap," I said. Having everyone see me with my mom in the hallway at school would have been bad, but having Leslie Preston see me here, in this shirt, with Connor, was worse—much, much worse.

"Don't swear," Connor whispered. I guess my use of the word mattered more to him than why I was saying it.

I didn't know what to do, so I looked down, hoping she wouldn't recognize me. The chances of that were slim, seeing that anyone given the choice of looking at Connor or me would have to choose me, especially if that person was about to eat.

She walked to the cooler and grabbed a Diet Pepsi—probably her dinner—and slapped it on the counter like she was killing a spider.

"Is that all for you this evening?" Connor asked in his disgustingly happy customer-service voice.

Yeah, I thought, *until she notices me and rips me a new one. Just this Diet Pepsi and a side of humiliation served cold.* I kept looking down, but I knew she could see me, knew she was looking at me and thinking all the snobby things she always thought about me and now that she had validation for them, thinking them even more.

"Do you take fifties?" she asked, pulling out a crisp one. She held it by the edge like she had just gotten her nails done, perfect pink gumballs at the ends of her fingers.

"You're not trying to pull one over on us, are you?" Connor asked in his singsong *I am the best employee ever* voice.

She looked at him like his face was made of puke. That was how Leslie Preston looked at everyone, though I couldn't blame her in this case.

"Watch how I make the correct change," he said to me, and I knew I was in for it. She was totally going to let me have it. Tell me what a loser I was, what a joke my life had become, ask me how I could even show my face after what had happened.

I must have looked like I was praying, and in some ways I was—praying that I could truly hide, unlike the symbolic type that Daniel had accused me of.

Maybe Aaron would come in and take me away from

all this. He had found me before. I pictured his voice in my head—*she's the loser*—as I steeled myself for her first strike.

"See?" Connor said, but I wouldn't look up.

Forget correct change. I was about to have my ass handed to me by the Homecoming Queen.

"That's ten, twenty, thirty, forty, and fifty."

She knew just how to torture me, making me wait, my heart beating like a fish dying in my chest.

"Have a Gas-N-Go night," Connor said.

As I closed my eyes and prepared to be annihilated, the bell above the door rang and I realized she was gone.

"Now did you watch me there?" he asked, crossing his arms over his chest like he was my father teaching me how to ride a bike.

Why hadn't she said anything? Was she just trying to torment me? Preparing to come back with the whole Homecoming Court to laugh at me? Waiting to text everyone she knew that *Amy Fleishman the druggie criminal* was not only a druggie criminal but was also working at crappy, dirty Gas-N-Go?

"I feel sick," I said, took the bathroom key, and ran toward it. I locked myself inside and lit a cigarette.

I needed Lila and Cassie. They haunted me like a smell that reminds you of something. Like when I would smell gasoline and think of riding in the motorboat at summer camp. I'd crave that feeling, just from the smell; could even see the lakefront, sun-sparkling water rapping against the dock, making the sailboats and canoes that were tied up dance in the shallows.

I thought about Cassie and Lila and how it used to be. How for a short while this town, which we considered the world, felt like it was ours for the taking.

I thought about how, if they had been next to me, I wouldn't have cared that Leslie Preston had ignored me. That if they had been next to me, I would have ignored Leslie Preston.

Now that they were gone, it wasn't cool to reject everything we were supposed to embrace. Without them beside me, I couldn't deny that I wanted to keep chasing the impossible dream of teenage-girl perfection, even though I was further away from it than I had ever been.

Without them beside me, no one would understand why I'd made the choices I had, why they'd seemed like my only choices at the time.

When presented with mediocrity or failure, I'd chosen failure. I'd chosen to be the best failure I could be.

I guess I'd finally succeeded.

· · ·

"I thought you were going to call me," Aaron yelled as I stepped out of Gas-N-Go after work.

I didn't know it was him at first. It was dark and I didn't see the black convertible idling at the far end of the lot until he beeped the horn.

Maybe he had felt me calling for him, or maybe he just needed cigarettes.

I walked over to him. It was a warm night. He was wearing a T-shirt and shorts. The lights on the dashboard tinged his skin ghostly green.

I had thought about calling him, but the whole having to talk because we were on the phone thing, the whole having to fill the weird silences thing, kept me from going through with it.

It was much safer to know that I could call him if I wanted to.

"What are you doing here?" I asked.

"Waiting for you," he said.

He'd said exactly what I wanted him to say. Maybe talking to boys wasn't that bad. Well, as long as they were doing the talking.

"Cool shirt," he said.

I looked down. I was still wearing my red Gas-N-Go polo. Why did I look like such a dork every time I saw this guy? "It's for work."

"Just another monkey suit," he said.

"Nice car," I said, totally spazzing out. I couldn't help it. It *was* nice, way too nice for him to be driving and way too nice for him to be waiting for me in.

"My dad's. He lets me borrow it at night sometimes. Get in."

He didn't have to ask twice. I was supposed to come home right after work, but what were my parents going to do, arrest me?

We drove out of the parking lot and onto Main Street, the top down, my hair blowing around. I kept trying to pull it back, but it kept coming loose, so I gave up and just let it fly.

I looked at Aaron. Damn, he was cute, like a guy in a garage band cute. So cute that I never would have considered talking to him first. So cute that Lila should have been in the car instead of me.

But *I* was in the car.

From his profile, I could see he was smiling, one hand on the wheel, the other on the shifter. Red hairs had escaped his ponytail and were flying around his head like they were electric.

I put my head back and watched the streetlights rush past like a movie on fast forward, blurry and buzzing. He turned up the music. I had to remember this feeling. Remember it so I could feel it later, but it was fleeting, fast, like the car. I knew it would stop when we did.

We parked up the street from my house. I realized I hadn't even told him where to go. "You know where I live?"

"It wasn't hard to figure out."

I wondered what else he knew about me. I wondered what else he wanted to know.

"I didn't think you were ready to go home yet," he said.

I shook my head and looked at Joe's house. Hopefully he wouldn't walk by and ruin everything, embarrass me with his letterman jacket and geek hands.

We reclined our seats back and looked up at the sky. I waited for Aaron to say something about the stars, but he didn't, so I didn't, either.

"I drew something for you," he said, reaching into the backseat and handing me a piece of paper.

It was *me*, wearing my suit, riding on his skateboard. He'd done it in pastels, so that it looked blurry at the edges, like I could have been skating to anywhere.

"So you could see what you were missing." He smiled.

"Wow, thanks," I said.

"No big deal," he said.

Maybe it wasn't to him, but I wasn't used to cute boys giving me things. Phone numbers and pictures they had drawn of *me*. What was next?

"You have cigarettes?" he asked.

I gave him one and put one in my mouth, and he lit them both with his Zippo. "I like your lighter," I said, spazzing out again. I didn't like his lighter. I liked the way he held it, like anyone who saw him with it would know it was his.

He leaned over and kissed me. He tasted like smoke. It was my first kiss with a cigarette in my hand. I tried not to drop it as he pulled me closer. I could feel it burning in my hand, could feel the ash growing. His crooked tooth pushed against my bottom lip, but it felt good, like he was telling me a secret.

He kept kissing me as he threw his cigarette over his shoulder onto the street. I did the same, hoping it didn't hit anything that would ignite. His hand was flat on my back, the hand that had held his cigarette resting on my knee.

I tried to think about what bra and underwear I was wearing. I tried to think whether I had shaved my legs that day, but I couldn't stop wondering why he was kissing me. I was wearing a shirt that smelled like deli meat and gas-station-bathroom air freshener. My hair was tangled and flat from the drive. He'd barely even talked to me. He didn't even know me.

Maybe that was why.

He was such a good kisser. I kissed him harder; his tooth pierced my lip. His hands gripped me like I was the safety bar on a roller coaster. I could feel his nails digging into my knee. Maybe it didn't matter why. It all felt too good to stop. It all felt too good to question.

I should have known better.

Eighteen

Dick Simon decided that trash cleanup wasn't good enough. He said I also had to show I had a deep caring for other people; besides, my mother was still complaining about not being able to get the smell out of her car.

I protested that the quiz the social worker had given me had clearly shown I was meant to work with trash, but he said something about having to convince the judge I cared about the well-being of others.

All this supposed self-improvement was not about improving me at all; it was for the benefit of some judge. Forget about being a better person, like Daniel kept telling me I had to be—my personal growth was less important than impressing some guy who essentially wore a dress for a living.

"The elderly," Dick Simon said.

"How about kids?" I asked. Kids I could deal with. Old

people scared the crap out of me.

"No one wants you near their kids," he said.

I guess old people had nothing left to lose.

I was sent to Blooming Maples, the old folks' home down the block from my house. It had that hospital-like, boxy brick outside, that sterileness that it seemed to emit into the air around it like a force field. The sidewalk surrounding it was as white as a nurse's uniform, which I guess was meant to prepare the residents for seeing that stark white on a daily basis.

This was way worse than trash. Nursing homes are where old people gather to die. It's almost like they think that if they store themselves together, maybe someone who has a little more life left will be able to spare some.

Old people made me sad. This was going to suck.

I found Mrs. Mortar lying on her bed with three pillows supporting her back so she could sit up. She wore a red kimono with red lipstick to match, as well as enough blush to stop a car. Of course, I had to give her props for wearing a red kimono. Other than my Gas-N-Go polo, I didn't own anything red. Red scared me almost as much as old people.

She was applying, or rather trying to apply, nail polish. She wasn't really putting it on her nails so much as she was putting it on her whole fingertip. She had that shaking thing so many old people do; it looked like her fingers had been slashed with knives and hot-pink blood was coming out. She lifted her left hand to show me.

"Nice," I said, trying to be the cheery, helpful visitor I was supposed to be.

"It's amazing what a little color can do for a girl," she

said, and then looked at me more closely, as if realizing for the first time that she had no idea who I was.

"Do you need help?" I asked, though I hoped she would say no.

She either ignored me or didn't hear me. Thank God some people are too proud to wear a hearing aid.

"So tell me about you," she said, putting the cap back on the bottle and blowing on her nails.

After the arrest, there was the sitting, the listening, and then the people like Daniel, who wanted me to tell them about myself. Talking about my life had never been my favorite topic of conversation, and it wasn't any better now.

She sat and waited.

"My name's Amy," I said, realizing it was the only safe thing I could really say. Even my last name was incriminating, if she could do a Google search.

"Go on," she said, in that way old women talk when they're trying to sound like young women. In a voice that says, *I'm still sexy.*

"I'm seventeen," I said, thinking maybe that would appease her. As far away from seventeen as she was, I thought it had to be something.

She grabbed a fur stole from the hospital-grade metal headboard and wrapped it around her neck. I think it was fur. It looked more like a snake of dust bunnies from a vacuum bag. "And?"

She was worse than Daniel. At least he let me sit there staring. Of course, that might have been because she wasn't asking me these things for my own benefit. She was bored and old and my visit was probably the most interesting thing to have happened to her in the past month.

I suddenly felt sorry for her, especially for expecting anything from me. I guess I could have told her about my steamy make-out session with Aaron, but that was mine. He was mine. I didn't want to share him with her.

With anyone.

I looked around the room. She had dried roses hanging on her wall in bunches, at least twenty of them. The red of the petals was covered with green, which also made the room smell like rot. At least, I hoped that's what it was.

"My first husband used to give me roses when we fought. I divorced him because he loved hot weather. I," she said, indicating the wrap, "did not."

"Tell me more about you," I said. Maybe she wanted to know about me, but I wanted to know about her. Staring down the barrel of incarceration was scary, but staring down the barrel of death had to be terrifying. Maybe she had some secret.

"No, no, you don't get to do that." She pulled the wrap tighter around her neck and in the process covered it with nail polish and coated her nails with pieces of gray fuzz. "I've been through seven presidents, almost as many wars, two husbands, three kids, and a hysterectomy—you tell me about *you*."

"I have a pet bird," I said.

"Wow," she said, "you're a regular Amelia Earhart." She closed her eyes, which let me know she was bored. Even *she* thought I was boring. "Haven't you ever done anything crazy?" she asked, pulling her stole off and throwing it across the room. "Maybe something that doesn't involve a pet bird?"

I thought about Aaron again. We had made out until my lips were chapped and raw, but that didn't feel crazy, it felt right. I didn't need to explain myself to him. Our lips were too busy to talk anyway.

"Not really," I said. There was also the arrest. Sure, it seemed like exactly the kind of thing you would tell people about years later—*you can't believe the crazy thing that happened to me in high school*—but sitting in the middle of it took away any glamour.

"Fine, let's make this easier," she said. "What will you do after you leave here?"

I thought about it: Did I need to work? What appointment did I have? I realized I didn't know, which I took to mean I had nothing to do after this. I was actually pretty excited about that.

"Nothing," I said, loving the plain blissfulness of the word.

She shook her head and heaved herself out of the bed and into a pair of slippers that was sitting on the floor.

Maybe I should have told her to sit down. I should have said, *Don't overexert yourself,* but I was kind of hoping she would tire herself out enough that she would fall asleep and I could spend my remaining mandated time listening to her snore and rummaging through her room for the flask I knew she must have. The way she was acting, it was probable she had more than one.

"Bring that over here," she said, motioning to the dresser. "I'm not about to be the only woman in the room wearing lipstick."

Her makeup looked like it was from the Stone Age. I was positive I didn't want it on my face and that if any of it *did* get on my face, it would probably cause a rash requiring immediate medical attention. At least there were nurses on staff.

"Make like you're giving your beau a kiss," she said, puckering her own lips, which looked like that part in the movie when the protagonist's aunt is about to give him a kiss and all you can see is puckered, quivering lips coming toward you on the screen.

I could have protested, but she seemed to really be enjoying herself and at least she'd stopped asking me questions. Then she picked up the eye shadow and blush. She looked like she was having an epileptic fit and who knows—the way my face turned out, maybe she had one.

I needed to stop letting people put makeup on me.

I turned and looked at myself in the mirror and felt that strange sensation you get when you're walking down the street and you see someone who looks just like you, and for a second you think you're looking at yourself and then you realize it's just someone else, with a completely different life, who has your hair, or nose, or eyes.

She stood behind me with her finger on her chin. "Something's missing," she said, and went to her closet. "This." She handed me an old, silver-sequined flapper dress, which would have actually been pretty cool if it weren't covered with huge brown rust spots. "Arms up," she said, and she waddled behind me with the dress. At least she was letting me wear it over my clothes—whatever bacteria it housed would have to travel through a layer of fabric before it could reach my skin and turn my nerves into children's paste. "Perfect," she said, sitting on the bed to catch her breath. "Now at least you look interesting."

That would not have been the word I would have chosen. I looked like an extra from Michael Jackson's "Thriller" video.

"You're worse than that kid they sent me last week. President of the chess club. Sure, chess is boring, but at least he was passionate about it." She waited, probably so I could tell her what I was passionate about.

But there was nothing, had been nothing since I was little and wanted to be a bird. After that, I just wanted a friend, a best friend, and after I had those friends, I didn't hope for anything else. I thought if I did, they would get taken away, but they got taken away anyway.

"What I've learned about you in the past twenty minutes is that your name is Amy, you are seventeen, you have a pet bird, and you do nothing," she said.

I looked down. Was she right?

"You have your whole life ahead of you and that's all you have to say about it?"

It was exactly the sort of thing old people say to young people, when it appears to those old people that those young people are wasting their lives. But I wasn't one of those young people anymore.

This was my life, arrest or no arrest. I had done very little and wanted even less. It sounded a lot worse when she said it back to me, though, even with the arrest tacked on.

"I might as well call the chess wiz back in here," she said, closing her eyes again.

I started to feel angry. Started to hear the words that usually would have stayed in my head come pouring out. "What do you want from me? I got arrested. I don't know what I'm going to do with my life because I don't have a life anymore, okay?"

She put her hand to her throat and sucked in hard. I had rendered her speechless. For once that day, she had no more questions, so I kept talking.

"It's easy for you to tell me that I'm wasting my life. You think I don't know that? You think I don't know there's nothing that makes me special? That the only thing I may ever do that makes news is, as far as my parents are concerned, the *worst thing I've ever done*?"

I watched her, waiting for a reaction. I'm not sure what reaction I wanted, but the one I got certainly wasn't the one I expected. She gurgled and started turning blue.

I ran into the hallway screaming for a doctor, a nurse, anyone to help.

I hadn't rendered her speechless. She had been having trouble breathing and I hadn't even noticed. The person I'd finally chosen to tell everything that Daniel had wanted to hear, couldn't hear me anyway.

As I watched from the corner of the room, hoping they could resuscitate her, I couldn't help thinking that maybe there was something to that personality test after all.

• • •

Mrs. Mortar had really gotten to me. Walking home, I tried to think about Aaron, tried to tell myself that he didn't feel the same way she did, couldn't feel the same way she did.

But how did I really know how he felt?

Maybe he'd realized after last night ʰ had thought I was, that I was boring. Mayʊ. I would never see him again.

I had spent all of ten minutes with Mrs. Mortaɾ she had dismissed me as a nobody, a loser. I had to ask someone who knew me if she was right.

Instead of going home, I stopped at Joe's. His house looked the way it always did: small, olive green with chocolate-fudge trim, with a rainbow daisy spinner, spinning like something was chasing it, stuck in the front yard.

The only difference was that, for the first time in three years, I was going to walk up the driveway that we used to draw all over with chalk. I was going to ring the doorbell that we used to treat as a musical instrument, driving his mother and dachshund Spud crazy. I was going to stand on the porch we used to hide under.

I rang the bell. I tried not to think about how long it had been since I was able to walk in without even knocking. How long it had been since I had even been inside. How hopeless I really must have felt to ignore all that and ring his doorbell anyway.

I heard Spud start barking, that familiar yippy sound. I rang the bell again, hoping to drown it out.

"Oh, are we talking again?" Joe asked as he opened the door. I heard Spud come up behind him, his nails scratching on the linoleum as his little legs ran toward the door. Joe looked at me like I was back from the dead. I guess in some ways I was.

Amy, what the hell?" he asked.

"Sorry, I know, I shouldn't have come here."

"No, what the hell are you wearing?"

I looked down. In all the commotion at the nursing home, I had forgotten to take off Mrs. Mortar's dress. "Trick or treat," I said, shrugging. It was easier than explaining my zombie-wear.

"Are you on something?" he asked, squinting.

Considering how I looked, the odds were probably PCP. Joe held Spud at his side with his leg as the dog started to whine.

"Do you think I'm boring?" I asked, itching my cheeks. I *knew* Mrs. Mortar's makeup was toxic. Well, at least there was the possibility of me dying before I had to hear Joe's answer.

"What? Amy, what is wrong with you? If you're on drugs or something, you need to leave."

Spud continued to whine, giving me big brown eyes that I knew were begging for a pet. I put my hands behind my back, trying to fight the urge.

"Joe," I said, opening my eyes wide so he could see they were clear, could see I was sober. "Do you think I'm boring?"

"What are you talking about?"

"Just answer the question, please."

He sighed. "I think you're annoying. I think you're frustrating. I think you're exhausting. But no, not boring."

"You're sure?" I knew I sounded desperate, but at that moment there was little I could do to contain it. I couldn't hide behind my mean girl when I was the one who had rung the doorbell.

"Um, yeah." He started to laugh.

"What?"

"Amy, I mean, you haven't been to my house in years and you finally come here and you look…" He laughed again, harder.

"I know," I said. I guess I'd hoped he wouldn't mention the part about me being the one to actually ring his doorbell.

He picked up Spud and held him. "So, why are you here?"

Why was I there? I looked down. Mrs. Mortar's dress was so long it covered my sneakers. I couldn't move. "I guess I just wanted to ask you that," I said.

"You're acting weird, and not the way you usually act weird. Like, bald Britney Spears weird."

"Sorry," I said. *Not like I usually act weird.* I assumed he meant toward him.

I wanted Joe to say something else. I wanted to say something else. But what did he want to hear? What did I want to hear?

"Are you okay?" he asked.

I was so far from okay, but how could I explain that to Joe? After his father left, he'd made it his mission to pretend he was. At seven, having watched his father pack up his car and drive down our street and away from him, his mom, and Spud, Joe tried to convince everyone he was *fine*, just like I was trying to do now.

Joe waited for my answer. He held Spud tightly in his arms, even as he squirmed. Joe's hands were motionless, anything to be regular, anything to be normal.

My hands were still behind my back. I wanted to pet Spud. I wanted to let him lick my face the way he used to—well, once Mrs. Mortar's makeup was safely removed.

"No," I said.

He nodded. "Will you be okay?"

"I don't know," I said, feeling like I was going to start crying. I didn't want to cry, not in front of Joe. "I think I have to get home."

"Right," he said, stepping back, realizing that whatever truce we had fashioned in that strange, delicate moment was over.

"I guess I'll see you at graduation," he said, heaving Spud on his shoulder with one hand as he closed the door with the other.

He wouldn't, but I didn't want to tell him that. At least he could believe I would be there. At least he wouldn't know how bad things had gotten, not yet.

Nineteen

I came home to find Dick Simon sitting at the dinner table with my parents. He was in my seat, which bothered me a lot less than the fact that he was in my house. Forget about coming home to find one of your teachers sitting with your parents at the dinner table with a bib around her neck. Finding your lawyer is much, much worse.

I was hoping he hadn't been briefed on the Mrs. Mortar situation and wasn't there to tell me that not only was I up on drug charges, I had been accused of attempted murder, too.

My mother was in a pink-and-white-checkered half apron, and she was at the stove stirring a pot full of something I was sure she hadn't made. She never wore an apron and she never cooked. She must have called the caterer. Not a caterer, *the* caterer. She used him so often he was referred to as *the*. That night, she was "making" her famous heated-up whatever she'd ordered, and then everyone could rave about how exceptional she was at dialing a phone and how knowledgeable she was about the mysterious world of temperature.

Whatever. It meant this little visit had not been impromptu. They had invited Dick Simon over for a reason.

"No need to get all dressed up for me," he said, laughing.

"You're late," my mother said, turning away from the stove to look at me. "What on earth?"

I was still wearing that disgusting dress. I pulled it over my head and threw it in the trash. I didn't really want to get into everything that had happened, so I took a seat at the table and said, "I made a new friend."

"Was it a transvestite?" my mother asked.

Dick turned red and got that look on his face that a little boy gets when someone says the word *penis*.

She huffed and went back to stirring; it smelled like she was burning whatever food we were eating. My mother can even mess up food that's been cooked for her.

"It doesn't matter if it's a transvestite as long as it's a law-abiding transvestite," my father said.

"I guess anyone would be better," my mother said.

I picked up the fork from the left side of the plate and ran the tines along my lips, trying to keep in what I wanted to say about Lila and Cassie.

"Amy, your teeth," my father said, grabbing the fork from my hand.

"Dick, you saw those girls in court. You didn't even have to hear them speak to know they were bad news."

"Nope," he said. "I could spot them from a mile away."

"Not a care in the world for the rules they're breaking," she said, shaking her head. "I think I saw that Cassie girl spit on the floor in the courtroom."

"We've all been arrested. We'll all be punished," I said.

I was just like they were. Why couldn't everyone understand that?

"We'll see," my mother said. It was her way of saying that someone would get back at Cassie and Lila for what they had done to me. Or at least, what she thought they had done to me.

I guess I couldn't blame my mother for blaming them for what happened. I mean, I blamed her for a lot of the things that had happened to me. Did that mean that, according to her logic, she would get what was coming to her? Was *I* what was coming to her?

"Smells great," my father said, which was code for saying he was hungry.

I waved at the air in front of my face. It did not smell great. It smelled like burning paper, which is probably what it was, considering it's not beyond my mother to forget to take something out of its container before she reheats it.

I was tired of waiting for someone to explain why Dick Simon was there, so I asked.

"This is just a thank-you for all the hard work he's doing for you," my mother said.

I wondered why my full paychecks from Gas-N-Go weren't enough.

"Yes, indeed," Dick Simon said like some Southern gentleman. "Your mother is one gracious hostess."

I just about puked in my salad bowl. I found it interesting that they were thanking him when he hadn't really done anything yet—other than torture me—as far as I could tell.

Finally, dinner was served. Luckily, Dick was the kind of guy who didn't speak once food landed in front of him. He ate until his plate was clean, so this eliminated any chance of him asking me how I thought things were going, how my job was, whether I felt I was making progress in therapy, or whether I was ready to rip my hair out.

My father was one of these men as well. This left my mother and me to make conversation, so we didn't speak.

My mother got up from the table to get dessert and came back with a white-frosted cake that read *Thank You Dick* in blue icing.

I heard angry words in my head, cursing me for not making it home in time to find the cake in the fridge so I could have added *For Being A* in between the words that were already there.

"Why don't you two take a walk," my mother said, after Dick Simon and my father had inhaled the cake I refused to eat with after-dinner coffee.

Dick Simon got up and stood behind my chair, attempting to pull it out for me. I sat there for as long as I could, ignoring him while my mother glared at me.

"Amy, Dick is waiting," my father said.

"Fine," I said. As I walked out of the kitchen with him, I realized he hadn't told one joke during all of dinner. I should have known something serious was about to happen.

We went out the sliding glass patio door and into my backyard. Since we lived on one of those streets where everyone has a perfectly rectangular patch of backyard grass, we walked around the perimeter.

"Jail isn't pretty," he said.

I nodded. I didn't need to be told that. I could guess. And what I couldn't guess, I knew about from movies. It was inhabited by men and women who had one very noticeable defect or characterization. The woman with the scar that ran from the outside corner of her eye all the way down the corner of her mouth like the trail of a tear. A big fat guy who grunted and punched instead of speaking. The skinny little meth head with a face like a snake who helped people get things from some unknown source.

"You don't seem as scared as you should be," Dick said.

I stared at him. Of course I was scared, but I was also emotionally spent. If I had learned anything from my experience violating the law, it was that feelings are not a bottomless pit. You can run out of them, and I guess I had.

"Sit down," he said.

I looked around, but there were no chairs waiting for us in the yard. I sat down in front of a wild rose bush. He followed a minute later, falling to the ground in a way that made me wonder if he would ever get up again.

He went on to tell me horror stories, but most of what he said sounded like those tall tales your grandparents tell about how they would have to walk ten miles to school every day, uphill, in the snow. It was hard to take someone seriously who made you afraid that you might find a whoopee cushion every time you sat on a chair in his office.

"I know what I'm talking about," he went on, catching his breath. "I've had clients who've gone inside." And when he said this he squeezed his thigh, or at least the portion he was able to squeeze in his very-small-by-contrast hand. "Maybe you think you know what it's like in a general way, but you don't really know anything about it until you've been there day in, day out, folding laundry and cleaning toilets and praying while you're in the shower that you don't get jumped."

I looked at the swing set my parents had bought me when I was nine. It was rusty and the swings moved slightly in the wind. When I was little, I would sit on the swing in the center and pump my legs until they ached. Flying so high, being just like AJ, feeling nothing but pure, simple joy. I wished I were swinging now.

"Why are you telling me this?" I asked. I knew jail would suck. Like that was news? Knowing it didn't change anything. Maybe he should spend less time telling me about jail and more time working to keep me out of jail.

"I'm just doing my job," he said, closing his eyes and breathing. "My job is all about the truth. Sometimes it's a hard truth and sometimes it's a bend of the truth and sometimes it's a slight shading of the truth. You should know what can happen."

"I thought you said you could get me probation."

"I can," he said, unfolding a piece of paper from his pocket and handing it to me. It was typed on his letterhead—Richard Simon, Esquire—and had a bunch of *Sorry, so, so sorry*s and *I was in with the wrong crowd* and *I was making the wrong decisions* and *I am all different* *now.* It also detailed how everything that had happened the night of my arrest was the fault of Lila and Cassie.

"What the hell is this?" I shook the paper. I couldn't help it.

"Your get-out-of-jail-free card," he said, handing me a pen.

"No," I said, even though what I really wanted to tell him was where he could stick that pen. There was no way I was turning on Lila and Cassie.

"This is the deal my buddy is presenting. Sign it and you get probation. I would suggest you take it."

"What does he want with Lila and Cassie?"

"It's not about them," Dick said, waving away my comment. "It's about scaring them enough to testify against other, more connected people, and on and on up the line."

I wondered how even the Assistant DA knew that Lila and Cassie were more popular than I was. I shook my head.

"Perhaps the real owner of the evidence you were found with, perhaps his or her compatriots," he said.

Brian, I thought. Lila would kill me.

"You could get a year inside if you don't sign it."

"Then what am I paying you for?"

"For this," he said, still trying to hand me the pen. "I'd take the chance while I still had it."

"What will happen to Cassie and Lila?"

"Do you think they would ask that about you?"

I didn't have to answer. They were my best friends—that had to mean something. I had to be able to count on someone other than AJ.

"You'll change your mind. Everyone does," he said,

struggling to stand.

"Well, maybe everyone does," I said, standing before he could, "but I'm not everyone."

"Sure you are," he said. "Everyone is someone until they're faced with a traumatic situation, and then they become everyone. You're not special, you know."

I stood above him. What was with everyone needing to tell me how ordinary I was? Other people were allowed to go on being ignorant and boring and regular and plain, without it being shoved in their faces every five minutes.

"I'm having a little trouble getting up," he said, reaching for my hand. The back pocket of his pants had gotten caught on one of the thorny rose branches and I could hear the seam tearing as he struggled.

I grabbed his hand and helped him up. Then, I ripped the paper he'd given me into little pieces and threw it across the yard. He stayed behind, picking them up.

I found my mother sitting at the kitchen table looking anxious. Like the decision I was supposed to make was a baby she was waiting for. "You'd better go get Dick," I said.

"What have you done now?" she asked, running toward the door, not even giving me the chance to respond.

Considering how that question had been answered lately, I couldn't blame her.

I went down to my basement hovel to call Lila. I doubted that my mother had gone after Dick because she cared about his well-being—I knew it had to be because if anyone saw him scavenging around on the lawn with his pants falling off, the Collinsville rumor mill would have been up and running for new business.

AJ chirped from his cage as I opened the basement door. Maybe Mrs. Mortar thought having a bird was lame, but at least I knew AJ would never rat me out. Well, *could* never rat me out.

As I picked up the phone, I wondered what I would say. If I called Lila and told her what Dick had said, would it give her ideas? Would telling her what my lawyer wanted me to do help her to see a way out that she may not have had before?

I dialed her number. Maybe she wouldn't answer. I could feel satisfied that I had at least tried to call her to tell her what was going on. And then spend the rest of the night smoking and trying to forget.

"How's the job?" she asked, without even saying hello. It was obvious that her caller ID was working, and that she was screening her calls. It seemed odd that it was the first thing she would ask me about, too. Like a family member who doesn't know you well, asking about something so basic and universal.

"How do you think?"

"I've seen you in there when I walk by," she said, as I heard her light a cigarette.

She'd walked by and hadn't stopped. I felt my stomach turn. Where was she going? Why hadn't she taken me?

I heard her inhale, waiting for me to talk. Was she mad at me?

"What have you been doing?" I asked. *Other than walking by and not stopping?*

"Nothing. I'm so bored," Lila said, sucking in hard on her cigarette.

"Yeah," I said, though I was hoping for an excuse. I was the one with forty-seven appointments every day, but even I found the time to pick up a phone. But it's not like she could have called me. I didn't have a cell anymore. And maybe she wanted to stop when she walked by Gas-N-Go, but her lawyer had also told her to separate herself from me.

"Brian and I got back together."

"Seriously?" Only Lila could resnare a guy she'd essentially just stolen a thousand dollars from.

"I blamed it on Cassie." She exhaled. "He's been so sweet to me. He feels really bad. It's so nice to have someone to talk to about everything."

I had tons of people to talk to about everything, but none of them understood. Well, Aaron understood. I considered telling Lila about him, but I knew I couldn't risk it. If Lila knew I was hanging out with Aaron, she would do her Lila thing and take him away.

"Brian calls me every morning to wake me up and then every night before I fall asleep," she said with an actress's sigh.

"You won't believe what my lawyer just said to me." I couldn't believe I'd actually said it, but I would have said anything to make her shut up about Brian.

"Your lawyer," she said, exhaling sharply, waiting.

"He wants me to testify against you guys." I whispered the last part; I don't know why. It just seemed like the sort of thing you would whisper to someone.

"Why are you telling me this?"

"Who else am I going to tell?"

"I don't know; your therapist?"

It was mean, but I ignored it. "Lila, calm down, I'm not doing it."

"I don't even see my lawyer. I can't even remember his name," she said.

"I told you, I'm not going to do it."

"The whole thing sounds pretty sneaky to me."

"That's what I said."

Silence.

A drag in and a drag out. "I don't even think I would have told *you* about it. I wouldn't have needed to."

"I wanted to be upfront with you," I said. "He told me it wasn't even about you. It was about scaring you into turning on other people."

"What other people?"

"I don't know," I said, even though I did know. Brian and then whoever was above Brian.

Silence.

"Lila."

A drag in and a drag out. "Listen, we probably shouldn't even be talking. I bet this line is tapped or something. Maybe I'll come and see you at work sometime this week."

Which I knew was her way of saying she would never come by.

I could have called Cassie after that, but if I told her what I had just told Lila, she would probably come over and kick my ass. Though, considering the way I felt after talking to Lila, having my ass kicked would have been an improvement.

Stupid Dick. That confession didn't mean anything. I knew my real confession wouldn't have been about the arrest at all. It would have been about that little girl on the swings in my backyard, and the way she felt when she was in the air. How it made her believe that she could be anyone and do anything. How it made her forget everything else.

My real confession would have been to apologize to her for turning into me. For letting her dreams drain out, until I became someone she wouldn't even recognize.

Twenty

"You're late," Connor said. I looked at the *It's Always Time for Pepsi* clock and realized that even though 7:15 p.m. meant it was time for Pepsi, it also meant I was fifteen minutes late for my shift.

The thing about Connor was that it looked like someone had given him mouth-to-mouth and the air had just stayed inside him, like his body had been floating around Lake Erie for three weeks and when someone finally found him, they hadn't bothered to wring him out or dry him off.

Weirdly, his bulk was the thing I liked best about him, because he made me feel thin.

"Sorry," I said easily, which meant I probably didn't really mean it.

He picked up his clipboard. "I need to do inventory," and he said *need* like someone in the desert says they need a glass of water. In that case necessary, in this case pathetic.

I rolled my eyes. I couldn't help it.

"What if someone comes in here and wants something, and we don't have it?"

I shrugged. They'd probably just go somewhere else, which would make my life a hell of a lot easier anyway.

"Listen, I know how much you hate being here," Connor said, motioning to the store around him, "but you don't have to make life unpleasant for me, too."

"Fine," I said. I could give him that. Even though I hated it there, Gas-N-Go might just be his one refuge. That was only slightly less sad than my current situation.

He started to walk into the back and then stopped. "Why don't you do some dusting until a customer comes in, if that's not too much to ask?"

By dusting, I knew he meant the food. I took the feather duster from behind the counter and started on the dry goods. The food needed to be dusted because it sat for so long without anybody buying it, which kind of unraveled Connor's whole "need to do inventory" claim. Not only was it dusty, but the boxes of cake mix, or instant rice, or crackers had been there for so long that they looked weathered. Like they'd been sitting out in the sun for years, or like someone had dipped them in a vat of bleach. They looked like Connor. He had the same paleness and flatness about him.

He'd washed his Gas-N-Go shirt so many times it had started to turn pink. Well, not pink, but that faded red color that's just a little more red than pink. There's nothing sadder than faded red, because it always seems like it's trying so hard to be red again.

I wondered if I looked that way now, and if not, I feared it was only a matter of time. The scary thing was that Connor seemed happy with the way he looked, the way the store looked, the way the world looked.

The only time I could ever remember being happy was when I was with Lila and Cassie. Same for being happy with the way I looked or the way the world looked. I was able to see the beauty in things, even in myself. With them next to me, the negative voices in my head were drowned out.

Lila and Cassie had given me that and now Dick Simon was asking me to betray them, was telling me that if I didn't, they would probably betray me. It was hard to decide which would make me feel worse.

As I was dusting the chip aisle, a few of the bags fell from the shelf. For some reason, it felt really good watching them fall and then stepping on them as I moved, hearing the crunch beneath my feet.

I decided to make a game of knocking over as many food items as I could before a customer arrived. I got to about twenty. I was working very slowly.

The guy who came in was on his way home from work. His tie was hanging out of the front right pocket of his pants like a red and blue tongue, and his hair looked like it'd had quite a few runs of his fingers through it, in that way men brush their fingers through their hair when they've had a stressful day—less an act of vanity and more an act of waking up their brain for whatever is ahead. He was looking around furiously.

When I saw a customer acting like this, I was supposed to ask how I could help him, but that night I didn't feel like it. I watched as he walked across the food items on the floor and crunched a bag of Doritos with his foot.

I wanted to run over and join him, to jump up and down on the bag like a trampoline, but I figured I could just wait until he left.

"What happened in here? It looks like there was an earthquake or something."

"Rats," I said, and shrugged. "We set the bait, but every so often a few big ones come out and climb the shelves."

He shook his head and went back to looking for whatever he was looking for. Even the threat of massive rodents couldn't deter him. He came up to the counter almost a full five minutes later with a bag of Cheetos and a Mountain Dew. These were the items he had been searching for.

I was not impressed and I guess I showed it with the look I gave him as I rang him up, because he said, "They're the cheesiest," and then sort of growled.

"How do you know?" I asked, even though I knew he was just reciting from the cardboard display with Chester Cheetah, smiling like a crocodile, at the back of the store.

I'd stared at it while Connor trained me on the deli meats, and I'd wondered how exactly Cheetos knew they were the cheesiest and if I would ever know what the cheesiest was if I had never tried them. Apparently if I hadn't had Cheetos, then I did not even know what cheese tasted like. Without Cheetos I was incomplete until I ate them and then after I ate them I would see that they were so very much the cheesiest that I would become addicted to them, and like I needed another vice, Chester; like I needed one more thing that whispered to me while I was trying to sleep at night.

Thanks a lot.

The guy just shrugged. He was obviously not as affected by it as I was.

He dug around in his pants for the last six cents he owed me, even though I knew that he probably had a ten in there or something that he just didn't feel like breaking. One of the things I'd learned about people while working at Gas-N-Go was that they were either deathly afraid of receiving change or they saw it as some kind of accomplishment when they had it exact. The look in their eyes as they were searching their pockets, part pleading, part apologetic, and then the look they got when they found it, was the look a dog gave you when he fetched something.

As he rummaged, he said the stupid things all people say, like, "I know it's hiding in here somewhere," and "Why do you only find pennies when you don't need them?" He then proceeded to take out everything he had in his pockets and put it on the counter, which included his tie, his wallet, a pack of gum that looked like it had been soaked in water, a Starburst wrapper, a bunch of wadded-up pieces of paper, and a cell phone.

"I just cleaned this counter," I said. I probably wouldn't have said it if I hadn't thought he was the type of guy who would take it. I probably wouldn't have said it if I hadn't wanted him to leave so desperately, so I could go back to crunching chips under my feet and not thinking.

"This just isn't my night," he said, and he returned everything except for the wallet back into his pockets. "Just take it out of this," he said, and gave me a ten.

I knew it.

I also knew that if Daniel had been there, he would ask me why I was so angry and why I was taking it out on this guy. Why I wasn't realizing that I was really angry at myself for being in this situation, for having to choose between myself and Cassie and Lila. That it had nothing to do with this Cheetos-loving, change-hating, small-talk-making guy who was just trying to live his life.

But Daniel wasn't there.

When he leaned in to accept his change, I smelled chlorine on his hair and realized that he swam. I pictured him in his goggles and his cap that fit over his head. I saw him diving down into the blue-green pool water, his feet kicking like a paddleboat motor and swimming back and forth between the shallow and deep ends, getting nowhere. Just like me.

Maybe that was why I was so angry at him.

• • •

Aaron was waiting in his black convertible again when I got off work. Mrs. Mortar had been wrong. Walking toward his car, I couldn't help feeling tingly, like someone was watching me live my life and giving me a high five. It was a feeling I wasn't used to, but one I had felt when Lila, Cassie, and I were hanging out. I'd always thought it was them, but maybe it was just what it felt like to not be ignored.

"Hey," he said. Maybe this was becoming a thing. Maybe *we* were becoming a thing. Lila might have had Brian, but I had Aaron. That had to be worth something.

"Hi," I said, putting a cigarette in my mouth and giving him one. *Hi.* I obviously wasn't getting any better at talking to him, even after our make-out session.

He lit them both, the flame illuminating his face in the darkness. A face that I still couldn't believe he wanted *me* to kiss.

I got in the car without him telling me to. Maybe I was getting better at some things.

Instead of parking on a street by my house, we parked at the back of Gas-N-Go by the big green Dumpster I emptied the trash into every night after my shift. I made up some excuse about Neighborhood Watch, but really it was Joe. I didn't want him to see us together. Things were weird enough between us after my front-porch freak-out.

"I missed you," Aaron said in between kisses.

I chose to believe that, rather than what I knew it probably was—the way he got me to take my bra off. It was in my pocket and his hands were up my shirt, cupping my chest like he was climbing a fake rock wall. But he *missed* me, and I was getting to second base for the first time. Not that I would have anyone to tell about it.

"Me, too," I said, kissing him back, trying to ignore how hard he was squeezing.

I had missed him. Missed this, this escape to a place where I didn't have to think about the arrest or Lila or Cassie or my parents or Dick or Daniel. Where all I had to think about was the feel of leather seats, the taste of smoke, the sound of a car when it's just turned off. *Click, click, click.*

He pulled away and gestured to me for another cigarette. His Zippo snapped open and closed. "How's it been going?" he asked.

"Fine," I said. I didn't want to ruin the mood with all my crap, even though there was a lot of it.

"You hang up the sketch I gave you in your room yet?"

"Yeah," I said. "It looks really good." I hadn't. I didn't have a room to hang it up in. I kept it in my pillow along with his phone number. Like the opposite of *The Princess and the Pea*, I *wanted* to feel it under my head as I slept. Every morning, the pastels had smeared a little more, turning my pillowcase into one of Daniel's tie-dyes.

"That's how I see you," he said.

I didn't know how to respond. The girl in that picture was fearless, was free; she was anything but the way I saw myself.

"I just want you to know," he said. "I'm not sure exactly what you're dealing with, but I've been through this before. I can help you." His hair was a mess. He took it out of his ponytail holder and combed it with his fingers, the cigarette still in his mouth.

"Thanks," I said.

"I mean, if you want my help." He ran his finger up and down my thigh.

"Sure," I said. It came out like a breath. I wanted anything he wanted to give me—help, his tongue, whatever.

"Your lawyer will say he's trying to help you, too," Aaron said, taking one last drag of his cigarette and throwing it at the Dumpster. It sparked like a small firework when it hit.

Why was he talking about my lawyer? How did he even know I had a lawyer?

"That's what mine did," he said, taking a long drag.

I looked at him. He was trying to help me. He was trying to tell me what it had been like for him.

"Said he would take care of everything." Aaron shook his head.

"When you did what you're not supposed to talk about," I teased, picturing the day of my arraignment, his finger shushing his lips. Lips I could kiss whenever I wanted.

"This isn't a joke," he said.

"I know," I said, trying to ignore how much he sounded like Dick had in my backyard the other night.

"Your lawyer will try to make you do whatever he says."

"Like my parents," I agreed.

"Yup." He nodded. "Lawyers are soldiers for the monkey man." His finger traced a circle on my knee.

"Well, really for my mom, I guess."

"The monkey man can sometimes be a woman," he said, his hand playing with the bottom of my shirt.

I leaned in to kiss him again.

"My advice would be not to listen," he whispered into my lips. "You're stronger than that."

I thought about the girl in the picture he'd drawn. Maybe I was. "Why are you being so nice to me?" I asked, finally having the courage he said I had.

"I like you."

"I like you, too."

"Well, I guess that's settled," he said, kissing me again.

I thought about Dick, his stupid jokes, his way of dismissing everything I wanted. "My lawyer is an idiot," I whispered.

"Exactly," he said.

"I won't listen," I said, my eyes closed.

"Just to me," he said, kissing me like I really was the girl in that picture, making me believe it, too.

I guess Aaron was the only one I could trust.

Twenty-one

One good thing about living in the basement was that I didn't have to make my bed anymore. That was something my mother had always insisted on when I was living upstairs. Even if I had gotten out of making it all day, she would still force me to make it at night before I went to sleep, as a way of teaching me a lesson about making beds. She didn't bother teaching me that lesson anymore. She didn't bother teaching me anything anymore.

What she did do was make my life hell. She woke me the next morning when I had no appointments other than working at Gas-N-Go that night. There was absolutely no reason for her to come and wake me at six thirty in the morning. No reason, except that she was crazy.

She stood above me. I could hear her breathing, could hear AJ flying around his cage as if he were warning me that she was in the room.

"So what do you plan on doing about this, then?" she asked, like we had been having a conversation. In reality, she had just kicked my mattress and yelled like a madwoman.

I guess this was her new question. She had given up asking me how this could have happened. Asking how didn't get her anywhere when what she really wanted to know was what I was going to do about it.

"Mom, I'm sleeping," I said, putting the pillow over my head and hoping she would leave so that I could be asleep again soon.

"I'm not leaving until you come to your senses," she said, falling back on her tried-and-true colloquialisms.

My answer was still no. I wasn't any closer to agreeing to turn in Lila and Cassie than I had been when Dick presented it to me. I wasn't sure what it would take to make me go along with it, but the fact that my mother wanted it so badly certainly wasn't helping. Aaron was right; they were all just trying to get me to do what they wanted me to do.

Even though Dick was the one who told me about it, it had definitely been her idea. It was like her way of making sure they would never want to be friends with me ever again.

"Go away." I wasn't in the mood for one of my mother's talks, with her sentences that flew around and around like flies, never really landing on anything. I could hear her standing there, watching me. Then I could hear her gnawing on her thumbnail. "Please," I said, and meant it. I wanted her to leave. The only time I ever got to truly forget what was happening was when I was sleeping.

"You need to take Dick Simon's offer."

"I don't want to talk about this right now," I said.

"It's your best chance," she said, starting to cry.

"Mom, stop."

She continued. "You never listen to me. Fine, I've accepted that, but Amy, this is not for me. This is for you."

It wasn't that I hadn't thought about what Dick had suggested, but if I did what they wanted, it would be like my life was a house on fire, and I was leaving Cassie and Lila inside it to burn. I would be pushing them out of the way even as smoldering beams fell on them. And maybe that didn't mean anything to my mom, but it meant something to me.

No one but Aaron really understood. I turned away from her and pulled the covers over my head.

She ran upstairs and slammed the door before I could say anything else. At least there was one good thing about her recent weakness for uncontrollable sobbing fits; I could keep what secrets I had left.

I was almost back to sleep when my father came down. My mother was sending in the big guns. She knew it was hard for me to deny anything my father asked, and as much as I hated to admit she was right about anything, she was certainly right about that.

"Dad, please, just let me sleep," I said, sitting up and looking at him, hoping that if he saw my bloodshot eyes and pleading face, he would be his usual amenable self and leave me alone.

"I was hoping you might join me for a walk," he said

shyly, like he had an ulterior motive that he was embarrassed about. It made me think of those douche commercials where a mother and daughter are walking on a beach and the daughter finally gets up the courage to ask the mother if she ever gets that "not-so-fresh feeling," only in my case I guessed my father and I were not going to talk about my smelly lady parts.

"How about in a few hours?" I said, hoping it would placate him enough to make him go away.

"I'll be at work," he said. "Besides, your mother would like the two of us to talk."

"Then the answer is definitely *no*."

"Fine," he said, looking down. "*I* would like it."

I pulled the covers off and followed him up the stairs. Maybe he meant it and maybe he didn't, but maybe that didn't matter.

• • •

My father and I hadn't taken a walk together in years, but when I was a kid, we took a walk almost every night that it was warm enough, as soon as we finished eating dinner. When I was little, our walks were all about escape. We were escaping our house and my mother and her rules. My father would smoke a cigar and give me all the sugarless gum I could consume before we made it back home.

He would tell me about Scribbles, the dog he'd had as a kid, and I would always ask him if we could get a puppy. Then he would pretend that we already had one, because he didn't want to say no like my mother always did. He would pick up a stick and play fetch with the imaginary dog we were only allowed to have on our walk. He would bend down and pretend to pet it and when we were back at our driveway he would tell it we would see it again next time.

But on our walk that day, there were no cigars and no sugarless gum. We didn't talk about Scribbles; we talked about Dick's offer. My father in his dress pants, pressed white shirt, and tie that he wore to work every day, and me in my pajamas.

As we walked, other parents in our neighborhood were leaving to go to work or were waving from behind their screen doors, and other kids were still sleeping.

"Have you come to a decision yet?" he asked, like my mother hadn't told him what I'd just said. Maybe he hoped he'd get a different answer if he asked.

"Dad, I can't."

He nodded. "All I want you to do is what's best for you," he said.

I wanted that, too, if I could figure out what it was.

"I miss our walks," he said, and I could tell he meant it. I knew he wasn't just saying it to get what he wanted. I knew because I did, too. Our lives had been so much simpler then.

"Yeah," I said.

"We could still take them," he said.

"Sure." For some reason I thought about spending a year locked up. If I was convicted, we wouldn't be able to take walks anymore. We wouldn't be able to do anything anymore.

"When did you stop being happy?" he asked.

I wondered if it was the same thing Joe had tried to

say to me, just in a different way. I used to be happy. I used to be nice. Maybe my father just hadn't noticed until now. Being at his office so much, he hadn't watched me turning from his happy little girl into whatever I was now. He hadn't seen it coming.

"I never really was," I lied. Lied so hard it made my stomach hurt. It was easier than telling him the truth—that I didn't know the answer. That he was right. That Joe was right. That there was a before and an after, but the middle was a mystery.

"It makes me sad to hear that," he said, stopping to look at me.

I shrugged because I couldn't respond. He probably didn't want the real answer, anyway. As a dentist, my father wasn't in the business of being a conversationalist. His business was shoving stuff in people's mouths so they *couldn't* talk. It was easier that way.

We circled around. A few more houses and we would be in front of Joe's. Even from here I could see that the windows were still dark. He and his mother wouldn't be up for hours. I knew Spud was still sleeping, too, under Joe's covers, spooned up next to his legs.

I wanted to go hide under his porch. Hide from my lie and from my father having to hear me tell it. But what if Joe found me in my pajamas, crying? Would he be nice to me? Or would he tell me I was a druggie loser and to get lost? Who was I to him now? I guess I didn't want to find out.

"I've got a bicuspid that's been bothering me," I said, changing the subject.

"Call Peggy and make an appointment. If I'm booked, she'll make time for you." He put his arm around me and gave me a sideways hug.

We walked in silence back to the house. I couldn't help wishing that for my father's sake at least, like our imaginary dog, I had never existed.

Twenty-two

Seeing how things had gone at the nursing home, Dick finally realized that forcing me to work with people was a mistake.

"Animals," he said.

Whatever—I liked animals, and they were definitely better than trash.

Even though I'd begged to go plenty of times while petitioning for that puppy as a child, I'd never been to the Humane Society in my town. They called it Lollipop Farm, which I guess was supposed to make you forget that the unpicked animals would in all likelihood be killed.

I found the owner mopping up an empty cage. I decided to think good thoughts about that empty cage, even though the paperwork hanging on it told me otherwise.

"You must be Amy," she said, and held out a hand for me to shake.

What was with being arrested and then having to shake people's hands? After I got arrested, everyone wanted to shake my hand when they met me. Like being arrested turned me into an adult overnight, like I was on one long job interview.

She didn't introduce herself, but she was wearing a nametag that said Annie. Her hair was old-newspaper blond and as fluffy as the head on a badly poured beer. She looked like a zookeeper, one of those women who were so natural and comfortable and grounded that they could wear cargo shorts without even worrying about how they made them look fat.

"Thanks so much for helping out," she said, sounding like a cheerleader leading a pep rally where no one was listening. "We don't get many volunteers here."

"Sure," I said. "I love dogs." This conversation was about as interesting as her Birkenstocks.

"Your lawyer already told me your story, so you don't have to worry about going through all that," she said.

It was something, anyway. At least I wouldn't have a repeat performance of what had happened with Mrs. Mortar. I waited for Annie to continue over the sound of barking dogs echoing through the cement hallways.

"I know you've probably heard it all before," she said, taking my shoulder, "but you'll get through this."

I looked at her skeptically.

"I was just like you; scared, alone, unsure. Now look at me." She nodded in that way sober people nod when they're trying to make you see how much better their life is now that they are sober.

She thought all my problems came down to drugs. If only they could be explained away that easily.

"Thanks," I said, not really knowing how to respond. It was definitely possible that she had been arrested, like me, but I doubted that her father had just asked her when she'd stopped being happy. I doubted that she had been told to turn on her two best friends.

Then again, maybe she had, and did, and that was why she was here, alone with a bunch of dogs.

"Here you go," she said, handing me the mop and indicating the other empty cages down the line, and I realized quickly that I wouldn't be working with animals at all. I would be cleaning up their crap.

She left me to work while she went to feed the dogs that were alive—dogs that still had a chance to get out of there. From what I could tell, Lollipop Farm was a small, poorly run operation, with very little in the way of funds. I came to this conclusion because Annie appeared to be the only employee and because they only had one mop.

Before the arrest, the small things I did every day to survive felt like they had meaning and purpose in them, but now, being forced to stop and think, I started to wonder what I was doing. I couldn't help remembering that I was on a planet hurtling through space, that I was just one girl, in one town, in one country, with little choice in the matter. I felt like I had said a word over and over again and it had lost all its meaning.

As I mopped, I held my breath. The cages were totally disgusting. It smelled like I was at the zoo. It smelled like the zoo was in my nose. This was worse than trash; it was worse than defending my life to Mrs. Mortar; it was worse than cleaning the bathrooms at Gas-N-Go. I was picking up actual poop with a shovel and scrubbing cement floors free of pee, and there was nothing I could do but keep cleaning.

To try to keep my mind off the stench, I sang "It's the Hard-Knock Life for Us." Probably because the owner's name was Annie, but also because for once in my life, being an orphan seemed like an interesting prospect.

After I finished cleaning the cages, I found Annie out in the fenced yard. She handed me a bag of food.

"These are the troublesome dogs," she said. "That's why they're out here, so be careful."

Apparently, they made so much noise and were such a nuisance that they couldn't be kept inside with the other dogs. They barked and yipped as we came by with our bags of food.

"Go loudest first." She opened the cage of a Saint Bernard whose bark sounded like the impatient hooting of an owl. "Trust me—your ears will thank you."

I headed for the next loudest, a Pomeranian who sounded like someone impatiently beeping during a traffic jam. As soon as I poured his food, he stopped barking and licked my hand.

"You got any pets?" Annie asked.

"AJ," I said, "a parrot."

"Cool," she said. "Birds are smart, much smarter than we give them credit for." She squinted. "I hope you don't keep him in a cage."

"No," I lied. I'm not sure why.

"Birds need to fly," she said.

I decided to focus on how lame that sounded, rather than think about how AJ had been in an essential jail forever and would never know any different. How I would always keep AJ in a cage. If I didn't, he might fly away.

I went on to the next loudest pen; it held a Husky with ice-colored eyes I would have killed for. She howled like a werewolf but quieted as soon as I delivered her food.

I showed Annie my empty bag. "More in the shed," she said.

I let myself in and turned on the light. I could hear the dogs that were waiting to be fed still barking. I wondered if these dogs were really troublesome, or if they were just like Daniel had said I was: craving, needing attention. With all those other dogs around them, what else were they supposed to do?

Twenty-three

That night at work, I stood behind the counter and stared. Connor had given me another chance to see if I could man the Gas-N-Go cash register all on my own. Well, all on my own under his watchful eye.

He still ran out of the back room like a woman with a towel on any time he heard the bell above the door ring. When I got sick of staring at nothing, I walked over to the door and opened it just to see him run from the back, out of breath, looking humbled when he saw that no one was there.

And when he looked at me with his sad face, I shrugged, a shrug that said, *Beats me*, and went back to staring.

If my mom and dad had their way, at the end of the summer I would be heading off to stare at the wall of a dorm room instead of the wall of a cell. But I would still be staring at a wall. I knew why it mattered what building it was in, but I also knew it was because I was scared out of my mind and thinking about what else I should be doing, wondering how the hell I could get out.

I guess, even after you die, even if you think you've been happy your whole life and have been moving too fast to even stare at a wall, you'll still be forced to stare at the top of your coffin for eternity, wondering why you never realized this was what it all meant.

I went over to the front door again and opened it, to clear my head and laugh at Connor's elephant-stampede run to the sales floor.

He looked at me and sighed, taking the door from my hand and closing it when he found the store empty. "I know you're under a lot of stress right now, but your job should not suffer for it."

"Don't worry, there's no one here anyway—it's not suffering."

"There are other things you could be doing. Other things *I* could be doing."

Of course there were other things I could be doing. I could be with Aaron. I could be in my room with AJ, smoking. "Relax, Connor, it was just a joke."

He shook his head. "I know, Amy," he said.

"You know what?"

He reached for my hand. "It's okay. Your mom told me."

I shook his hand away. "How do you even know my mother?"

"She just needed someone to listen to her. She's very upset."

Who didn't she have working for her? "Yeah, apparently

her feelings are on the eleven o'clock news."

He looked at me in a way that said, *I am so glad you are not my daughter*. "We thought it would be best if you came to prayer group at my church."

"I'm Jewish, Connor."

"You can be any religion to ask for Jesus's help and guidance," he said, looking up.

My mother was actually willing to put my life into the hands of Jesus—that was how bad she thought things had become. If only I had known that getting arrested could have been the thing that made my parents get a Christmas tree when I was a kid.

"We feel you are scared and think a circle of peers might help you make the right decision."

"Your church freaks are not my peers," I said, realizing I shouldn't be taking this out on him. It was all coming from my mother. Connor was just a pawn in her game.

"Call them whatever you want now—after tomorrow night you'll call them friends." He paused to see if I would agree, and when I didn't, he continued. "My wife and I will pick you up. We'll have dinner beforehand. How's Denny's sound?"

"I'm not going."

"You have no choice."

I stormed over to the counter and started cleaning it. I wanted to do anything other than look at him, anything other than realize that my life and my decisions were still being run by my mother. Connor was right: I didn't have a choice. I didn't have a choice about anything anymore.

Didn't anyone see that maybe this was why I wasn't just

going along with everything? I mean, besides not wanting to screw over Lila and Cassie, and Aaron's hot breath in my ear. I finally had a decision that was mine to make.

"So that was all I had to say to get you to do some work?" he asked, smirking.

I glared at him.

"Come on, Amy. I just want to help."

"You're only doing what my mother is telling you to do," I said, rubbing the counter hard enough to start a fire.

He stood there watching me. There was nothing else to say. My mother had him doing her dirty work. She was probably paying him, too.

"Please, just go away," I said, still scrubbing, scrubbing, scrubbing.

"All right, all right," he said, holding up his hands and walking away from me and into the back room like a gun had been raised at him.

I wished I had one.

The bell above the door rang to announce a customer's arrival. Connor didn't even run out when he heard it, which meant I had to deal with whoever it was. I turned away from the counter and fiddled with the cigarette rack, hoping that if I ignored the customer, he or she would go away.

I heard someone walk up to the counter and the drumming of her nails against it.

No such luck.

"Salem 100's."

I turned and found Cassie's mother standing on the other side of the counter. Her hair was shorter and darker, oil black.

I touched my own hair. I was barely even bothering to brush it anymore.

"Oh, it's you," she said, her eyes squinting.

"Hi, Mrs. Wick," I said, feeling my legs start to shake. It was what I always said to Cassie's mom, but I doubted it would fly this time. I reached for the emergency bat under the counter.

"What are you doing here?" she asked.

"I work here," I said, indicating my shirt. Though it probably wasn't really what she was asking. She was asking, *What are you doing in my line of vision? And how long until you are out of it?*

"How's Cassie?" I asked before I could even stop the words from coming out of my mouth.

"How do you think?"

I knew how I was doing, but I wanted her to reveal some secret about how Cassie was surviving. I wanted her to tell me anything.

I saw her turn and glance at her parked car. Cassie was sitting in it, her head down. I dropped the bat and made a move to go outside.

"Stop right there," she said. "Don't bother. She doesn't want to see you."

It couldn't be true. Could it?

"Just stay away from her." She put her hand on the huge pickle jar that sat on the counter. Maybe she was looking for a weapon. Thinking she could break it over my head so that when I fell to the ground, my skull would be haloed by a briny, bloody puddle like a fertilized chicken egg.

"Is she okay?" I asked.

"Yeah, she's great," she said. "How about those Salems?"

"I miss her." I wasn't sure why I was bothering. It sounded more pathetic than I had planned. I guess I was lonelier than even I thought I was.

"Good for you," she said. She handed me a twenty.

"Everything will be fine," I said, which was what I wanted everyone to say to me.

"Maybe for you, maybe not," she said, taking the cigarettes and her change.

"I'm sorry," I said, surprising myself. Wondering why I could say it so easily to her when I couldn't even really say it to my own parents, other than thoughtlessly repeating it because I hadn't known what else to say the morning after the arrest. Maybe because saying it to Cassie's mother didn't have to mean anything.

"Right, that's what Cassie keeps saying, too," she said, walking out of the store.

As I watched them drive away, I tried to picture Cassie saying it, wondered where she found the strength to keep saying it. Maybe she didn't know what else to say, either.

• • •

My mother was waiting for me when I got off work that night. Which meant Aaron wasn't. His car wasn't there. He'd probably been scared off by her suburban-mom minivan. She was really racking up reasons for me to be pissed off at her. I passed her, determined to walk home alone. Dealing with Cassie's mom had been enough mother for one night.

She drove up next to me and rolled down the window.

"Ignoring me is not going to make this go away."

She had a point, but I didn't care. "I can't believe you told Connor." I didn't say what else I wanted to say, which was that in telling him, she had taken away the one place I could go where I could act normal, like nothing was wrong. Even Aaron knew I had been arrested. As good as I felt when I was with him, I couldn't pretend.

"I wish we could talk," she said.

I wondered if we ever had. Wasn't that why she had gotten me AJ, so I would have someone to talk to, even if that someone was a bird?

I kept walking while she drove next to me at a crawl. "What did you expect me to do?" she asked, and I could hear tears in her voice. But at least I didn't have to look at her.

I lit a cigarette.

"Put that out," she said, the tears subsiding under her stern parental voice.

"Why are you doing this to me?" I asked.

"Amy, I just want to help you. That's all I've ever wanted."

"You can't, okay? You can't." It was mean, but it was also true.

I heard her tears coming back. "Amy, I'm your mother," she said, putting the car into park. "I love you."

I stopped walking and looked at her. I could have just repeated those words, said them easily, like I used to when I was little. I could have said what she wanted me to say and done what she wanted me to do. But it wasn't that easy. I wanted it to be that easy, but it wasn't.

Eventually she gave up and drove past me, her red taillights bright and hot as coals at the bottom of a fire as she made her way down the street.

As I walked home, I couldn't help thinking about Cassie being reduced to a girl sitting in a car with her head down, waiting for her mother. Saying she was sorry over and over again. Cassie was the tough one, the stubborn one.

I was the one who should have been able to apologize. Who should have been able to tell my mother the words she wanted to hear. Maybe I was more stubborn than I realized.

Twenty-four

The following night was Moons Over My Hammy for Connor and his wife and chocolate milkshakes for me. Connor had been right—I didn't have a choice. I had to go to dinner and to their church group with them, just like I had to do all the other annoying things my mother told me to.

I'd never admit it, but it was mostly because I didn't know what else *to* do.

I called Aaron as Connor beeped in my driveway, hoping he might come to my rescue, but he didn't answer his phone. He probably didn't know it was me. I called again as my mother banged on the basement door. It went straight to voice mail and I hung up. What message was I supposed to leave? *Meet me at Denny's?*

I sat across the table from Connor's wife, trying to figure out what she saw in Connor. Not like she was any prize, but she was female and she was breathing. Considering the age of their children, they must have met in high school. I wondered if he used to surprise her in parking lots, if they used to have hot and heavy make-out sessions in cars parked in dark places.

She had a chin-length bob and apricot-blond hair. The color you get using an at-home color kit, which, other than usually turning out orange, illustrates like nothing else that you are completely uncomfortable with yourself. I knew that because I'd used them.

She wore one of those plaid flannel overall dresses with a yellow turtleneck that made her look like Big Bird from the neck up. I couldn't help feeling like I looked pretty good sitting next to her. Maybe she could be my new best friend. I tried not to wonder whether Lila had thought something similar the night we first met.

I looked over at the blue daisies Connor's wife had brought for me. I guess blue daisies signified a last-ditch effort with a burgeoning convict, like red meant love and yellow meant friendship. I considered going back to Blooming Maples to give them to Mrs. Mortar, since then, at least, I wouldn't have them around to remind me that the only person who had ever bought me flowers had been Connor's wife.

"You could at least be grateful this whole prayer circle is for you," Connor said between bites of his sandwich.

I sipped on my milkshake. "Don't they have anything better to do? Like drinking strychnine or speaking in tongues?"

"That is very closed-minded of you," he said.

"I'm Jewish, Connor," I reminded him again, in case he'd forgotten.

"Well," he said, wiping his mouth, "look where that has gotten you."

"This night is not about converting me," I said, spooning up chocolate ice cream from the bottom of the glass.

"The night's not over yet," he said.

His wife stayed silent, but she ordered me another chocolate milkshake.

"Do you guys eat like this all the time?" I asked, starting on my second milkshake, even though I felt like I might puke. I really hadn't eaten much since the arrest. It felt good to have a stomach full of chocolate.

"Only on special occasions," his wife said, finally breaking her silence, turning to look at Connor and rubbing his shoulder.

Hopefully this prayer circle really did drink strychnine, so I could kill myself as soon as we got there.

• • •

I hated to admit it, but part of the reason I didn't want to go to Connor's prayer circle was because I was afraid of churches. Any time I went to one, I was immediately made aware of my *otherness.*

Sure, every church I'd been to looked the same as my temple at first, brick on the outside, waxy tiled floors on the inside, hallways flanked by classrooms and offices, and school-grade public bathrooms. But then I would enter the sanctuary and see that big cross hanging on the wall, and

I'd realize it was all different and I was all different. There was nothing more terrifying than being completely unlike everyone around you.

I felt that enough in my secular life.

Luckily, the prayer circle was in the rec hall, so at least I could pretend I wasn't in a church—that is, until they started praying.

Connor paused for a second before we entered, just long enough for me to see that all the women were dressed exactly like his wife. Like they had taken a big pile of those overall dresses that were on sale and had them all blessed.

Connor put himself between his wife and me, then put his arms around both of us. I elbowed him. "I was forced to agree to praying, not to touching."

"Touch is one of the most powerful healers."

"So is morphine. I'll take that instead." I walked ahead of them to a seat in one of the metal folding chairs they had arranged in a circle in the middle of the room. I crossed my arms and legs and harrumphed, letting everyone know I was not a willing participant.

A woman in a blue-and-green-plaid overall dress sat next to me and said, "You must be Amy."

I wanted to say something smart, but I couldn't figure out what, so I just nodded.

"We get strangers here, but not too often," she said, like some maid in a haunted mansion taking you up to your room, where you'll be killed that night. "We are just so glad to be able to help you with this decision."

"I don't know how much help you'll be," I said.

"Well, not us. Him," she said, looking up.

The craziest thing about all of this—and there were many crazy things: the fact that I was in a church, the fact that I was with Connor and wasn't at work, the fact that I was with a bunch of Dress Barn rejects, the fact that within minutes I was going to be praying to Jesus to ask Him for guidance—was the fact that this was my mother's idea.

My mother, who was an image Jew, which is a Jew who only cares as much about her Judaism as the person she is trying to prove it to, was sending me to the feet of Jesus for help. She must truly have run out of options.

"Let's get started," some guy said, cupping his hands around his mouth to make sure everyone could hear. I guess this was supposed to include the Man himself.

Everyone sat down in the circle of chairs, alternating man, woman, man, woman, and I felt instantaneously uncomfortable. Not because it was obvious I was the only one here who was not adhering to God's Perfect Plan, but because my stomach hurt and not in the *tummy hurts* sort of way. It hurt in the *dysentery* sort of way.

Someone said something about taking your neighbor's hand, but I was afraid that if I let go of my stomach, which I was clutching like a ball in my lap, it would explode, and by explode, well, just guess.

Then Connor said, "Jesus, we come to you today for guidance for our sister Amy."

I think I groaned, because everyone looked over at me—either that, or they were trying to picture me as their sister, superimposing an orangey bob and my own overall dress.

"She seeks your wisdom in making a decision with

immense gravity over the rest of her life."

I groaned again, and Connor whispered, "It's okay." Pulling me to him and shaking me, like an older brother giving your whole body a noogie.

It caused whatever had been struggling to escape from inside my stomach to start coming loose. I got up and ran for the bathroom.

"Where are you going?" Connor yelled after me.

I didn't bother explaining. I was afraid that if I took the time to stop, my soul wouldn't have been the only thing this congregation was cleaning up.

I practically pulled the bathroom door from its hinges as I ran inside, saying my own little prayer, thanking whoever was responsible for putting the bathroom right next to the rec hall.

As I sat on the toilet, I couldn't help wondering whether God was punishing me. Not that everything that had happened already hadn't made me consider it, but until that night I hadn't actually been purposely taunting Him. Maybe this was His way of telling me that I had even less control over things than I'd thought.

There was a knock at the bathroom door. It was Connor's wife, asking me if I was all right.

"Fine," I said, even though my stomach was saying something very different.

I heard someone come up behind her and heard her whisper, "Just a case of the Loosey Gooseys," and then, "Hell hath no fury like lactose. That's why Connor and I stay away from it."

Then I heard that someone chuckle.

Connor's wife opened the bathroom door. "Do you need anything?"

I didn't answer. I couldn't. I just groaned. Even if I could talk, I was not about to have a conversation with this woman while I was on the toilet.

"Some water, some juice?"

I said nothing, just answered with the sounds of someone whose large intestine is turning to liquid.

"She'll be okay. We'll just move everyone out here into the hallway," she said as she closed the door.

To which I answered by puking onto the floor in front of me, which seemed more than appropriate.

I sat there, dying on the toilet, as a group of Christians I didn't even know huddled in a circle in the hallway outside of the bathroom and prayed that their Lord Jesus would give me the wisdom to make the right decision. If that isn't enough to turn someone into an atheist, I don't know what is.

. . .

Connor called my mother and told her what had happened. Which was why I was surprised that, when I found her waiting for me at our front door, it was with a scowl instead of with a bottle of Pepto Bismol. I was glad Joe wasn't out on his bike. At least my humiliation would be reserved for family members and a few select members of God's assembly.

She was yelling before I even got inside the house. I could see her through the storm door, her mouth moving like a fish out of water gasping for breath. "This is real, Amy. As much as you like to play around, this is real."

"Mom, I'm sick."

"I'm tired of your excuses."

I thought about something to say in response, but I didn't really have the energy. Well, maybe I had the energy, but I certainly didn't have the time. I ran past her to the comfort of my bathroom.

"What? Do you think it will be *cool* to go to jail?" my mother yelled from outside the bathroom door. She leaned into it and turned the handle. I was glad that even in my hurry to get inside, I hadn't forgotten my habit of locking it.

"Mom, go away," I said. Not like I would have responded to this anyway. It was my mother's favorite chorus during a bitchfest—*If everyone jumped off a bridge, would you?*

"Why is this locked?" she asked, like she always did.

Usually I would have been in there smoking, or putting on way too much makeup, or trying on the thong Lila had given me, but now my mother was attempting to barge in on me when I was food-poisoning sick because she wanted me to turn on my best friends to avoid my own punishment.

When had things gotten so crazy?

"I already told Dick Simon and you and Dad and now Connor and everyone he knows—I'm not interested."

Why were they all making such a big deal out of this? I mean, I knew it was a big deal, but it felt like everyone cared a lot more about it than I did.

Like everything else.

"Fine. Get convicted, then. See if I care."

"Mom, you're making things worse," I said.

"*I'm* making things worse," she said. "That's a riot." She

started laughing.

I didn't respond. This was what she always did. Why bother talking when she didn't listen anyway? I grabbed the trash can next to the toilet and threw up.

She was supposed to be getting me a warm washcloth and some toast; she was supposed to be asking me if I was okay, if I needed anything, like Connor's wife had.

But maybe there were things I was supposed to be doing, too.

She knocked. "Open the door. I want to talk to you," she said.

"Mom, gross," I said.

She knocked again. "Amy, I mean it. Open the door."

I flushed the toilet, if only so I could shut out her voice.

"Amy, are you still there?"

I wasn't sure why she was asking. Did she think I'd flushed myself down the toilet? The sad thing was that if it were a possibility, I might have considered it in that moment. Gone down the pipes and floated up again into a new life, with a new me and new parents and two new best friends.

"Honey," she said, "I know you're scared."

"I'm not scared. I'm sick," I said, retching into the trashcan. Sick was truly the only thing I felt for once.

"How can you be so ill?" she asked.

I put my head into my hands. "I'm detoxing from heroin, obviously," I said sarcastically.

She didn't get the joke. She screamed my father's name as she ran down the hall. I had just two minutes of reprieve before he knocked on the door.

"Heroin, Amy? What's next?" he cried.

"Dad, come on, I was kidding," I said.

"Try telling your mother that."

"Dad, please, I feel really sick."

I heard him exhale.

"Dad." I wanted to say something else, but I didn't know what. I wished that whatever sickness I had would make the words that usually stayed inside come out, too.

He sighed. "Your mother and I hope you will come to a decision soon."

I heard him walk down the hall and slam their bedroom door. This was life in our house now.

The only decision I could be sure of that night was *never* to go to Denny's again.

Twenty-five

The next morning, I took AJ out of his cage and perched him on my finger. His yellow feathers were as bright as the sun I would barely ever see if I did end up in jail.

"What should I do?" I asked, peering into his little black eyes.

Everyone could ask me as many times and in as many ways as they wanted to about whether I would turn on Lila and Cassie. The only person's opinion I trusted was a bird's.

AJ was rarely silent, especially after prompting, but he didn't say anything—he didn't move. He just kept staring at me with those tar-colored eyes. It seemed like he was telling me it was my decision to make.

That was why I liked him better than most people.

I put him on my shoulder and called Lila. I guess I wanted to make sure that even though we hadn't talked about it, we were still standing together. I guess I wanted to make sure my indecision wouldn't leave me behind.

Her phone rang and rang. I couldn't help thinking that maybe she wasn't answering because she could see it was me.

That maybe I had already been left behind.

Even though I wasn't ready to admit it to anyone else, I was worried. I called Aaron. He had been through this. I took his number from my pillow, even though I didn't need to; I'd memorized it. Taken the numbers and used them instead of counting sheep to lull myself to sleep at night.

"What's up?" he asked, after I said hello.

He knew my voice. Or—I let myself believe the even spazzier thought—he didn't give out his number to that many girls.

"Nothing," I said. I guess even with him the words were hard.

"Sorry I didn't answer last night," he said. "I was at the skate park and my phone was in my bag."

"It's okay," I said.

"So, what's up?" he asked again, not in a mean way. I guess he could tell I was holding back. I heard laughing and music in the background.

"Where are you?" AJ still sat on my shoulder. I could feel his claws digging in.

"You know, just hanging out at my friend Brian's."

Brian's. I wondered if Lila was there. I wondered if they were talking about me. I wondered why he couldn't have just been there on prom night.

I heard him walk down the stairs, go outside, and close the front door. "It smells like piss out here," he said.

Cassie. It smelled like Cassie's piss out there. She would kill me if she knew I was even talking to Aaron after what he had done to us. Sleeping with the enemy. Well, not yet.

"Did something happen?" he asked.

Since I'd last seen him, yeah, a lot had happened. I'd been called on my bluff and my colon had basically fallen out, but other than that, just your average day.

"Not really," I said.

I heard his Zippo snap open, heard him light a cigarette, heard it snap closed. I wanted to listen to that sound forever.

"You want me to come get you later?" he asked.

I saw myself riding in his convertible, the top down, feeling the feeling I'd tried to solidify into concrete memory, but I knew I couldn't act like that girl, not tonight. The night before had scrubbed me raw.

"It's okay," I said, not wanting to say no.

"All right, later." He ended the call before I could say anything else.

It's okay, it's okay, it's okay, AJ repeated, flying back to his cage.

I looked up at the basement window. The sun was bright. So bright, it made me blink. It was the kind of beautiful summer day when, in my old life, Cassie, Lila, and I would have made our way down to the rocky shores of Lake Erie.

It was a whole forty-five-minute drive away. There were closer places to go, but we liked that no one knew us there. That we could be whoever we wanted to be.

We lay next to one another in the sun, waiting for some boys that Lila knew to meet us, the smell of dead fish and suntan lotion and hot sand all around. Lila was in a black bikini. I was wearing jean shorts and a blue tankini top, and Cassie had a flannel over her one-piece bathing suit.

"Aren't you hot?" Lila asked, leaning on her arm to look at Cassie. Her skin was shiny with suntan oil.

"Aren't you cold?" Cassie sneered. She drank from a plastic canteen. Then she passed it to me.

"I feel just right," I said, opening the cap and sniffing. It was strong, like ammonia strong.

I'd gotten used to our routine. Cassie was brash. Lila was beautiful. I was quiet and plain. Like human versions of the porridge in *Goldilocks and the Three Bears*. Being ordinary was exactly what had made me feel out of place around other people, but Cassie and Lila wanted me to be that way.

I braved it and took a sip. It tasted like spoiled apple juice. I coughed. "Yuck, what is that?"

"Seagram's, I think. My dad has had it hidden in his underwear drawer since the day I was born," Cassie said.

I passed it over to Lila. She took a drink, her mouth puckering. "It tastes like crap."

"You're going to start being picky now?" Cassie said.

Lila shrugged and took another swig. "I had a cousin who used to drink mouthwash to get drunk."

"Are you serious?" I asked.

She nodded, her sunglasses pointy like cat eyes. "I caught him on Thanksgiving one year. I never told anyone."

"That's so weird," I said.

"I know, right?" She laughed. "I would have to be so hard up to try that."

I doubted Lila would ever be that hard up.

"Your family is so fucked up," Cassie said, grabbing the canteen back from Lila.

"All the best ones are," Lila said, smiling devilishly.

"Right." I laughed. "The Mansons."

"Burn," Cassie snapped.

"The Kardashians," I added, bolstered by Cassie's encouragement.

"Ha!" Cassie laughed. "Double burn."

"Funny," Lila said, not laughing, which I knew meant she didn't think it was.

"Where are they?" Cassie asked, lighting a cigarette and looking around.

"They'll be here," Lila said. She could get away with saying things like that. She put her sunglasses on her forehead.

"Maybe we should go," I said. We had been waiting all day. My skin was hot and pink. The SPF 45 suntan lotion I had put on at my house had more than worn off. I hadn't had the nerve to bring it with me.

"We're waiting," Lila said.

"Whatever," Cassie said.

I knew we were. There was nothing Cassie or I could say to change Lila's mind. She actually liked the boy who was coming for her. I never knew what Cassie thought of her partners, but mine always seemed like leftovers.

Maybe I seemed like leftovers to them.

"We should come here every day," Lila said.

"Totally," I said. Sunburned or not, boys on the way or not, I would rather be there, far from Collinsville with Cassie and Lila, than anywhere else.

"You got the gas money for that?" Cassie said, shoving her spent cigarette in an empty soda can.

"They're here," Lila said, squinting and putting her sunglasses back on.

It was Kyle, Chris, and Nick. The guys who seemed to wave like cattails as they smoked cigarettes every morning before school on Farber Lane—taunting the administrators, daring them to do something about it. I'd never talked to any of them. Of course, Lila had. Or more likely, they had talked to her.

I watched as they walked over. They looked like variations on the same theme: clothes that hung on their scarecrow bodies, hair that was too long to be accidental.

"Stop drooling, Amy. You want them to know we've actually been waiting for them?" Lila asked.

"Sorry," I said, looking away.

"Kyle's mine," Lila whispered as she stood up. He was the cutest: dark brown hair and eyes, skin the color of caramel. There was no doubt he was hers.

"Hey," Kyle said, smoke leaking through the gaps in his teeth as he smiled.

"Took you long enough," Lila said, putting her arm around his waist and walking away with him.

Chris kicked at the sand like a stubborn horse. Some of it landed on Cassie. She stood up and pushed him. "What's up, slut?" he said. He was tall, gangly; he reminded me of a giraffe.

"Not much, fuckface," she said, but it was obvious she was smiling. "See you losers later," she said as the two of them walked in the other direction.

Nick stood there. His bathing suit hung so low that I could see a sliver of his underwear. Who wore underwear under his bathing suit?

Someone who wasn't going to the beach to swim.

"Hi," he said, his cheeks blooming pink.

"Hi," I said, trying to tell myself he was cute—cute enough.

He sat down next to me and handed me a McDonald's cup, the straw as gnawed as a nervous child's pencil. "Want some?" he asked.

"What is it?"

"Vodka and orange Hi-C," he said.

I gulped it down. Anything to help me get ready for what was about to happen. It felt like an old woman's hand traveling to my stomach, her brick-colored nails and costume rings clawing at my insides. "Yum," I lied.

He leaned over and started kissing me. At least he didn't waste any time, so we didn't have to sit there feeling uncomfortable. So we didn't have to try to fill the dejected silence.

We kept kissing. That was the whole point. Why Lila and Cassie had walked in opposite directions. So they could have privacy to do more than kiss.

I was used to it. Lila got the hot guy. Cassie got the mean guy. I got the guy who blushed the minute he saw me, whether we were in the sun or not. It was fine. What would I have done with the hot guy? What would I have done with the mean guy? What would the mean guy have done to me?

When it felt like Nick and I had kissed for long enough,

we watched the sunset, passing his McDonald's cup back and forth—the sun a bright orange circle, like a tea bag being dunked into the water. After that, we stared off into space and waited for our friends.

I dealt with the weird quiet, because I knew I could be more interesting later. Lila and Cassie would tell me about their boys on the ride home while we passed truckers and got them to honk their horns for us.

"His tongue tasted like honey," Lila would say.

"His body wasn't the only thing about him that was tall," Cassie would sneer.

Then, they would tell me more in Lila's backyard, as we lay on her lawn under the skim-milk stars. They would tell me about life through the feel of a kiss and a hand and a breath, with the goose-bump tickle of grass at our necks and the hum of mosquitoes in our ears.

They would fill me up with their secrets. They would make me feel like my silence was a choice. Like being left over was a choice.

Twenty-six

I found Daniel standing in the doorway of his office with his arms up like he was doing a jumping jack. He was wearing yet another tie-dye. It looked like a purple bull's-eye radiating from the center of his chest. "I'm not letting you in until you assure me you are clean and sober."

"You don't look like *you're* clean and sober," I said, indicating his shirt.

He didn't answer me. I walked under one of his arms. He didn't try to keep me out.

Apparently he had been briefed on the heroin I was phony-detoxing from. Was everyone that gullible, or was I really that much of a screw-up?

I sat on the couch and waited for him to follow. "You found me out. I'm on the dope, the hard stuff, the smack, the junk, the p-funk. I do it all day long and I hide it in my mattress," I said, shrugging.

"If you're really doing this to yourself, I can no longer treat you." He sat back in the beanbag chair and crossed his legs.

I was tempted to tell him I was on heroin, if only to end our annoying appointments once and for all. But then there really wouldn't be anyone besides Aaron who listened to me.

"Fine. I'm not hiding heroin in my mattress, but if my mother asks, don't tell her that."

"I don't tell your mother anything you say to me."

"What have I said to you?" It was a serious question. I couldn't remember where my thoughts ended and my words began. What he knew about me and what I let him know about me.

"You need to stop diverting attention away from what you should really be focusing on." He looked at me like he was a cat and I was a mouse he had been chasing, and he had finally been able to back me into a corner.

"I know, I've heard, turning on Lila and Cassie," I said.

"Yes, making the decision whether or not to testify," he said.

"It's not a decision, it's a mandate, and I've said no. It's not good enough."

"Why did you choose to say no?"

"Because Lila and Cassie would hate me forever," I said. *Because Aaron would think I was weak*, I didn't say. I looked at Daniel's shirt, each circle of purple a little darker than the one inside it, like the layers of a Gobstopper.

"Don't you care about what happens to you?"

"Of course," I replied, but as I said it, I realized it was

more a reflex than a statement with much feeling behind it.

I guess he realized it, too. "There is very little I can do if you won't let me help you."

"Fine, help me, then," I said.

Help me like you help your daughter, I thought. *Tell me what you tell her to make her smile the way she does in her softball picture, to make her want to play softball, to make her want to get out of bed every morning.*

I waited. He had to know something, to be able to share some little scrap of knowledge that would make everything better.

He shook his head. I'd finally asked him for help and he couldn't even respond. I thought about AJ looking at me silently the day before. Maybe no one knew the secret.

"Your fly is open," I said. It wasn't, but I wanted him to look in any direction but at me. If he couldn't help me, I didn't want him staring at me, studying me, analyzing me.

"I know it's hard for you to believe that people care about you, but they do."

"They care about what I'm going to do."

"That's the same thing."

"It really isn't," I said, feeling my throat catch, close up. Feeling the rest of the words I didn't want to say fall back down it, the letters scrambling in my stomach like Scrabble tiles.

"Whether people care about you or not isn't really the issue," he said, and he took off his glasses. "The issue is whether you care enough about yourself. So, do you?"

"Signing that paper doesn't prove anything," I said.

"That isn't what I asked," he said.

"Fine. I care about what happens to me."

"They're just words, Amy. I can say anything and pretend I mean it."

Maybe *he* could. It wasn't like that for me. I lived in a house without words. He had no idea what hearing them meant, what saying them meant, even if they didn't actually mean anything.

But maybe he was right. Was caring about myself the secret? But even if that were true, how was I supposed to get there?

He looked at me, his eyes going little-girl sad. "I know you're having a hard time without your friends."

"What do you mean? I'm fine. I just talked to Lila," I said, fast, fast, fast, so I didn't have time to think it wasn't true.

"That's a lie," he said.

How he knew this I wasn't sure, but I hoped he hadn't seen me flinch when he said it.

• • •

The minute I got home I tried to call Lila again. Well, not the minute I got home—first I had to deal with my mother slamming the front door in my face and telling me I could sleep on the street with the other junkies.

After having a cigarette and deciding that dealing with my mother was in fact better than holing up under the nearest underpass, I went inside, though I did reconsider when I found her in the basement ripping apart my mattress with a steak knife.

"What are you doing?" I asked.

"Getting that monkey off your back." She picked up

a handful of stuffing from the inside of the mattress and compared it with a book in her hand. It was called *Heroin: Not a Horse You Want to Ride*. She must have gotten it from the library while I was at my appointment with Daniel.

"Mom, this is ridiculous," I said, taking AJ from his cage.

"I'll tell you what's ridiculous—that you would put poison into your body. That you would bring"—she paused and turned the page—"that Lady H into my house." She picked up another pile of mattress stuffing, studying it.

Lady H, AJ squawked. *Lady H*, he squawked again.

"Where is it, AJ?" my mother asked, like he was Lassie or something.

"Mom, there's nothing in there. It was a joke," I said. I thought about Daniel's claim that he didn't tell my mother anything I said. Well, apparently he'd told her about the mattress.

She pulled out another handful of stuffing and compared it with her book.

AJ perched himself on my shoulder and bit at my hair. *Snow*, AJ said, *snow, snow, snow.*

I knew he meant the white beads of stuffing my mother was throwing into the air as she searched, but luckily she didn't hear him, or she probably would have thought I was on cocaine, too.

"Why don't you just buy yourself a microscope?"

"Don't tempt me," she said, dragging the mattress up the stairs, the corner of it smacking each step, so she could do in private whatever tests she needed to do.

I closed the door behind her, put AJ back in his cage, got underneath my heap of blankets on the floor, and called Lila. My hand glowed green from the buttons on the cordless phone as I dialed the number. I didn't really know what I was going to say, but I needed to hear her voice. I needed to hear her words, whether she meant them or not.

But instead of her voice on the line, or even the phone ringing and ringing and ringing, I got the punch in the stomach of a recorded operator telling me the number I had dialed was no longer in service and no other information was available. The only way I could reach Lila no longer existed.

I wanted to ask the operator if she knew why, to ask her if Lila had been forced by her parents to disconnect it, or whether she had chosen to disconnect it herself. I kept listening, as if she would give me the answers I was looking for.

I needed that woman in the phone. I needed to know why no other information was available. Why I was in my basement, under my covers with a phone to my ear, and only her recorded voice to turn to.

That day I realized that insanity isn't just about being crazy; it's also about being lonely.

I brought the phone upstairs and saw my mother in the backyard through the kitchen window. She was next to the swing set. She doused my mattress in kerosene and then lit it on fire.

As Cassie would have said, *She must be really fucking lonely*.

Twenty-seven

With my mattress incapacitated, I slept on the couch in the living room that night. I sat AJ's cage on the floor next to me and couldn't help keeping my hand on it, like a little kid falling asleep holding a stuffed animal.

Throughout the night, I would wake up to AJ's cage shaking beneath my palm and find him flying around in circles. This was not different behavior for him, but I suppose it was different for me to notice it. Notice it and realize that if I were convicted, I would be just like AJ, flying around in circles in my very own cage.

I smelled my father making breakfast before I saw it, smelled butter and warm batter. I picked up AJ's cage and brought it to the kitchen table with me.

"Bon appétit," he said in a faux French accent. "May I interest you in some cakes made in a pan?" He was standing in front of the stove with a spatula in his hand and

wearing the pink-and-white-checkered apron my mother had worn the night Dick Simon had come for dinner.

"I can make them bird sized, too," he said, trying to flip one in the air like the pros, but he ended up whipping it behind him, where it hit the wall and stuck like a suction cup. "Look," he said, pointing with the spatula, "wall-cake."

I smiled. At least he was trying. "Where's Mom?" Seeing as he was making breakfast, I was hoping the answer was something like *Istanbul*.

"Still sleeping," he said, turning back to his sizzling pan.

I looked at the clock. It was ten o'clock a.m. Usually if she wasn't up by seven we were checking her breathing with a spoon. "Guess it's tiring playing narcotics detective."

"Let her be. She had a rough night."

"Not as rough as my mattress," I said, pointing through the window to our backyard, where my mattress lay like a burned marshmallow. I was sure Joe and his mom had seen it, had smelled it. Bald Britney Spears weird? Um, yeah.

"She just cares about you." This is what my father said every time my mother did something crazy. My mother's definition of care was a mental disorder. "Besides, you're the one who lied," he said.

"I didn't lie. I was joking."

"You say *pancake*, I say *poncake*."

"I've never heard you say *poncake*."

"I hope you're hungry," he said, walking toward the table with a plate piled high.

"Does she know you're making breakfast?"

"I didn't make it for her. I made it for us," he said.

Such was my life: my mother went arsonist on my

belongings like I was a felon; my father made me pancakes.

I had to admit, that morning I liked it. It was nice sitting with my dad, eating terrible pancakes and listening to him talk about proper mastication techniques for better dental health. I should have known something terrible was just around the corner.

My mother ran down the stairs, yelling, "What did you do now?" I thought she was referring to the smell of my dad's pancakes, but then I heard two car doors slam in our driveway.

I found my mother standing at our front window. She had the curtain open a sliver, like a scared old lady.

"Who is it?" I asked, and then answered my own question by coming around behind her and looking for myself. I saw two policemen leaning on the side of their squad car. One was flipping through a wallet-photo-size notebook. The other was looking over his shoulder at our house and nodding.

"What are they doing here?" I asked. Was there some new law I didn't know about where they could come and haul me away at any time? "You didn't call them, did you? About the stupid heroin?"

"Why, should I have?" she asked, squinting at me.

"Maybe they're here about the mattress," I said.

My father walked up behind us from the kitchen. "What's going on?"

"Ask your daughter," my mother said, crossing her arms.

The policemen rang the doorbell and my mother jumped like she had been burned by the sound. I heard AJ squawking from the kitchen. "What is that bird doing at the table?" she asked.

"Aren't you going to answer it?" I said.

"Why should I? It's not for me." She didn't move.

I matched her stance, a younger, shorter, saner mirror image.

"Which one of us already has a criminal record?" she asked.

"I haven't been charged yet."

"Exactly—*yet*."

My mother and I stood across from each other like two cowboys ready to draw in a duel. Maybe I couldn't always say what was on my mind, but I could stand and stare like a ninja. The bell rang again.

"Is someone going to get that?" my father asked.

My mother and I didn't move.

One of the policemen started knocking, loudly, and yelling about getting a warrant. That was enough to make my mother give up. She went for the door like she was the explosive at the end of a fuse their words had lit.

"Sorry, I was in the shower and didn't hear the bell," she said, trying to sound her most law-abiding and innocent. Even though it was *so* obvious she had not been in the shower, even though my father and I stood on both sides of her.

"I'm Officer Kavanagh, and this is Officer Teesdale," he said, indicating himself, then the shorter guy next to him. "Does Amy Fleishman live here?" he asked, looking down at his pad.

"For today she does," my mother said.

Officer Teesdale asked, "Do you know a Lila Van Drake?"

"She does," my mother said. "Well, she *did*, anyway. Amy chooses not to see or speak with her anymore."

"Is that true?" Kavanagh asked.

With my parents standing there and two policemen staring at me, I couldn't really do anything but agree.

The policemen looked at each other and Kavanagh wrote something down. "Have you talked to her at all lately?"

"She just told you she hasn't," my father said.

"Then you don't know she's missing?"

I heard what he said, but I didn't understand it. "What do you mean, *missing?*"

"Maybe we should come inside."

We moved out of the way so they could enter. Kavanagh had to duck to make his way through the door and Teesdale knocked on the side of the doorjamb as he crossed the threshold. They were different from the guy who had arrested us. Who knew Collinsville was so well protected?

"Can I offer you some pancakes?" my father asked as they sat at the kitchen table.

"No," Kavanagh said.

"Coffee," Teesdale said, and then gestured for me to join them in one of the free chairs.

It wasn't until then that I realized I'd been standing. I couldn't feel my legs. I couldn't feel anything except hot, buzzing panic.

"Nice bird," Kavanagh said, pointing at AJ's cage.

"Did something happen to Lila?" I asked.

My father brought the coffee and bowed slightly as he placed it on the table. He looked down and realized he was still wearing the apron. "I don't usually cook," was how he decided to explain it.

"She's probably on some bender, sleeping one off on someone's couch," my mother said.

"That's certainly a possibility," Teesdale said, latching his hands together on the table and leaning closer, like he was asking me to deny it.

"Is Lila okay?" I asked, feeling like she had been standing right next to me and I had lost her in a crowd.

Lila, AJ squawked, *Lila, Lila, Lila*. I put my hand on his cage to quiet him. It was strange, having him repeat out loud the way her name was pounding against the inside of my head.

"Did she tell you whether she was planning on going anywhere?" Teesdale asked, watching me over his coffee cup.

"Where would she go?" I asked. *And why wouldn't she take me?*

"Has she contacted you at all in the last four days?"

"No," my mother said, glaring at me, daring me to prove her wrong.

"She's been gone that long?" I asked.

"Give or take. Her parents only reported her missing yesterday. I guess they thought she might come back."

"They usually do," Kavanagh said, and both of them nodded.

My father came up behind me and put his hands on my shoulders.

"Well, are you looking for her? She could be hurt, or lost, or tied up in some maniac's garage," I said, my voice escalating.

"I'm sure they are doing everything they can," my father said.

"It's hard to find someone who doesn't want to be found," Teesdale said.

"What's that supposed to mean?" I asked.

"He means she skipped town," my mother said, sounding like Lila had spit in her face.

"She wouldn't do that," I said.

"Really?" she replied, snapping her head hard enough to sprain her neck in order to look at one of the cops. "How often does someone get kidnapped just as they're about to go to trial?" She was doing her best *I guess I look like I was born yesterday* expression.

"She wouldn't leave me," I said.

"Well, she did," my mother said. "She was smart enough to know that her life was more important than your friendship—something you should have realized by now."

My father just rubbed my shoulders, I think less out of comfort and more because I was there and he could. I was there and Lila was gone.

"If you don't mind, we'd like to set up a tracking device on your landline," Kavanagh said. "Just in case she tries to call you here."

"Yes, whatever you need," my father said.

"Someone has been calling over and over again and hanging up," my mother said, sounding very sleuthy.

"That was probably Lila," I said. "She might need help." *Lila,* I thought, *or Aaron.* I tried not to think who I would rather it had been.

Lila, AJ squawked again, *Lila, Lila, Lila.*

"Could you identify anything from the calls? A sound? A location?" Teesdale asked.

"Why didn't you tell me?" I asked, putting my hands on the table and leaning toward my mother.

"How could I have known?" she asked.

But then I wondered when she would have been able to tell me. We yelled about the arrest, we fought about the arrest, we stewed about the arrest. There wasn't much room for anything else.

"Do you have a cell phone?" Kavanagh asked.

"She hasn't used it in weeks," my mother said.

"Do you mind if we check the phone records on it?"

"Whatever you need," my father said again.

Who knew what they would find on those phone records? Would they be able to find *anything*, considering it had been turned off and hidden up on the high shelf? At least what my mother had said was true. I hadn't used it in weeks.

"Looks like she made your decision for you," my mother said, tearing up. "I'm calling Dick." She wiped her eyes and left the table.

"We have some forms you'll need to sign for the tracking system," Teesdale said, looking at my father. "Why don't you come outside?"

"Don't worry," Kavanagh said, "we'll find her."

My father squeezed my shoulder and followed the officers out, still wearing that apron. I knew they'd taken him outside so they could talk to him privately, tell him to watch me, to make sure I didn't follow Lila's lead and try to go anywhere.

Those calls had to have been Lila, checking in from the road. I could see her. In the distance was a green highway sign. The air smelled of gasoline and cows. Maybe there was the sound of crows cawing, or crickets thrumming, or corn growing. Maybe Lila wanted to apologize but couldn't. Maybe she wanted to say good-bye without words.

While my mother was upstairs plotting Lila's murder and my father was in the driveway with a frilly pink apron on talking to policemen, I grabbed the cordless phone and AJ and went down to the basement to call Aaron. Taking my chances before the tracking system was installed.

"Do you know where Lila is?" I asked as soon as he answered.

"Who?" he asked.

"Lila." I paused. "Brian's Lila." I wondered if anyone would ever refer to me as Aaron's Amy. It was doubtful, considering no one had ever seen us together.

"No," he said. He had me on speaker. I heard music in the background. I heard him spinning a wheel on his skateboard, but no laughter. He was probably in his room. It was only then that I realized I had never seen his room, had never even seen his house.

"The police were here," I said. I was out of breath, like I had just run a long distance. "She's missing. No one knows where she is."

"Wait, what?" he said. I heard him take the phone off speaker. "Police?" he whispered. "Where's Brian?"

"I don't know." AJ stared at me from his cage, his eyes like shiny black beads. "They say she's been missing for four days."

"Did you tell them anything?"

"I don't *know* anything." I pulled my comforter off the

floor and wrapped it around me.

"You didn't say something to the police?" he asked again.

"No," I said. I was starting to feel defensive and I wasn't sure why.

"Well, why would she just leave?"

"I don't know," I said.

I heard Aaron put me back on speaker. I heard him opening drawers, heard him breathing and texting.

"Aaron?"

"I have to go," he said.

"Are you going to look for them?" I was hoping he would say yes. I was hoping he would say, *Yes, I'll pick you up, and we'll go look for them together.*

"Just call me later, okay?" he said.

"When?" I asked before he could hang up. I didn't care how desperate I sounded. He might be the only one who would be able to tell me that Lila wasn't really missing, that she was just hiding out at Brian's house. That she hadn't really left.

When, when, when? AJ tweeted.

"Later." He paused. "Or tomorrow," he said. "Just don't do anything without calling me first, okay?"

What did he think I was going to do? I could hear footsteps upstairs in the kitchen, my dad throwing out all those pancakes, pouring hot coffee down the drain.

"Amy?"

"Yeah," I said, "okay."

"Don't worry," Aaron said as he ended the call.

I picked up AJ's cage and put it on my lap, holding it

to my chest like a pillow. Lila was gone. Cassie wasn't allowed to talk to me. AJ really was the only friend I had left. At least he could never leave me. I thought about Annie saying I shouldn't keep him in a cage, but this was why. I knew if I ever gave him the choice, if I ever took him outside and opened his cage, he would just fly away, too.

Twenty-eight

When I woke up the next morning, it was silent, so silent I couldn't fall back asleep. Something was different; something was wrong. As AJ snoozed in his cage, I crept upstairs. I checked the kitchen first—empty. The family room, living room, computer room, and dining room were all empty.

I listened for noise above me. It was possible my parents were still asleep. I tiptoed up the blue-carpeted stairs to find their bedroom door open, bed made, pajamas folded like small presents on top of it.

My parents were gone, together, without me.

I brought AJ up from the basement and put him on the kitchen table while I made coffee and eggs. I hadn't eaten anything since my father's pancakes the morning before. I hadn't even left the basement.

After I'd gotten off the phone with Aaron, I smoked

and cried and watched AJ breathe, watched the yellow feathers on his chest move up and down like a tiny rising and setting sun.

The police were wrong. Lila couldn't have just taken off into the night. Rappelled down from her window with her bed sheets and hopped into a running maroon van with a back window in the shape of a star, lugging a backpack with her green Chuck Taylors hanging from it, spinning like a baby's mobile as she pulled the door closed behind her.

But why could I see it so clearly if it weren't true?

I think my father had tried knocking at one point, but I ignored him. I wasn't ready to talk to anyone about Lila. I wasn't ready to say what I knew: she had left. She had left without me.

Good morning, AJ squawked as the eggs sizzled in the pan. *Pretty Amy, pretty Amy,* he tweeted as I fed him toast crumbs.

I wondered how much longer I had before my parents got home and I was bombarded by their questions about what I was going to do. Their demands about places I had to go and people I had to see.

I took a bite of eggs and washed it down with a big gulp of sweet, creamy coffee.

"Where are they?" I asked AJ.

Good morning, AJ squawked in response.

I didn't know, either, but at least they weren't here.

I decided to take the chance while I had it to grab my phone from the cabinet on the high shelf. I could call Aaron and see if he'd found her, without fear of the stupid tracking device. Maybe Lila had sent me a text. Maybe she had called me. Maybe Cassie had called while her mother wasn't looking. If the police were going to know about any of that, *I* wanted to know it first.

It wasn't until I pulled out the desk chair to use as a step stool that I realized exactly where my parents were. I saw it, written on the calendar in my mother's script. It was Sunday. My parents were at my high school graduation.

They had actually gone without me.

I felt myself go cold and start to sweat, the way you feel when you overhear someone talking about you.

I threw the eggs and toast down the garbage disposal, grabbed AJ, and went to the basement to try to go back to sleep. It was obvious I had made the wrong decision in even attempting to be conscious. I lay down in my sleeping bag, closed my eyes, and tried to forget, but I couldn't stop thinking about how weird it was.

My parents were at my graduation without me.

Everyone at my school was there without me.

Everyone at my school knew I wasn't there.

Just like the prom.

I put AJ on my shoulder and went back upstairs. If I couldn't be there, at least I could see it.

I turned on the computer. *You've got mail*, it said.

You've got mail, AJ repeated.

I logged on to the school website. My username and password still worked. Even if they had gotten rid of me at school, they had forgotten to erase me from cyberspace.

The camera was fixed on the auditorium stage. The thick, red-velvet curtains were open, a mouth framing Mr. Morgan and selected dignitaries. Mr. Morgan stood at the center of the stage, smiling and hand-shaking and passing out rolled-up diplomas. The ceremony was almost over.

A line of my classmates waited next to the stage, each wearing the cap and gown I'd had to return for a refund. Ready to accept the diploma I would get by mail. They looked like they actually cared for once about what Mr. Morgan was going to say, because it was their name and his saying it signified something. Their being there signified something.

They were on the *T*s: Jeffrey Tate, Margaret Thistle, Holly Tolle, Scott Trafer, no *U*s, Becky Vackworth, Kyle Vaughn, Frank Vicksburg, Gloria Vining, Joe Wright, Julie Yablonski.

No Lila Van Drake, no Cassie Wick; he skipped them as if they didn't even exist. I was sure he'd skipped me, too.

That's what words or the lack of them could do, Daniel—they could make you disappear.

I was invisible again. Just as I had been during freshman year before I was friends with Lila and Cassie; from nothing to nothing in four years flat.

I watched Joe walk off the stage. He held his diploma with both hands, maybe so they wouldn't shake, but maybe because he finally felt like he had done something his father's departure couldn't take away. He wanted to hold on tightly to that feeling. He had to have noticed I wasn't there, but he was probably the only one.

The audience clapped as Mr. Morgan announced they should applaud all the graduating seniors. He congratulated the parents and families for making these special, amazing, wonderful kids, who were about to go out into the world and do special, amazing, wonderful things. Then he congratulated my classmates for all their hard work, for making it this far, for being special, amazing, wonderful kids who were about to go out into the world and do special, amazing, wonderful things.

I could hear them cheer, could see their caps being thrown up in front of the camera like migrating birds.

Congratulations, AJ squawked. *Congratulations*.

Maybe it didn't matter. Like Mr. Morgan had said, I was getting the same diploma. I was still graduating even if I wasn't there. Maybe it didn't matter, but I still pulled the power cord before I had to see any more.

I couldn't help thinking back to the question my father had asked me, back to what Joe had said. Would I have been happy even if I had been there? Sure, with Lila and Cassie by my side, but what if I had never met them? What if I were still the girl with the half-blue face?

Would the pictures from that day have shown me smiling, attempting to hide how afraid I was? Pretending I felt normal and pretty and fine, because that's what my parents wanted to see. Doing what I thought I was supposed to do and being who I thought I was supposed to be and knowing it would never be enough.

Twenty-nine

Instead of going to work that night, I went to Hully's Tavern. I needed a drink. I needed several drinks.

I told Connor I was sick, and I was: sick of Dick and Daniel and my mother, and sick of the *I told you so* chorus I knew I would soon be hearing, sick of Connor and his frown-upside-down mentality, sick of working for money I never saw, sick of my father looking at me and seeing misery, sick of acting like I didn't care.

Besides, I couldn't risk being at Gas-N-Go on graduation night. If anyone from my class came in to buy beer and saw me, I was going to kill myself.

Of course, I couldn't even get out of my neighborhood without spotting Joe. I could see him starting to walk down the street. He was wearing his varsity volleyball jacket and carrying a plastic grocery bag that was badly camouflaging a six-pack, Collinsville South arched in white letters on his back.

"Hey, can I have one?" I yelled, walking faster to catch up.

Maybe I wouldn't have to go anywhere. Maybe he would give me some beer and I could hide under his porch drinking while he went to whatever party he was going to. Then I could stumble home later and actually sleep that night.

"I don't think that's a good idea," he said. His hair was still wet from the shower. His ears were still pink with warmth.

"I have money," I said.

"You can do whatever you want," he said. "I'd just rather not be involved."

It was the kind of thing he'd said the day we stopped talking during sophomore year, when he told me I was changing, I was different, and because I'd wanted exactly that, I didn't care.

"You can just say no; I don't need the lecture." He was allowed to drink, but I wasn't because he thought I did more than drink, because I drank more than he thought I should.

"Fine," he said. "No."

"Thanks a lot."

"You did this to yourself," he said, shrugging. "Don't get mad at me." His left hand was in his pocket. His right was gripping the grocery bag tightly.

I thought about the last time I had seen him, when he'd asked me if I was okay. Something had changed since then, something that made him not care about the answer to that question anymore.

"So you saw the police in my driveway?"

He shrugged. He didn't even bother asking why they

were there. It was assumed they were there because I was me.

"Noted, I'm a druggie loser," I said. "I've also had a horrible day and would really like a beer, please." I looked at him the way I had on prom night, when I was begging for him to let me in. When I was trying to say, *Just do* me *a favor*.

My backpack felt heavy on my shoulder. I heaved it to the other side as his phone chirped with a text.

He took it out and looked at it.

"Leslie?" I asked. "She can probably have all the beer she wants, right?"

He didn't say anything, just punched buttons on his phone with his left hand. The beers clinked in the six-pack in his right.

"If you really want one, just take it," he said, shoving the bag toward me. "I don't want to fight with you."

"I don't want to fight with you, either."

We could say that, but we *were* fighting. Or maybe only I was.

I looked at the bottles through the plastic, like shiny green jewels sticking to the side with condensation. I thought I wanted one, but maybe I just wanted to have a beer with *him*, to talk to him the way I used to, to have things be normal again—to fall into our old, easy routine. But that was something I didn't have the words to ask for.

"Just forget it," I said, walking away. He hadn't even asked me why I wasn't at graduation. He probably hadn't even noticed. I was such an idiot.

• • •

Hully's Tavern was so old that it leaned to one side like a wrestler frozen in his rocking stance. As I walked in, I realized that my life had gotten pretty bad if I actually felt relieved just to be there. It was a bar people visited as a last resort because other bars wouldn't take them. I had been there once before with Lila and Cassie and the bar's leniency when it came to drinking age was exactly what I needed that night to get me good and smashed.

I went into the bathroom to change out of my work shirt. Even though I hadn't been going to work, I couldn't let my mother know that. So I'd acted like—even though I felt like my heart had been clawed out—I was ready for another night of providing mediocre customer service at Gas-N-Go.

Done in the bathroom, I swung my bag over my shoulder and walked toward the bar like a girl who was used to swinging a bag over her shoulder. Like a girl who had a bag over her shoulder all the time, a girl who moved easily between the personas of student and runaway.

I sat at the bar and waited for the bartender to take my order. There were two guys sitting next to me already enjoying their drinks. One of them looked like the coughed-up lung of a giant: red-skinned, sweat-covered, shaped like a blob. The other one wore a maroon windbreaker, a baseball cap, and white sneakers. He looked into his beer like a fortune-teller reading a crystal ball and twisted his glass back and forth. His other arm rested on the bar, his head in his hand, cocked sideways as if he was about to fall asleep, which was probably what happened to most people while they were waiting for someone to get them a drink.

Even though the bartender's back was turned, I was sure he saw me waiting. There was a dirty mirror behind the dusty bottles on the filthy bar, but still he made me wait. He made me wait so long that my face got hot and I started to sweat, like I was feeling a kind of claustrophobia from time pressing down on me.

I scanned the rest of the bar and found that the only other female was a waitress who was filling endless bowls of pretzels that she stacked on top of one another for some supposed later patrons. She looked at me in that way you look at someone that says, *I used to be just like you and in a few years you're going to be just like me.*

"What does someone have to do to get a drink?" I finally asked. Customer service in Collinsville was dying on the vine without any help from me.

The bartender turned, smiled, and said, "You're not old enough to know." He filled a glass with beer and swung it back and forth in front of me like the pendulum in a grandfather clock. "What will you give me for it?" he asked, his eyebrows like drawn arrowheads piercing his forehead as he wiggled them up and down, waiting for my answer.

I was pretty sure I was the only seventeen-year-old ever to have been asked this question in a bar. I didn't know what to say. Maybe just saying what I had wanted to say to Joe would have been easier.

Usually Lila or Cassie would come to the rescue in a situation like this. When I had been at Hully's with them, I'd sat at a table and waited while they went up to the bar to get our drinks. They had gotten them without a problem.

Had he asked them this question?

I took a deep breath. It seemed like the best thing to do. It was either that or run out of there screaming.

"Exactly what I thought," he said, pouring the beer down the sink behind him. "Get out of here. You think I can't smell underage snatch?"

"I'm not underage," I tried, sliding the ten-dollar bill my mother had given me for dinner that night across the bar.

"You're not worth getting fined for, sweetheart," he said.

I guess that meant that Lila and Cassie were. There it was. Cold, brutal evidence that without Lila and Cassie, I didn't matter. Put that in my manila folder, Dick.

"I've been arrested," I said, thinking maybe I could scare him into giving me a beer.

"Really?" He laughed. "For what?"

"Selling drugs," I said. Even though it wasn't true, it sounded better than what had really happened.

"Who'd you sell to, My Little Pony?" He laughed again, slamming his hand on the bar with each *har, har, har* that came out of his mouth.

People saw me no differently than they had before the arrest. I was still a joke. The only difference was, I had no one to hide behind anymore.

I took my ten dollars off the bar and left him there, laughing.

It was almost nine and I walked along the quiet streets of Collinsville, wondering what the hell I was supposed to do. I couldn't go home—not that I wanted to, anyway. I couldn't go to work, and I definitely couldn't take the chance of going anywhere I might be seen by my celebrating classmates, especially Joe.

I called Aaron from a pay phone. He was right—it did smell like homeless ass. He picked me up and we drove in silence to one of the new housing developments under construction on the other side of Main. The street was dark and bordered by big wooden frames waiting to be filled in with walls and floors and windows and doors, with moms and dads and sons and daughters.

With boys like Aaron.

With girls like me.

He parked the car and lit a cigarette. He didn't lean in to kiss me right away like he usually did; he just stared straight ahead.

"Did you find Brian?" I asked. I knew the answer was no, that he would have told me if he had, but I couldn't think of anything else to say.

Aaron shook his head.

"Do you think they left together?" Maybe I wanted to plant an idea in his head, or maybe I was just trying to keep him answering questions so he didn't have a chance to say whatever he was about to say. I didn't think I wanted to hear it. I was pretty sure it involved breaking up with me. Though I wasn't even sure if we were officially together enough to require a break-up.

"What a dick," he said, blowing out smoke with the force of a steam whistle.

"Yeah," I said. I guess that meant they had left together. Even on the run, Lila had a more romantic love life than I ever would.

"At least I still have you," he said.

I looked at him. I guess he wasn't breaking up with me. Maybe my love life *was* more romantic than I thought. Maybe I *did* want to hear what he had to say.

"I do, right?" he asked, turning to me. It was dark, but I could see his eyes. They were wide, pleading.

"Sure," I said.

"I mean, I can count on you," he said, taking a drag. The end of the cigarette flashed like an amber crosswalk light.

"Of course," I said.

"I'll wait for you," he said quickly. "I mean, it will only be a year, maybe less."

"What are you talking about?"

"Well, with Lila gone and now Brian, too," he started. "I mean, I'm sure your lawyer has told you."

I thought about Dick, about the paper he wanted me to sign, about what he'd said about the real owner of the evidence we were found with.

Aaron.

He *had* followed me from the courthouse. He had known who I was, had chosen me not because he liked me, but for this. My eyes started to burn.

"You'll wait for me," I repeated. I didn't know what else to say.

"Yeah, sure, I mean, it's the least I can do," he said. He breathed out, started to smile. "It's awesome of you to do this for me," he said.

"So, that's what this was," I said, the words in my head coming out before I could stop them.

I looked at the car around me; the open, sparkling sky;

him. Those times with Aaron had been just like riding on my swing set as a child: a fake freedom, an illusion of happiness.

"No," he said. But I knew he was lying. It was easy to lie with one word. As easy as it was to lie with no words.

"You used me," I said.

"No," he said again.

"Stop lying."

"We only kissed, Amy."

"You know what I mean," I said, my eyes tearing, making everything in front of me blurry, everything except the ability to see that he was one of the people up the line that Dick had been talking about. How could I have been so dumb?

"No," he said. "I mean, you haven't really even done anything yet."

"But you want me to," I said, "for you, and you'll wait for me." I repeated his words. All he wanted, like Lila, was a person he could train.

"Amy, stop," he said, putting his hand on my knee.

"No," I said, pulling away from him. "Just admit it." I thought about the picture he'd drawn. He hadn't seen me that way. He had seen me as someone he could exploit, could lie to, someone he could hurt.

He shook his head and lit another cigarette: *snap, sizzle, snap.*

It was true. I really only had AJ. I got out of the car and ran. I heard Aaron calling after me, heard his car start, but I didn't stop, wouldn't stop.

Aaron's Amy. I was even more of an idiot than I thought.

I kept running through backyards and down side streets. I ran and ran until I got to Gas-N-Go. I could have kept running toward home, but there was nothing for me there. There was nothing for me anywhere.

The lights were off in the store; it must have been after eleven. I went around back and sat next to the green Dumpster, catching my breath. I leaned against the door and looked up at the stars; they hummed and throbbed. What I hated to think, but couldn't deny, was that Lila and Cassie could live life without me. What did it mean that I found it so hard to live life without them? What did it mean that I couldn't even see what was right in front of me, without them there to show me?

Aaron had never liked me. He was the mean boy. Maybe Cassie could have handled him, but he had fooled me. Cassie would have known Aaron was full of it. Lila would never have let herself have actual *feelings* for him.

I closed my eyes and saw Lila at a thruway rest stop. She was with a guy wearing light denim jeans, a black leather belt, and no shirt. I saw him lying on top of her on a grassy hill by the restrooms, her delicate head poking out from underneath his shoulder, her eyes looking up, her pupils filled with the same sky I saw.

I thought about how in movies when you are missing someone, you are supposed to think about how they see the same stars you see. This is supposed to make you realize that the world may be big, but you are both still a part of it. It is supposed to make you realize that they are not that far away.

I fell asleep, thinking about what a crock that was.

Thirty

"Don't worry about saying thank you," Connor said as we got into his car the next morning.

I guess my parents had called him when I didn't come home and he'd gone out looking for me — or, more likely, he had come to open the store and found me sleeping in a pile of trash behind it.

"Thank you," I said, not wanting him to have anything to hold over me, "but I can walk home from here."

"You're not going home," he said, starting the car.

I felt my stomach drop. "Where am I going?"

"You'll stay with me for a while," he said, like the words coming out of his mouth were normal instead of totally freaking bizarre.

"Why?" I asked. My face was getting hot. It's not like I wanted to go home, but that was a very different thing from being unwanted there.

"Because your parents won't take you," he said, looking straight ahead as he started the car.

"But you will," I said, still not quite believing what was happening.

"Sure," he said. "I care about you."

"Why? Why would you care about me?" I asked. I'd generally been civil with Connor, sure, but I'd never been *nice* to him. He had no reason to care about me.

"You're a human being," he said. "You need help."

I stared out the window so I didn't have to look at him. Why couldn't everyone just leave me to rot in peace? If I had to deal with one more person saying they cared about me, I was going to scream. Especially because the one person who I'd thought actually did had been a complete illusion.

"I'm not going to be able to pay you rent or anything," I said, wanting to say easy, direct things so I didn't start to cry.

"Sure you will. I doubled your hours," he said.

"This day just keeps getting better and better," I said, feeling my eyes go watery.

"You smell," he said.

We drove to Connor's apartment with all the windows down. As part of our rental agreement that I had not been given the option to disagree with, I would be staying with him so he could make sure I went to work and, being sure I made it to work, he could be sure I would be able to pay him rent. It sounded more like I was an indentured servant than someone he "cared about."

"What about AJ?" I asked, realizing I had forgotten him. Realizing I might just be as crappy as everyone thought I was.

"Who?"

"My bird," I said, picturing him alone in his cage in the basement, probably hungry, lonely, and sad.

"Don't worry, we can go get him later," Connor said.

I guess I could have jumped out of the car and run down the street, away from him and all of this, but with my parents having given me up to a virtual stranger, Joe thinking I was an out-of-control druggie, and Aaron just wanting me as his puppet, it was clearer than ever. I had nowhere else to go.

· · ·

Connor had more rules than my parents did and most of them were about the way I acted or what I said in front of his children. I wasn't allowed to disrespect him, his wife, or his religion. I wasn't allowed to drink, smoke, or cause any other "moral destruction" to my body while I was under his roof. Staying at Connor's might just be worse than I had it in my parents' basement.

Connor and I walked into his apartment and found his family sitting around a kitchen table with more breakfast food on it than was available at most hotel buffets: eggs, bacon, sausage, hash browns, pancakes, doughnuts.

His wife looked much the same as I remembered her, but in her own surroundings she seemed happier, less nervous. The kitchen was decorated in sunflowers: sunflower napkins, sunflower clock, sunflower utensil holder, sunflower dishtowels, and most likely sunflower shelf paper.

"This is Christopher and Cayla," Connor said, his arm moving like a weathervane pushed from a slight wind. "And you already know Tiffany."

I realized it was the first time Connor had ever told me his wife's name. I guess now I knew why.

"I'm hungry," Christopher said, holding his knife and fork like a steering wheel and banging them against the table.

Both kids looked the same as they had in the Christmas photo Connor carried in his wallet, just in summer clothes instead of winter.

"You're just like your father," I said. I couldn't help myself.

Connor held up one finger to indicate my first strike. "Why don't you go take a shower?"

"I don't want to impose," I said, doing my best timid houseguest impression.

"It's not an imposition," he said, grabbing my shoulders and leading me out of the kitchen. "It's an order." He pointed at the bathroom.

"Daddy, what's wrong with her?" I heard Christopher ask as I left the room.

"P.U.," Cayla said, clapping and giggling.

"Eat your breakfast," Connor said.

I wondered if things could get any worse. Not only had I been disowned, I was also being made fun of by kids.

Connor's apartment wasn't a home to write home about, but I had to admit the shower felt pretty good. Even though the only shampoo he had was Prell. I guess wayward teenagers couldn't be choosers.

I got out, combed my hair as well as I could after the deep-conditioning treatment, and changed into a bathrobe that hung on the door. I twisted my hair up into a towel. My clothes were ripe and I was happy to find a laundry basket to throw them into, even if it did have a scallop shell on it that matched the bathrobe, the towel, and the pieces of pink soap that sat in a shell holder on the sink.

I opened the door, steam from the shower wafting out, and saw Cayla standing there.

"You work at my daddy's office?" she asked, playing with the ruffles on her hot pink shorts.

"Is that what he told you?"

She nodded, her eyes wide, waiting.

"Yes, I work at your daddy's office," I said, holding up the towel turban on my head.

"Wow," she said, "you're lucky."

I nodded. Smiling like you do with kids when they seem so happy that you don't want to change it by saying anything. You nod, smile, and nod at their shiny, smiling faces. I was lucky to work at Gas-N-Go with Connor.

Whatever.

"What do you guys do there?"

"Hmmm," I said, buying time. I didn't want to destroy whatever image he had created for her of his work life. As I thought about what I was going to say, I realized that I hadn't fully understood what she'd meant. She actually meant I was lucky I got to be at Gas-N-Go with her daddy; that I got to be with him, while she was here at home. I felt an odd pang in my chest. Like the string breaking on a guitar.

"He wishes he could be here," I said. "With you," I added. Saying what I would have wanted someone to say to me at her age, sounding lamer than I would ever let anyone above her age hear me sound.

"I know," she said, twirling and dancing down the hallway.

She knew. She knew what I never had.

I went back into the bathroom, closed the door, and sat down on the floor on the other side of it. Apparently Cayla knew the secrets I had been begging everyone else for. I guess I didn't have to tell her not to believe a mysterious boy's kisses and lies.

I needed AJ. It felt like a cigarette craving, that same kind of anxious needle.

I walked out of the bathroom to see if getting AJ later could turn into getting AJ now, and found Connor standing on the other side of the door, his hand in the air pre-knock.

"You have an appointment with Daniel in twenty minutes," he said.

"Are you kidding me?" There was a word I wanted to say before *kidding*, but that was a no-no in Connor's house.

He held up a page copied from a calendar.

"Where did you get that?" I asked, grabbing for it, the towel on my head falling off from the force. Again, what I wanted to say before *did* was censored for Connor's house.

"Your mother gave it to me."

Of course she had. "I'm not going." I walked past him and sat on the couch in the living room, pulling the robe tighter around me.

"You can go see Daniel, or you can live on the streets,"

he said, following me.

"Connor, come on," I said.

"I mean it," he said, crossing his arms and standing above me.

"Fine, but we're getting AJ right after," I said, walking back to the bathroom to get dressed.

Why was I talking to him like that? I felt like a child.

My clothes were gone, taken out of the laundry basket. Tiffany must have come and tossed them into the washing machine. At least I wouldn't need to wash them in Prell.

I ended up having to borrow something from Tiffany and I was blessed with one of her pre-baby outfits. A denim jumpsuit, probably not unlike what someone would wear in jail. Except it was acid-washed and the sleeves and ankles had elastic around them so that it looked like the suit was filled with air when I put it on. As a bonus, it had gold studs along the collar and American flags placed endearingly on each breast pocket.

I looked like a homosexual fighter pilot.

I was standing in their bedroom, looking at myself in their full-length mirror, when Connor came up behind me. "If you tell me I remind you of your wife in this outfit, I'm going to lose it."

"Not at all. She looked way better in that than you do."

I took it as a compliment. I pulled the fabric out at the sides of my thighs. "Well, she's got the hips for it."

"I'll be waiting for you outside of Daniel's office when you're done. No funny business."

"You think I'd try to go anywhere wearing this?"

• • •

Daniel was silent as I walked in. Apparently my outfit had rendered him speechless. It was odd, considering some of the things he actually left the house in—that day, a long, white linen tunic and shorts.

"I know, I know. I look like an ass."

"You said it; I didn't." He wrote something down on his pad, probably, *Note to self: acid-washed is out.*

"So just say it already." I sat down in the rocking chair across from him.

"Say what?"

"That I am in destruction mode."

"You said it; I didn't," he repeated with a sad smile. "You don't look so good."

"Of course I don't look good. Lila's missing. I mean, she could be dead, or hurt, or worse."

I didn't even want to get into how I was feeling about the whole missing my graduation thing, and then on top of that the whole I have a more insecure outlook than Connor's three-year-old daughter thing. And, of course, the whole Aaron thing.

"It's pretty sad that you'd rather think she was dead than face the alternative."

And it was, so I didn't say anything.

"I know you're angry, and you should be. She abandoned you."

"Everyone has," I said. It was really true. Everyone but AJ.

"You mean your parents," he said.

He had no clue.

"They're angry. Besides, staying with Connor was my idea," he said.

"Of course it was."

"They need space from you. Considering everything you've indicated to me, I'm not sure why you're upset."

"I'm not upset," I said. "Not about that." I wasn't, really. But even though I couldn't ignore that I had done a lot of crappy things, none of them had made my parents kick me out of my house.

"Uh huh," he said, writing something else down.

We sat there for a minute, his way of telling me he didn't believe anything I was saying.

"Would you kick your daughter out?" I asked.

"Absolutely," he said, without even thinking about it.

"What would she have to do?" I asked.

"Are we talking about me or about you?" he asked.

I looked down at my legs, the acid-washed denim spreading out like I was wearing clothes in a pool.

"This is why action matters, why choice matters. Anesthetizing yourself from your feelings has consequences," he said.

"Everything has consequences," I said. "I'm tired of consequences."

"Then sign the paper," he said, as if he had caught me.

"You have a copy of it on you?"

"More jokes." He shook his head.

It wasn't a joke. If he had a copy I probably would have signed it, just to screw over Aaron.

"You really are hurt," he said.

"I miss AJ," I said.

"Your bird," he said, like he was reminding me. Like he wanted me to understand that I was talking about something that couldn't really miss me back. That AJ was safe because I could think he felt anything about me, and he could never act or tell me differently.

"You need me to relay something to your parents?" he asked.

I knew what they wanted to hear, what they all wanted to hear, but I wasn't there yet, at least not for the right reasons. I balled up my body like a fist and closed my eyes. Without my parents there pushing me to turn on Lila and Cassie, it was finally only my decision to make.

I kept bitching about everyone just letting me make my own choices, but the truth was, I was too much of a chicken to make one anyway.

Thirty-one

Connor took me straight to work after my appointment with Daniel. He let me know that my mother had dropped off AJ and some of my clothes at his apartment—conveniently, I thought, while I wasn't there.

Connor brought me one of his Gas-N-Go polos to wear, but he forgot to bring my pants, or at least that was what he claimed. My guess was that, more likely than forgetting, he just didn't want to go through my clothes and run the risk of seeing a pair of my underwear.

I stood behind the counter and pulled his shirt over the top of the denim pantsuit. I looked at my reflection in the front window. I looked enormous.

It reminded me of when I was a kid and I had to wear my Halloween costume over my coat and snow pants. I hated that feeling. I closed my eyes.

I couldn't believe that after all this, after everything,

looking like I was fat still bothered me more than any of it. I guess it wasn't necessarily true, but I suppose it was better to focus on that instead.

I heard the bell above the door ring and opened my eyes to find Ruthie Jensen walking in. She hadn't lost her sixth sense for knowing when your life was sucking. And mine was beyond sucking now.

Feeling like I was fat was about to become the least of my problems.

I knew it wasn't a coincidence that she was there. In true gossip-monger fashion, she liked nothing better than to talk to people who were directly affected by the gossip she spread. Lila's departure was just that sort of thing.

Joe had been right. I should have stayed at the prom—he should have let me stay at the prom. Or maybe I should have listened to him sophomore year when he tried to warn me. Should have cared when he'd told me it was him or them. I wondered where I would be right now if I had.

Ruthie walked down each aisle with her arms outstretched, touching the surface of every item her hands came across.

I swore that I could feel the fluorescent lights singeing my hair and burning the skin on my scalp. I could feel the ceiling pushing down on me, getting closer and closer every time I looked up. Like in those movies where the spy is stuck in a room that starts to push in on itself, the ceiling and floor like the right and left sides of a vise.

I wished it were really happening—that the ceiling and floor were drawing together like magnets. That before Ruthie could say anything to me, Gas-N-Go would flatten to the pavement, our blood and bone oozing out.

But my only consolation for the fact she was there was that she was probably touching more germs than she would be exposed to in a lifetime.

She looked like Laura Ingalls in that beginning scene from *Little House on the Prairie* where she throws out her hands and spins through the field of wildflowers, but only in the arms. In the face, I realized, she kind of looked like an anteater.

I tried very hard to ignore her, but I was so freaked out by seeing her, and trying so hard to ignore her, that I ended up looking right at her. Not like I could have avoided her, anyway. I knew I was the reason she was there.

"Haven't seen you for a while," she said, smiling, her lips like two small snakes slithering on her face.

I nodded; maybe if I didn't talk to her she would lose interest and go away.

She walked toward the counter and waited for an answer. She was not going to make this easy.

Ruthie had never spoken to me directly before, and I didn't know if I was more afraid that she might know who I was or might not know who I was. If she confused me with a friend of mine and told me about my own arrest, I was going to lose it.

So I said what my mother said when she ran into people she hated. "Yeah, I've been busy." Then to prove it, I dusted the counter and fiddled around with the gum rack. It was probably the most work I had ever done in my whole time employed at Gas-N-Go.

"I can see that," she said, in that condescending way

that means, *Yeah, right.* She tapped her hands on the counter. "Summer job?" She looked around the place, like the answer was written in pieces on the walls.

I nodded. It was not technically a lie—it was summer and it was a job.

"Nice," she said, which I knew meant she thought it was anything but.

"Are you here to buy something?" I asked, trying to seem very disinterested.

"I saw you in here and just wanted to stop by and say hi," she said, smiling with those slithery snake lips again.

She was obviously there to tell me something—tell me something or find out something. She had plenty on me already. I was working at a convenience store and not doing a very good job at a job you'd have to be an idiot not to do a good job at. Oh, and because of Tiffany's jumpsuit, I looked like I had gained a good fifty pounds since the fateful prom night that had started it all.

I prayed for Connor to come out of the back room. To fly out on his customer-service wings and barrage her with questions about how she was doing and what he could do for her today until she got freaked out and left. But I guess my living with Connor made him want to avoid me at work. Of course the one good thing that had come out of being his reluctant roommate was now coming back to bite me.

"How's Cassie doing?" she asked.

I froze. What was she asking me? How was Cassie doing since Lila had gone? How was Cassie doing since the arrest? How was Cassie doing in general?

I didn't know how to provide the answer to any of those

questions. I thought back to the night Cassie's mother had been here, when I had tried without success to find out the answer myself.

I figured saying, "Fine," covered me, so that was what I said. I hoped it might be all she needed to hear so she would get the hell out of my store and the hell out of my face.

"Good, I was worried about her," she said, her snake lips quivering slightly. As horrible as my parents ever thought I was, I could see that Ruthie was a truly evil person. She wanted bad things to happen to people so she would have stuff to talk about.

"I sure hope she's taking care of herself," Ruthie said, her eyes darting back and forth as if she were looking for a weakness in the wall that I had made of my face.

I just kept nodding, even though I wanted so terribly to ask her why she was worried about Cassie, why Cassie needed to take care of herself, but then she would know that I hadn't been talking to Cassie and would have more information than she had come in with.

I started unpacking cigarette cartons, picturing myself smoking every one, sitting in an open field on a sunny day with a pothole-size ashtray next to me. Smoking my mind into an empty page, my only thoughts inhale, exhale, inhale, exhale.

"Well, it happens," Ruthie said, still eyeing me.

"Yes, it does," I said, making sure I emphasized *it* so she would know that I knew what *it* was, even though I had no idea.

"If you're going to have a baby shower for her, I would

love to be invited," she said, letting the words *baby shower* seep out, then appear in front of her and dissolve into shadows of themselves, like she was the Caterpillar from *Alice in Wonderland*.

She had to be lying. Cassie was pregnant? She would have told me. At the very least, Lila would have told me. I looked down, too ashamed to admit I hadn't known. Too sad to say that we were all so far away from each other that I had to hear from the human grapevine that one of my best friends was pregnant.

"I know; I was shocked, too," she said, winking. "She works nights at Pudgie's Pizza if you want to see how she's doing."

Hearing Ruthie say that, I could see Cassie clearly, her stomach rising like the pizza dough she kneaded. The small cells inside her being tossed like the chicken wings she covered in hot sauce, one-handed, in a silver bowl.

"Who told you?" I asked in a voice I didn't recognize. A voice that sounded like someone had squeezed my lungs together like an accordion and forced the words out of my mouth.

"I don't even know," she said. "I've heard it so many places I can't remember where I heard it first." She leaned her elbows on the counter and rested her face on top of her hands, like we were buddies or something. "I can't believe she didn't tell you. I thought you guys were good friends."

Best friends, I thought, *just like Lila and I were best friends*. But now that didn't mean anything.

Ruthie leaned in so close to me that I could see the blackheads on her nose. I stared into them, hoping one would open up and swallow her face and then her neck, then her shoulders and her whole body, so that nothing would be standing in front of me but a big, black hole.

"I guess Lila doesn't know, either," she said, acting like she had to think about it. In reality I knew she'd had this script written long before she came to see me. "When did she leave, a week ago?" Ruthie asked, smiling again.

"She didn't leave," I said, still trying so hard to believe my lie.

"Really? That's what I heard. I also heard her parents aren't even looking for her," Ruthie said, one sentence spilling out after the next. "I don't blame her for leaving, though; I would probably run away, too, if I were facing what you guys are facing, but everyone deals with that sort of thing differently, I guess."

"How do you know all this?" I asked.

She didn't answer me, just kept pushing forward with the rumors she wanted to spread. "Gosh, poor Cassie, with everything she's going through already, to get pregnant right in the middle of it. I'm surprised she hasn't killed herself."

"I'm surprised she hasn't killed you," I said, and watched Ruthie's face go slack. It wasn't what I had planned on, but the minute it came out I realized it was the perfect thing to say. For once, the words came easily. "When she finds out you're telling everyone, I mean."

"Everyone already knows," she said, walking toward the door. "Just like everyone already knows that you're going to end up in jail, like the druggie loser you are," she said. "Cassie's telling everyone how stupid she thinks you are. That you were going to turn her in, but you couldn't even go through with it. I heard Lila said the same thing."

"You don't know anything," I said, my body going tingly. It was hard to breathe. I grabbed onto the counter; it was the only thing keeping me from falling to my knees.

The store around me went fuzzy, and my breathing got heavy.

I was pretty sure I was having a panic attack. My vision turned to tunnels, my head felt woozy. I was cold and hot, shivering and sweaty. I knelt on the floor and closed my eyes to keep myself from collapsing.

I heard the bell above the door *ding* as Ruthie left, probably on her way to tell everyone in town what a freak I was.

For once she wouldn't be lying.

Thirty-two

"Your parents want to talk to you," Connor said, standing above me. I had been asleep on his couch, AJ's cage crooked under my shoulder.

I guess Connor had called my parents and told them how he'd found me the day before—down on my knees, hyperventilating and sweaty in the middle of Gas-N-Go. For once I was glad to be tattled on. It meant I finally got to go home.

"Come on," he said, jingling his car keys.

"Can't I change out of my pajamas first?"

"We don't have time for that. Your dad has an early appointment."

I shrugged. I could get dressed when I got home. I grabbed AJ's cage and walked out to Connor's car.

I kept AJ on my lap for the drive and leaned my chin against the metal dome on the top of his cage. Maybe things weren't as bad as I'd thought. If my parents forgave me, maybe everything could go back to the way it used to be—well, after I figured out what to do about Lila and Cassie.

We pulled onto my street. It was early, quiet. Newspapers still sat in plastic bags on people's dew-wet lawns.

"Good luck," Connor said as I got out of the car.

I walked up the driveway, AJ's cage swinging in my right hand. The porch light was still on, or maybe it was on for me. I turned the knob, but the door was locked. I rang the bell and waited.

The door stayed closed.

I rang the bell again, trying not to think how similar this felt to prom night—my hope high in my throat as I waited for the door to open.

I heard a car pull up in the driveway and turned to find Dick Simon's coffee-ice-cream-colored Cadillac. Something wasn't right.

"Mom!" I yelled, banging on the door. "Dad!" I rang the doorbell over and over—the way wind chimes might sound during a hurricane.

My parents weren't answering the door. I was locked out. I was in my pajamas. I had nowhere to go. I thought about all the times I had locked my door to keep my mother out of my room.

I had to admit it felt pretty crappy being on the other side of it.

I looked at Joe's house, at his porch. I could run across the street and hide under it. Sit in a ball in my pajamas, the dirt below me, light leaking through the wooden slats above. There was no way Dick Simon would fit, but I knew that wasn't a solution. Without Joe there, too, I was just hiding, and how long could I hide? I couldn't stay down there forever. I would have to come out eventually.

My choices became sitting on the cement stoop until my parents calmed down enough to let me in, if ever, or seeing what Dick Simon wanted. Dick Simon won after five minutes because it started to pour.

I opened the passenger door. I was surprised he hadn't gotten out of the car, until I saw that his stomach was wedged under the steering wheel. I put AJ's cage on the seat.

My hand went to where my pocket would have been and where my cigarettes would have been if I hadn't been wearing pajamas. "I'm not going anywhere with you," I said, even as the rain saturated the fabric and stuck it to my skin.

"We can do this the easy way or the hard way. But decide soon, because you're getting my upholstery wet."

I looked at the sky. The rain wasn't stopping any time soon. I felt my shoulders deflate as I got in and moved AJ's cage to the floor in front of me.

He paused to look at me, his eyes puffed out like marshmallows. "You're soaked."

I sucked on my pajama sleeve, trying to get any water that I could; my throat felt scorched. "Where are you taking me?" I asked, because I wanted to know, but also because I was trying to estimate how many of Dick's horrible jokes I would have to hear before we reached our destination.

I rolled down the window. His car smelled.

"It's a surprise," he said, launching into a spate of jokes about surprises.

I closed my eyes and tried to fall asleep, listening to his windshield wipers squeak back and forth while AJ tried to imitate the sound. We drove for what seemed like forever, or maybe that's what everything feels like when you've been seemingly kidnapped in your pajamas by a guy whose car smells like ass covered up with pine air freshener.

Dick shook me awake. "You don't want to miss this part."

I opened my eyes. We were on the highway. I saw a brown sign that said CORRECTIONAL FACILITY NEXT RIGHT.

"That's us," he said.

"Why are we going there?" I asked, feeling helplessness tingle up through my fingers that were splayed out, bracing myself against the dashboard. I felt it move up my arms, to the center of my chest, causing my heart to race. It was exactly the way I'd felt the day before at Gas-N-Go, except now, I had a real reason to feel it. I held AJ's cage tightly between my legs, squeezing so hard the bars probably left indentations on my skin.

Dick didn't say anything, just hummed as we took the exit. The idle sound of it, the lack of fear it displayed, magnified my own.

The correctional facility didn't look the way I had thought it would. It didn't look like an evil fairy-tale castle. It looked like a school. Like a really well-secured school.

The guard at the security gate waved us through.

"Ready?" Dick asked.

"Did I sleep through my trial or something?" I tried

to act tough like Cassie, hoping her strong words would keep me strong, but I was terrified. This was *jail*-jail, the thing Dick had told me was a possibility that first day in his office, but which I was never prepared to believe—never equipped to believe.

We were here now. I couldn't deny it anymore.

"Just wait; it gets better," he said.

We drove on past the gate. I could see pens with barbed wire on the top, just like the barbed wire I had seen as a child when we would drive downtown to temple. Back then, I'd thought it was silver ribbon that had been pulled through scissors so it curled, like on the top of a wrapped present.

I took AJ from his cage and put him on my shoulder. If I was going to be forced to go in there, at least I would have him with me.

"No pets allowed," Dick said. "Put the bird back or they'll take him away." I rubbed AJ's head and locked him in his cage.

Dick parked in a spot marked VISITOR.

"What? You don't have your own?" I asked, still channeling Cassie, hoping it would actually make me feel unafraid, wondering if it ever worked for her.

"I try not to make a habit of coming here."

At least there was one unexpected plus if I was convicted—no more surprise visits from Dick Simon.

• • •

Inside, we were met by a female guard, who patted me down and ushered us through a metal detector. Then she asked for our IDs.

"Don't have it," I said, indicating my cold, wet pajamas, and finally starting to breathe again.

It looked like whatever Dick Simon's little plan was, it was about to blow up in his big, fat face. Until he handed her a copy of my birth certificate and my Collinsville South ID.

"How the hell did you get those?"

The guard who was attending us looked at me. "Do you always talk to your father like that?"

"This is not my father," I hissed.

Dick Simon laughed. "You just made my day." He slapped his leg. "And I didn't even get strip searched."

Once we made it past security, we walked through a locked doorway into the visiting area, which really just looked like a crappy high school cafeteria. There were signs on the walls that said things like: No Fighting, No Running, No Yelling, No Swearing. It was like a very intense swimming pool.

I took a deep breath and told myself that if we were in the visiting area, it meant we were just *visiting*. I would be back in the car with AJ soon.

Dick led me over to a table where a girl sat waiting for us. She was big. And when I say big, I mean watermelon-size breasts, elephant-size thighs, and a camel toe from a biologically engineered camel. So much for bread and water.

"I'm Stubby," she said, standing. She was so short that she looked like she was still sitting down. Apparently she thought I had other notions about the origin of her name, since she said, "Because I smoke so much."

For my own safety, I decided against telling her that was probably not the reason. She squinted as she looked at me, then she turned to Dick. "So, this is that brat you've been telling me about."

Fabulous. Not only was I being discussed among the Save Amy Brain Trust, I was also being discussed by random teenage convicts.

Wait. Was I a random teenage convict?

"What's your name?" She reached out to squeeze my cheek, and I pulled away. "You're going to have to be a lot friendlier than that if you don't want me to kill you." She looked at me like I was a piece of prime rib she was planning on eating with her hands.

"Tell her your name," Dick said.

I closed my mouth tightly and shook my head. I'd had no idea what not wanting to talk really meant. Daniel's office was a joke compared to this.

She leaned over the table, her hands palms down, her nails scratching against it as they closed into fists. Her face had turned bright red, so that it looked like she had a huge tomato on top of her body. "When I ask you a question, you answer it."

"Amy," I said very quietly. I was afraid if I talked too loudly, her head might explode the way glass did from a high-pitched noise.

"I had a girlfriend named Amy once," she said, looking wistful for a second. "I hated that bitch. She's not the reason I'm in here, but if anybody found out what I did to her, I'd never leave."

I couldn't help thinking that Dick Simon had hired this girl. That she was acting. That I was on *Punk'd*, or the new show I had wished we were on when we'd been stood up at Brian's house on prom night.

"I think I'll call you Brat," she said, like I was a puppy she had just been given.

"Well, I'd better be going," Dick Simon said, standing. Then he pulled up his pants and adjusted himself.

I stood, too, thanking whomever I had to thank for getting me the hell out of there before Stubby had a chance to give me another nickname. Maybe there *was* something to all that Jesus stuff.

"Not you," Stubby said, grabbing for me.

"My parents would never allow this," I said, looking at Dick Simon with all the fear I had been attempting to hide during the car ride. *Feeling* all the fear I had been attempting to hide during the car ride. Though I knew they had to be behind it all. "And AJ—he's still in the car," I said, grasping at any excuse to leave.

"Don't worry," Dick said. "I'll take AJ back home—I mean, to Connor's for you."

Home was now Connor's. I was now here. Now totally sucked.

Dick crossed the room and waved a little wave like his hand was working a paper-bag puppet.

Then he was gone.

"Now we can get to know each other a little better." Stubby smiled, her mouth as wide and jagged as a jack-o'-lantern.

She took me on a tour of the facilities, starting with her

cell. Well, really, she showed me her toilet, which was in the middle of her cell. Taking me by the hair and shoving my face into it, asking me if I'd ever been this close to shit.

Which I didn't answer, because what I had learned in the time I had already spent with Stubby was that if she wanted an answer from you, you would know it.

"Well, I sleep in it every night," she said, shaking my head harder.

I couldn't believe it, but I was actually counting the seconds until I saw Dick Simon again.

She was allowed to treat me this way. Apparently, along with this being my parents' idea, they had also given permission. They had signed some release that parents who are at the end of their rope sign that allows their misbehaving child to be taught a lesson by a criminal.

My mom was always looking out for me.

Then Stubby went through in more gory detail basically everything Dick Simon had already told me about being locked up. The whole time she talked, she smoked cigarette after cigarette.

I had asked her for one, and when I did she looked at me and smiled a smile that made her face look like the bunched-up end of a sausage. "What will you give me for it?"

It was what the bartender at Hully's had asked. I still didn't have an answer. I looked down at myself, thinking about what I could give her. My wet pajama pants stuck to my legs.

"That's the way we work things around here," she said, raising her eyebrows.

I let her voice become a low murmur and tried to inhale

as much secondhand smoke as I possibly could. I focused on the soft sizzle of paper and tobacco burning. I could see her mouth moving, but I just watched the smoke going in and going out, going in and going out, going in and going out.

I focused on the smoke, because if I had let myself listen to what she was telling me, to really think about what she was saying, about the fact that I was sitting there, next to her, on her bed, in her cell, and that as she inched ever closer to me, the bed groaning and squeaking like a dying pig, I would have finally started to cry and I think that would have really put her over the edge.

My parents were willing to do anything to keep me out of this place. Why wasn't I?

• • •

Hours later, back in the car with Dick, I was still voluntarily heterosexual. Thankfully, my mother hadn't added a line item on the release form allowing Stubby to violate me. Stubby had left me with a warning that if she ever saw me again, she would be the last person who ever saw me.

Dick dropped me off in front of Connor's apartment. AJ was waiting inside for me, along with a hot bath and dinner. As badly as I wanted all of that, I did *not* want my parents to know that Stubby had gotten to me. And if Connor saw me, there would be no way I could hide what I was feeling from him or from them. There was no way I could keep pretending that I was still strong enough to say no to everything they wanted.

I went to Lollipop Farm. I wasn't sure what I was going to do once I got there, but it was one of the only other places I could think of where I was still welcome. At least the dogs couldn't tell me if I wasn't.

Annie wasn't there. It was closed and dark and I heard the troublesome dogs howling from their yard in the back. The gate wasn't locked. I guess Annie figured that if someone wanted to come in and go to the effort of stealing a dog, they would want to take care of it, too.

I let myself in the gate and they went crazy, barking, wanting whatever I could give them. I grabbed some treats from the supply shed and distributed them down the line, stopping to pet that ice-eyed Husky on the head. She pushed into my hand, as if she were touching me back, saying thank you for giving her the smallest kindness.

I got that. I guess kindness was hard to come by, especially when you were stuck in a cage, or about to be.

I let myself in and sat with her, petting her, just petting her, as the sky went from gray to black, the stars glittery specks.

I remembered learning in Biology that pain was the only thing that could counteract fear. Like, if an ax murderer were chasing you, you wouldn't feel afraid once his ax sliced into you. The excruciating pain would cover up your trembling fear, or maybe it was the other way around. I guess it didn't really matter. I wasn't ready to give in to fear yet, so instead of thinking about my day with Stubby, I thought about Cassie.

If she had gotten pregnant before all of this happened, I would have been standing there with her, finding out at the same moment she did. Huddling with her and Lila in whatever was the closest public bathroom to the closest drug store where we'd bought the pregnancy test. The three of us, staring at the plastic stick and willing it to translate to negative in urine hieroglyphics—one vertical blue strip, a minus sign, an empty circle.

But now I was finding out from Ruthie Jensen, and Lila was gone and everything was different and wrong and terrible. Everything was just like it had been freshman year.

Everything was nothing.

Thirty-three

Finding myself in a cage the following morning, I felt a rush of raw panic in my first moments of waking up, until the Husky that was sleeping next to me started barking and licking my face.

"Look who's awake." Connor was watching me on the outside of the bars, standing with his arms crossed.

"What are you doing here?" I sat up and looked at him. Anything was better than the smell coming off the cement floor I was sleeping on. It hadn't been mopped in a while.

"Right back at ya," he said.

"What time is it?" I croaked.

"Why, are you late for something?"

I thought about it and honestly didn't know. I was sure I was supposed to see someone or do something. I shrugged.

"You're burning your bridges, Amy," he said. It sounded like something my mother would say—he'd probably already talked to her that morning.

"What are you doing here?" I repeated.

"Why didn't you come home last night?" he asked, grabbing the bars. I couldn't help thinking that he resembled an orangutan.

"You lied to me," I said. "You all lied to me."

"Oh, please," he said, reminding me that the things I had done were worse.

"How did you find me?"

"Your mother called. I guess the owner called her," Connor said.

Annie had called my mother to tell her I was asleep in one of her dog cages; that must have been a great conversation. But if Annie had called my mother, why wasn't my mother standing in front of me?

"Am I in trouble?" Had she really sent Connor, rather than have to face me herself?

"Not with Annie," Connor said, opening the cage to let me out.

I felt guilt fill my empty stomach. I'd had nowhere to go, but I probably shouldn't have broken into Lollipop Farm. I probably shouldn't have made this yet another place I would no longer be welcome, regardless of what had happened to me the day before.

"Is AJ okay?" I asked. I'd left him *again*. He was all alone in his cage, probably squawking for someone to feed him.

I wondered if, after receiving the call from Annie, my parents had seen me that way. And, in having still left me in Connor's care, how fed up they must have truly been to be able to ignore those feelings.

"Cayla's taking care of him," he said. "Come on, it's time to go to work." He handed me a Gas-N-Go polo to put over my pajamas. Once again, he had neglected to bring me pants.

On our way out, I stopped in at Annie's office to apologize. I felt like one of the troublesome dogs, looking down, ready to be scolded.

Annie watched me with her recovering-addict eyes and told me she understood, that she had been there, maybe thinking I would offer the kindness she was offering to some other utter failure someday. It was enough to make me want to lock myself back in that cage.

· · ·

I stood behind the counter at Gas-N-Go crunching on barbecue potato chips and drinking lime Gatorade. Trying to lose myself in the chew, chew, chew.

In salty sweetness. In tart, toxic green.

Connor was in the back doing inventory, *again*. I knew he was avoiding me. I could tell he felt guilty for his part in sending me to Stubby's cell for the day, even if he was just a pawn in my mother's and Dick Simon's game. Even if the things I had done really were worse.

The Save Amy Brain Trust had succeeded. I was officially scared. But was that enough reason to finally do what they wanted?

The bell above the door rang. I wiped my barbecue-powdered hands on my pajama pants, expecting to find a nameless, faceless Gas-N-Go customer, someone I could mindlessly serve and then send on his or her way.

Instead, I found Aaron, his skateboard under one arm.

"No," I said, coming around to the front of the counter. "Get out." I thought about what scared women say in movies to their assailants—*Get out or I'll call the police*— but I was not in the mood for the police.

I'd had enough of the police.

"Please," he said. He put his hands in front of him like he was trying to show me he wasn't going to hurt me. It was too late for that.

I shook my head hard, shut my mouth tight. I just wanted him to leave.

It was bad enough I had to think about what he had done without him standing in front of me with his skateboard and chalk-pastel-stained hands and terracotta ponytail and crooked tooth to remind me that I had actually liked him.

That I had actually believed he liked me.

"I have to talk to you," he said.

I looked at him. I couldn't tell if he was dragging it out because he was nervous or because he wasn't really sure what he was going to say yet. Maybe he thought that when I saw him I would run from behind the counter and jump into his arms, apologizing and telling him I would do whatever he wanted, whatever he needed.

I wished I could do that. It would have made everything so much easier. It would have been nice to have someone's arms to jump into.

"It was Brian's idea to do that to you guys on prom night," he said.

"I don't believe you." I shook my head again. Maybe he was telling the truth. I didn't know, but I also didn't care. Not anymore.

He stared at my pajama pants. I moved back behind the counter before he could ask me about them. Before he realized that what he had done to me was not even the worst thing that had happened in the last forty-eight hours.

"It was," he said. "I didn't even know you then."

"Why would he do that to Lila?" I said, unsure why I was even asking. Brian had left with Lila. There was no way he would have stood her up on prom night if he was willing to leave his whole life behind for her.

"I don't know," he said. "But that's the truth." He dug into his pocket for a cigarette and put it behind his ear.

"I don't care," I said. What had happened on prom night was nothing compared to everything else he had done. It was nothing compared to everything else that had happened. Aaron standing me up was one of the better things that had happened that summer.

"I did actually like you," he said, propping his skateboard against his leg and leaning on the counter. Putting his hands on it like he might have put his hands on me, if it had been weeks ago and dark and we were in his father's car. "Really," he said, making his eyes go soft, like they would just before he leaned in to kiss me.

I thought about that age-old story where the main character's friends bet him to go on a date with the dorky, ugly girl, and he realizes she's not so bad. I didn't want to be that girl.

Maybe it meant I wasn't.

"I'm still not doing what you want," I said.

"That's not why I'm here," he said.

"Then why?" I asked. I couldn't believe that I still kind of wanted to make out with him.

"To see you," he said.

"Well, you've seen me," I said, holding my arms out at my sides, trying to act like I didn't care. But I did. He was saying all the right things.

Too bad he was the wrong guy.

I looked at the door, trying to push him out of it with my mind—wanting *so* badly for that bell to *ding*.

"Okay," he said. He stood there. He picked up his skateboard, moved it from one hand to the other and back, the mountain range on the deck of it moving from east to west, from west to east.

I looked down at my deflated bag of chips on the counter, still waiting for the *ding*. Waiting until he was gone so I could try and pretend nothing that had happened to me had happened—starting with the night I'd met Aaron and going all the way back to prom night.

"Can't you at least think about it?" he pleaded.

I looked up. He was leaning toward me, his skateboard under his arm, his crooked tooth poking out over his bottom lip as he smiled. Aaron was as bad as my mother had thought Lila and Cassie were.

He was worse.

"Please, Amy," he said so softly that the words almost disappeared.

I gripped the baseball bat that Mancini kept behind the counter, though I doubted this was the kind of emergency he'd had in mind when he put it there.

"Just go," I said. The bat felt hot in my palm.

He touched the cigarette behind his ear—rolled it with two fingers like a tiny piece of Play-Doh. "I mean, you were my girlfriend and I asked you for a favor. That's not wrong," Aaron said, shaking his head.

Maybe it wasn't, if that was what he'd really asked for, but what he'd asked for…even Lila and Cassie hadn't asked for that.

"I wasn't your girlfriend," I said. I had wanted so badly to be. In spite of everything, the word made my stomach flutter.

"Then maybe you were the one who was using me," he said, squinting. "Ever think about that?"

"You should leave now." I showed him the baseball bat in my hand. I needed him to stop talking. I needed it all to stop.

"What are you going to do, hit me?" He laughed.

I shrugged. I didn't know what I was going to do. I couldn't feel anything except the smooth wood in my hand. I couldn't see anything except his face—that I had kissed and trusted and daydreamed about.

"I should have fucked you while I had the chance," he said as he smiled wickedly. "You would have done it, too," he whispered, leaning toward me. "You would have done *everything* I wanted."

I watched his lips. They opened and closed. Opened and closed—cruel words flowing out.

"You would have *liked* it," he hissed.

Hearing his words, it was like I could feel everything

that had happened to me: every loss of friendship and loss of freedom, every piece of me that had been chipped away by Daniel and Dick Simon, every bit of scar tissue that formed from the police and my parents.

I brought the bat up and swung angrily, smacking his arm hard enough to make him drop his skateboard. I hadn't meant to actually hit him, but it felt stronger than anything I could say.

"You crazy bitch!" He picked up his skateboard from where it had fallen and cocked it behind him.

I swung again, harder. But the force caused me to slip and fall, my chin hitting the counter on my way down, like one of those crash test dummies hitting a windshield. I guess Connor was right about keeping the floor areas clean for safety reasons.

I heard the bell above the door *ding* as Aaron finally left. In reaction to seeing my body doubled over on the floor, he got the hell out of there.

I guess that was how much he *liked* me.

I tasted metal and when I put my hand to my mouth and then inspected the contents, I saw blood and white specks like broken china. I didn't have to be a dentist's daughter to know that they were parts of my teeth. Daniel was right. I chose the people and things that populated my life. They didn't choose me. That was why I was here, on the floor of a convenience store all alone, with blood and teeth in my hand.

I know I'd always felt like I had to make the choices I made to survive, but the thing was—I made them. I could say the world forced me into it, but that would be a lie. It was me. It was all me.

I guess I started screaming because Connor came running out of the back room with yet another bat in his hand. Mr. Mancini must have had them hidden around the place like Easter eggs.

"What happened?" Connor yelled.

I opened my mouth to answer and was about to say something about having been robbed, because there was no way I was going to tell Connor what had really happened, but all that came out was a defeated moan and blood—lots of blood, like I had chewed on one of those red caplets that come in Dracula makeup kits.

"Mother of pearl," he said, coming up behind me and taking me by the shoulders. I guess for Connor to use that kind of language, I must have looked pretty bad.

He put a washcloth to my face, which quickly turned from white and green checkered to pink and green checkered. I was in too much pain to even care where it came from.

I watched him dial the phone, talk for a minute, and hang it up. Then he taped a sign on the door that said BACK IN FIFTEEN MINUTES. Connor was ever the optimist.

"Well," he said as he led me out to the car, "at least your shirt's already red."

"Whe re ga?" I asked, which in just-smacked-your-own-face translated to: "Where are we going?"

"Don't talk," Connor said. "Close your eyes and relax."

Seeing as my options were talk and possibly bleed to death in the process, or close my eyes and try to focus on anything but the gargantuan pain in my mouth, I decided to take Connor up on his suggestion.

I wasn't sure how I'd gotten here—to Connor taking care of me in an emergency instead of my parents. But I guess this was my life now: working at Gas-N-Go, staying with Connor, dressing like I shopped at Goodwill, until my trial, when someone else would decide my fate unless I had the guts to decide for myself.

I couldn't believe this was what I had been fighting so hard for.

I looked at Connor. He was so simple, so happy. He tried to make the best of things and his life was better because of it. He had a family to come home to, friends who cared about him, a job he actually liked. He had a life ahead of him that he could do anything with.

I closed my eyes and thought about what I had: my bloody pajama pants, my broken teeth, my broken relationships, and jail. That was all I had left now.

When I opened my eyes, we were sitting in the parking lot of my father's office.

"No fe we," I said. Which was just-bashed-your-own-mouth-in for, "No freaking way." If my father didn't want to see me, I didn't want to see him, either.

I guess I must have looked pissed off, because Connor said, "Well, where am I supposed to take you? Do you have money to pay for the emergency room? Because I sure don't."

He came around to my side of the car and opened the door for me. I was about to tell him that I knew how to use my hands, but then decided to show him by giving him the finger.

"What did I do?"

I knew it wasn't him I was really mad at, but I didn't care. "Di cu ot," which was make-him-feel-really-guilty for, "Didn't come out."

"I don't understand what you're saying."

"Wha ew?" I said as I got out of the car, which was look-who-took-his-Einstein-pills-today for, "What's new?"

• • •

We found my father waiting for us, playing Solitaire on his computer. So much for staring longingly at a picture of me.

My father's office had the general dentist's office feeling—white walls, chickpea-colored carpets, yellow and orange chairs, a little roulette wheel of small, tooth-sized drills, sinks like half-cantaloupes.

"Oh my God, what happened?" my father asked, running over and giving me a hug. I hugged back as best I could with my one free hand. "Are you okay, sweetie? Was there an accident?"

Connor was still standing in the doorway. Though I doubt he was intimidated by my father—a squirrel wouldn't be intimidated by my father—he may have been intimidated by my father's love for me. And if not intimidated, then definitely surprised.

"I think we got robbed," Connor said, shaking his head like he was saying, *You win some, you lose some.*

"Did you call the police?"

"Na pe," I gurgled, which meant everyone-was-totally-clueless for, "No police."

"What did she say?" my father asked, as if in the time I'd

been away I had developed a new language that escaped him.

"I don't know. I think she's delirious; she's been mumbling the whole way over here."

"Did they steal her clothes?" my father asked, as if seeing what I was wearing for the first time.

"E wih," I said, which was as-if-this-day-wasn't-bad-enough-already for, "I wish."

"Is she going to be okay?" Connor asked.

Though I couldn't tell if he was asking because (a) I was under his supervision when this happened, (b) he was afraid my parents would sue him, or (c) he really did care about me like he'd always claimed.

But, of course, it turned out to be (d) none of the above.

"Because I should really get back to work," he said. And when I turned to look at him, he continued. "They could come back and I don't want to leave the store unattended."

Right, like what would he do if "they" did come back? And then I remembered that "they" didn't exist.

"They" was Aaron.

"You go do whatever you need to," my father said in his calm dentist's voice, leading me to the nearest patient chair.

"Call me when you're ready, Amy," Connor said, waving good-bye.

"Ank u," I said, wondering why it was easier to say thank you when no one could understand me anyway.

My father sat me down, then reclined the chair and turned on his adjustable light. "Let's take a look," he said, which is what he said to every patient when he had one in this position. He probably didn't even think about it before he said it anymore. He pulled the hand that held the washcloth away from my mouth. "Does it hurt?"

Another patient-script question and one I would suggest he alter once I could talk again. If there's blood, it most likely hurts. In my case it really, really hurt. Describing it as just hurting did not do it justice at all.

"All right," he said, opening my mouth and getting in close. "Not terrible," he said, inspecting, "but not great. A little bleeding and swelling in the gums, two broken teeth. We'll have you fixed up in a jiffy."

Luckily, my father kept his office stocked at all times with a full set of veneers made just for my teeth; he was nothing if not pessimistic when it came to my mouth.

He pulled back and put his hand on my cheek, as if his touch would heal me. "You're a good girl. Your life shouldn't be this hard," he said, shaking his head and riding his stool over to the sink to wash his hands.

I guess my teeth being knocked out solidified for him what was happening to me. Gave him something he could see and understand.

I felt myself start to cry, huge heavy sobs that caused my father to run to me.

"Are you okay?"

I couldn't talk anyway, but I couldn't answer. I was anything but. I guess I hadn't been for a very long time.

"At least this I can fix," he said, as much to himself, it seemed, as to me.

"I orry," I said.

"I know you're worried, but you'll look fine. We can take care of that bicuspid while we're at it, too."

I didn't think I needed to translate what I meant, but I guess my father's not that sharp. Or maybe he had been waiting so long to hear that I really *was* sorry, that he couldn't even believe I was saying it.

I wiped my eyes. Bad girls like me weren't supposed to care about what happened to them. Bad girls like me were supposed to end up angry and broken and hurt. It was hard to admit that I was tired of being angry and broken and hurt. That maybe I wasn't cut out to be a bad girl.

"It's okay," he said, "we can fix it. We can fix it."

He gave me more of whatever he usually used to knock me out. I could tell because right before I closed my eyes, I saw four of him standing in front of me. One was more transparent than the next, as if someone had sliced thinner and thinner slices off of him, like deli meat.

I wondered if that was what was happening to me—if, as I grew up, as life got harder, there were pieces of myself that I placed in front of me to guard what was still me. I wondered if, after all this was over—if it was ever over— there would be anything left.

Thirty-four

I woke up to find AJ's cage next to me on my father's stool, his little yellow body watching over me like a sentry. I put my hand out and held it. The metal felt cool.

I turned and saw my mother on a stool on the other side, sitting in the dark. She was staring out the window and didn't notice I had woken up. I might have gotten away with closing my eyes again and falling back asleep, falling back into the nothingness of whatever my father had given me, but AJ started repeating, *Pretty Amy, pretty Amy, pretty Amy.* Even more evidence, considering how I must have looked, that AJ just said whatever I'd trained him to.

"Don't try to talk," my mother said, wheeling herself over. I was glad to be given the reprieve. There was really nothing to say anyway.

We had been in this position before, any number of times, when my father had to fix something that had gone wrong in my mouth, but until that moment, I had forgotten she had been the one to watch over me afterward to make sure I was all right.

I tried to sit up.

"Take it easy," she whispered. "Just rest."

I closed my eyes, because I was tired and because it was hard to look at her. I might have been able to say I was sorry to my father, but there was more I had to say to her, and I wasn't ready to say it yet.

"How did this happen?" she asked, though having told me not to talk, I didn't think she expected an answer. She might have been talking to herself, or she might have been talking to AJ. Wondering how things could have changed so much since the day she'd brought him home for me when I was eight.

When I was so happy to have a pet, so deliriously happy to have something to love, that I had sung, *I love you, Mommy*, over and over again as I danced around her. Perhaps she was commiserating with AJ, wondering how after that day, the three of us could have ended up here, like this.

She touched my forehead, petting it lightly like I was a cat in her lap. It was the first time she had touched me since the arrest, the first time she had wanted to and the first time I had let her. I tried not to think about how natural it felt. How easily I could fall back into just being her little girl.

"Here," she said, putting three pills into my hand. "They'll help you sleep."

I took them from her and gobbled them up like candy, closing my eyes again.

"What are you so afraid of?" she asked. A question she had never asked me when I could respond, probably because *she* was too afraid to hear the answer.

I guess to her it looked like I was more scared to be friendless than to be locked away.

That was true, but I had always been locked away; a confinement of caring so very much about what other people thought of me, the bars around me made up of my own perceived inadequacies. Lila and Cassie had made me not have to think about any of those thoughts.

Without them, I was locked up again, anyway, whether I signed the paper or not.

I heard the pill bottle shake as my mother stood. She handed me my cell phone. "You should check your messages," she said.

I turned on my phone, that familiar buzz and tinkle in my hand. I had messages. My mom had obviously checked them.

"I'll leave AJ here for you," she said as she locked the office door behind her.

It had been the first time in weeks that she hadn't yelled at me, that we hadn't started fighting, and I couldn't help thinking that maybe it was because I couldn't yell back.

I put the phone to my ear. Five voice mails. Was it Lila saying good-bye? Cassie saying she had something important to tell me? Was it Aaron having gotten my cell number in one last attempt to try to convince me to do what he wanted?

No. It was Joe.

All of them were Joe: that first night on my way home

from work, the day I was sitting on my porch in my suit smoking and he hadn't stopped, the night I was afraid he would see me in the car with Aaron, the day of my front-porch freak-out, and finally, the morning of graduation.

The first message said he was waiting under the porch if I wanted to meet. Each one repeated that, wondering if I was even getting his messages, wondering if I really did just want to be left alone. Until the last message, saying he wouldn't bother me anymore. That was why he had been so angry when I saw him on graduation night. He'd thought I didn't need him. That even as crappy as things had become, I was still choosing my new life over my old.

I pictured him leaving the messages, the wooden slats above him letting in lines of sunlight or porch light, the smell of wet earth, the only safe place he could talk to me, the only safe place I might be able to talk to him.

I put the phone in my lap. The only thing stopping my tears were the pills taking over.

Joe.

Thirty-five

I woke again to find Daniel, Connor, Dick, my mother, and my father standing over me. The light was on, and their heads were big, floating above me like a mobile made of beach balls. They looked at me like a newborn they were regarding through glass.

AJ's cage still sat on the stool next to me. He looked at me and tweeted, *Good morning*, his yellow feathers bright in the fluorescent office lights.

For a moment, I felt like I was in my own head, that all of them were figments of my imagination. That I had been pushed so far over the edge, I'd taken them on as my own personalities, and now they were left to fight with one another over who would get to tell me what to do next.

But then Dick Simon burped. Loudly. And I knew my supposed nightmare was all too real.

"I think she's awake," Connor said.

"How are you feeling, honey?" my father asked.

"Can she hear us?" Dick asked, waving his hand in front of my eyes.

"Of course she can. She got hit in the mouth; she's not deaf," my mother said with certainty, then looked at me and said, "Is she, Jerry?"

"Her hearing shouldn't have been affected," my father said.

"She could be in shock," Daniel said.

"She was fine two hours ago," my mother said, sounding worried.

"I think she can see. Her eyes are open," Connor said.

As fun as this was, I figured I should say something, because I knew if I didn't, there would be an ear, nose, and throat doctor added to the Save Amy Brain Trust. I couldn't bear having one more person wonder what was wrong with me. "I'm fine," I said.

"You're back here with us now," my father said, "safe and sound."

"What is this, some psychedelic *Wizard of Oz*?" I asked, looking specifically at Daniel's Technicolor tie-dye.

"I guess I'm not the only one she talks to that way," Dick Simon said.

"No," Connor said.

"No," Daniel said.

"No," my mother said.

No, no, no, AJ repeated.

"At least she's talking," my father said.

It was true. I was being snarky, but it did have that feeling. Connor as the Scarecrow, Daniel as the Tin Man, Dick as the Lion, AJ as Toto, and me as Dorothy just wanting to get back to Kansas, back to a life I could understand.

Of course, I was one punk-ass Dorothy.

I tried to sit up. My head didn't seem to want to comply.

"Everyone was worried about you," my father said. He was breathing heavily, his nostrils opening and closing slightly.

I figured I might as well play along. They were all being so nice to me; I kind of liked it. "I'm okay," I whimpered, covering my eyes with the back of my hand like some young woman who was prone to swooning, and probably British.

"Are you ready to tell us what happened, Amy?" my mother asked.

"Did someone threaten you?" Dick Simon asked.

I shook my head, but I couldn't help thinking about Aaron. He hadn't threatened me, but what he had done was just as terrible, maybe worse.

"She must be protecting someone," my mother said.

"If Cassie or Lila or one of their friends came after you, you need to tell us," Dick said.

Cassie, AJ squawked, *Lila, Cassie, Lila, Lila.*

My life was so much less interesting than they thought it was.

"It was me," I said. "I fell." It wasn't the complete truth, but how could I tell them about Aaron? I was too embarrassed. I was too ashamed.

"You fell with a bat in your hand?" my mother asked.

I nodded.

"No robbers?" Connor asked, looking disappointed.

I shook my head.

"None of this would have happened if she had just signed that paper," my mother said, starting to cry. Apparently she'd gotten over my self-inflicted injury and was on to the next drama.

"She still can," Dick said.

"She still should," Daniel said.

"She still might," Connor said, looking up.

"Hopefully, this makes your decision easier," my father said.

I wished it did, but the truth was, I could no longer deny that this wasn't about Lila and Cassie at all. That it really was about me trying so hard to hold on to this person I thought I wanted to be. This angry girl that I could hide behind, so I didn't have to look at myself, so no one else could look at me.

"Should we take her to the doctor?" Connor asked.

"There's a doctor right here," my mother said, pointing to my father.

"I can't say for sure if there's something wrong with her head. What if she has a concussion?" he asked.

I let them keep talking about me and thought back to the confession I would have written. I thought about that little girl on the swings in my backyard. All these people in front of me were trying desperately to help her. She would want me to let them. That girl was not alone. She had herself. She had me. And, hopefully, she wasn't too late to have Joe.

"Yes," I said. "I'll do it." Tasting the Y-E-S—positive, strong, the way I wanted to feel, even though I was terrified.

Yes, AJ tweeted, *yes, yes, yes.*

I'd wanted the words to be perfect. It seemed like they should be profound or something for as long as everyone had been waiting to hear them, but all I could say was yes. I guess sometimes saying what you mean is enough.

No one asked me if I was sure, no one said anything. I think they were afraid that if they started talking, I would change my mind.

Five pens were shoved in my face, waiting to be picked like kids on a playground. I took my father's and signed my metaphorical death warrant.

My hand shook as I wrote my name. It was scary enough to admit that I was alone, without having to admit I had no idea who I was anymore. I would deal with that another day.

Dick Simon took the paper and touched the back of my head, which for some reason I allowed. I hoped that my fall hadn't caused a form of brain damage that made me want to respect my elders, because that would make the rest of my life a major drag.

Thirty-six

Even though I'd signed the paper, I still had to go to the judge's chambers to hear my sentencing. "It needs to be made official," Dick said. "Nothing is definite until the fat lady sings, and my wife ain't much of a singer."

Basically, it meant that the judge had until the last minute to decide whether or not to give me another chance.

Was that what I was being given? It didn't feel that way. It felt like I was starting over, which I guess was the same thing, except starting over sounds terrifying by comparison.

Dick met us on the courthouse steps. The sun was so bright that the white concrete columns seemed to reflect light like mirrors. I could feel myself sweating under my suit jacket. Hope-fully this would be the last time I would ever have to wear it.

"It's too bad you didn't get to see me go to trial," Dick said. "It's the only thing I'm better at than telling a joke."

My parents just smiled. They had been smiling themselves silly since I signed that stupid paper. I was surprised that their cheeks weren't bleeding.

"Doing okay, Amy?" Dick asked.

"She's super," my mother said, smiling more, if that were possible. Basically it meant that I was doing everything they told me to. Everything could go back to the way it used to be. Well, everything that didn't involve Lila and Cassie.

I felt like I was going to be sick.

"You're not nervous, are you?" Dick asked.

I shook my head. I wasn't nervous. I wasn't sure what I was.

"How much longer?" I asked, looking at my phone. Joe still hadn't texted me back from the night before. Even though I'd apologized, maybe I was too late. Maybe a text wasn't enough.

"Ten minutes or so. Let's go inside and sit down," Dick said.

We sat in the marble-floored hallway on wooden-backed chairs that faced away from the judge's gold-lettered office door. My mother grabbed onto my father's hand, her diamond ring glinting in the overhead lights. They had been touching each other more since I signed that paper than I think they had their entire marriage.

"Amy, I'm just so proud of you." My mother looked at me and started to cry, like it was my wedding day or something.

My father pulled her in close and hugged her. "We both are."

I wished my mother hadn't been so busy being proud of me to remember to nag me into carrying that lame Liz Claiborne purse, because nausea was high in my throat.

I knew I was supposed to feel like I had been somewhere, or done something, or changed in some deep way, but mostly I just felt like I'd been treading water and while I wasn't looking, someone had come by and drained the pool.

"Do I have time to use the bathroom?" I asked.

"Sure," Dick Simon said, "just keep it to *numero uno*."

I wasn't sure what number was about to heave out of me. I left them sitting there and ran toward the nearest bathroom. I could hear their voices echoing behind me, peeping like ladies at a tea party.

I darted to the first stall, puked, flushed, and went to the sink. I turned on the tap and slurped water from it like it was a drinking fountain. Maybe I was nervous, or maybe I was just allergic to doing what my parents told me to.

I felt someone pull me away from the sink and throw me against the wall.

"You bitch," Cassie spat. "I didn't think I'd see you again, but I am *so* glad I did."

I looked around for a weapon. Then I looked at her stomach. I considered telling her I had fresh sutures in my mouth, but that was just the kind of nerdy thing that would make someone like her beat you even harder.

She kicked the wall next to me. "You sold us out," she said, her eyelids squeezed as thin as paper cuts.

Cassie was going to massacre me. At least there would be lots of police around to see her do it.

"I had to."

"Really? Well, I pleaded not guilty, because that's what innocent people do, Amy," she said.

"But my lawyer said guilt didn't matter."

"Your lawyer. You've got all these people telling you what to do and you're still a fucking mess."

Maybe I was, but I was trying. I felt like I was saying what I wanted to, doing what I wanted to, what I needed to. Well, at least starting yesterday.

"Did your mommy and daddy make you?" she asked.

"Shut up." I thought about Aaron and felt sick again. She had no idea.

"I guess you didn't know what to do without Lila around pulling your strings," she said.

"Or without you giving me crap all the time," I said, squirming under her weight.

"Oh, don't worry, I'm about to give you some crap." She smiled and lifted her fist.

"Cassie, please, I'm sorry," I said. Even though she was about to kill me, I was glad I had the opportunity to apologize. None of this had been her fault. She had been pulled into it, just like I had.

"Cassie, *please*," she mimicked.

"What was I supposed to do? Lila left. You got pregnant," I said. "What was I supposed to do, Cassie? Tell me."

She let go. "I am going to fucking kill Ruthie Jensen. I'm not fucking pregnant."

I looked at her. She was exhaling hard, hot, like a fire-breathing dragon.

I should have known Ruthie was lying. "I'm glad," I said.

"You really think I'm that stupid?" she asked, her face turning red.

"No. I mean, I didn't know what to think."

We stood there staring at each other, with our hands at our sides, waiting.

"So kick my ass already," I said. I figured I might as well get it over with. Pull the Band-Aid off with one clean swipe. Maybe the judge would feel bad for me if I had a black eye.

She reared up her fist. I closed my eyes and waited. I thought about how I had seen her do this to other people, other people who had wronged us, had talked about us behind our backs.

I couldn't believe I had become one of those people.

I heard her punch the wall next to me and start cackling.

"I'm getting rehab, just thirty days," she said. "Your lawyer isn't the only one who can make deals."

"You were screwing with me?" I pushed her into the sink.

"Ow," she said, pushing me back. "You deserved it. I mean, rehab is going to suck."

"I didn't deserve that," I said, pushing her again.

"You want to start something now?" she asked.

"Sorry," I said again.

"Me, too," she said. "Lila." Cassie shook her head. "What a crazy bitch. She made us look like serial killers or something."

I nodded. I guess I hadn't thought about how strange it was that she'd taken off. All I had been thinking about was that she had left me. That had been all I cared about.

"I guess Brian's gone, too," Cassie said. "You know his

friend, Aaron or whatever. He came to see me at work."

I felt dizzy. He had tried to get to Cassie, too. He was even more of an asshole than I thought he was. "Really," I said, waiting for her to tell me her story, my story.

"I threw a Pepsi in his face and told him to get lost," she said.

Cassie. She was so strong. That was why I loved her.

"There's no way I was going to fall for his bullshit," she said.

I guess I had fallen for some of his bullshit, but I felt like it meant something that I hadn't even considered taking the blame for him. Maybe I was stronger than I thought I was.

"Are you scared?" I asked.

"No," she said, but I could tell she was lying. I could tell that her tough words were just that.

"My parents didn't make me," I said, realizing that they really hadn't.

"Whatever," she said, fixing her hair in the mirror. "My parents made me."

I thought back to the night her mom had come in to Gas-N-Go, Cassie waiting in the car. Her mother had made her wait in the car. Her mother had made her stay away from me.

"What kind of person just leaves?" Cassie asked.

I shrugged. I didn't know. I guess Cassie and I were the kind of people who didn't.

"I forgive you," she said. "Lila's a bitch, but I forgive you."

"Thanks," I said, realizing she was doing easily what I had found it so hard to do. Throwing out apologies and forgiveness like candy coming from a piñata. "Are you going to forgive Ruthie Jensen?" I asked.

"No fucking way," she said.

I laughed. The kind of laugh I had thought I would never laugh again.

Cassie laughed, too. "See you," she said as she left the bathroom.

"Yeah," I said. "See you around."

Though I guessed I probably wouldn't. Without Lila, Cassie and I were like a two-sided triangle, our lines continuing on and on with nothing to connect them. And I knew that day that Lila was never coming back.

I felt my phone vibrate in my pocket. I took it out and a text from Joe flashed across the screen.

Welcome back, Amy.

I guess I wasn't too late.

• • •

I found Joe waiting for me under his porch when I got back from the courthouse. I didn't even take the time to change out of my suit. I ducked under the slats, smelling the wet earth, feeling the instant chill of being hidden from the sun. He handed me a juice box.

"Took you long enough," he said.

I sat on the ground next to him.

"Is it over?" he asked.

"Mostly," I said. It was, but there was still him, *us* to figure out. At least I hoped there was.

"You look like you're playing dress-up," he said, laughing.

"Yeah," I said, pulling at my pants. "I'm going to burn

this stupid suit."

We sat there listening to Spud bark in the yard, probably at a squirrel, maybe at a bird.

"I'm sorry," I said.

"For what?" he asked, casually taking a sip of his juice box. I was allowed under the porch again, but being allowed back into his life required more.

I shrugged. There was so much. Some had to do with him, but most didn't.

"I need you to tell me," he said.

Signing the paper had been easy, but Joe demanded words. He deserved them. I deserved them.

"For choosing them over you," I said quietly.

He looked at me, waiting. He knew me well enough to know there was more I wanted to say. Something I was building up to.

"For choosing"—it came out slowly, like someone checking the temperature of a pool with her toes first— "them over me."

He nodded.

That was all it had ever been—so simple, yet so hard to admit.

"It was always about you, Amy," he said.

Daniel had been trying to get the same thing out of me during all those sessions, but I hadn't wanted to tell him. I'd wanted to tell someone who understood that it wasn't just about the arrest—someone who knew what those words really meant and how important it was for me to say them.

I guess I'd wanted to tell Joe.

My eyes started to burn with tears. I took a breath,

pushed the air back out.

"Sorry I was kind of an ass about it," he said, looking remorseful.

"You really were." I laughed, wiping my eyes. "But I was, too."

"You really were." He laughed. He held his juice box in the air.

"What are we toasting?" I asked, copying him.

"This, I guess," he said, clinking his with mine. "You being you. Me being me. No more pretending."

We both drank. That familiar slurping sound—my mouth filled with grape juice, sweet and wonderful. It tasted like Joe.

"I'm glad you're okay," he said, and I knew he meant it. I knew the weirdness between us that had begun freshman year had been because we'd started having feelings that scared us, that made us want to pretend we didn't feel anything at all. That made ignoring each other safer.

"I am," I said, wiping my nose with my sleeve. "I will be."

"I almost failed English without you, Fleishman," he said.

"Spud never learned to talk?" I joked.

"No," he said, putting his hands on his legs and squeezing. They were shaking more than I'd ever seen them shake. Twitching like he was holding handfuls of bees.

"Are *you* okay?" I asked, feeling selfish. Maybe some of those messages had been because Joe wanted to talk to me, too.

"Same as always," he said, a slat of sunlight hitting his face as he turned to me. I hadn't been this close to him in a while. I had forgotten how green his eyes could get. How his eyelashes were the color of deer fur.

"You don't have to lie," I said. "Considering what I've been through, I think I can take it."

"There's time for that," he said, taking the last sip from his juice box, pressing it flat.

His hands started shaking again. I took them in mine—held them tightly, the way I had when we were kids. That familiar feeling, but charged with want. "What now?" I asked.

He shrugged. He looked at me, his mouth open slightly. "Should we kiss?" he said softly, like I was a mouse he was trying not to scare.

"We could," I teased, still holding his hands. I could feel his fingers stroking the insides of my palms.

"Do you want to?" he asked. "I mean, we don't have to," he said, stumbling over his words.

I leaned in and kissed him. We'd already wasted too much time pretending. His lips and tongue were cold from the grape juice. But I felt heat blooming on my face, in my throat, and then through each strand of hair, as he stopped and breathed onto my neck. It wasn't like kissing Aaron, when I'd kept wondering why. With Joe, instead of feeling uncertain, all I felt was sure.

All I felt was right.

"I missed you," he said. He touched the sides of my face; he touched my lips. His hands were still.

I kissed him again, harder. Punishing his lips for all the time we'd spent apart. I *had* missed him. I had missed me.

"Thanks for the messages," I said.

"You would have done the same for me," he said.

We kept kissing, until our mouths and stomachs ached. In the time we had spent avoiding each other, Joe had actually become a pretty good kisser. Maybe he had always been a good kisser.

"So, does this mean you're finally going to quit smoking?" Joe asked, laughing into my lips.

"Not going to give up on that, huh?" I asked.

"Not this time," he said, kissing me again.

Thirty-seven

Probation, a fine, and drug tests every month for a year. Dick said I was lucky. My parents just about wet themselves. I guess I did, too.

They never found Lila. She, like all attractive people, seemed to get away with things whether she tried to or not. There is a part of me that still wants to believe she was kidnapped. That she was taken by a wolf in the night, clenched between his jaws, struggling and bleating like a lamb. But that's only when I'm feeling generous.

Cassie went to rehab for thirty days. She'd made her deal by naming Aaron and some other people as the next ones up the line. I hoped they would have some anger management classes for her, too.

Connor was still happy. Daniel was still attempting to help reluctant patients, and Dick Simon still told horrible jokes. He sent them along with the seemingly never-paid-off invoice he mailed me weekly. The last one had a joke about a guy who had to pay his bills by candlelight because he always kept his electric bill for last.

As a self-imposed penance for breaking into Lollipop Farm, I volunteered to help Annie at night after I finished work at Gas-N-Go. I didn't mind. I liked being with the dogs and they liked being with me.

During the day, my father, Joe, and I were building AJ an aviary—a big, beautiful wooden structure the size of a sunroom—in our backyard. We would work before my father left for the office in the morning and during his lunch hour, the smell of fresh wood filling our patio.

My mother wasn't thrilled about having something imperfectly built by our hands in our yard for everyone to see, but I think she was starting to learn that you couldn't hide behind perfection.

Just like I was starting to learn you couldn't hide behind failure.

Unfortunately, I am only myself. I am scared and alone and unsure, but I am practicing. I am scared and alone and unsure, but that doesn't mean I always will be.

Like AJ repeating words, I can repeat being me, until I start to believe it.

Sometimes Joe and I will sit on the swings in my backyard and admire what we are building. It's just a skeleton of sand-colored wood and silver nails, but I can picture the day it will be ready; the day I will release AJ.

I can see him on that first flight. His little yellow body moving fast and hard like a tennis ball hit back and forth and back and forth. Choosing to land, or fly, or just be, and having the space to do so.

Sitting on the swings like I used to, with Joe next to me, pumping our legs until the chains creak, it's easy to believe that someday I will feel just like AJ unlocked from his cage.

That the bars I've put around me will fall away.

That I will feel like that little girl again, finally and beautifully free.

Acknowledgments

I am thankful to so many people who have supported me on the journey to publication.

To my agent, Susan Finesman, who asks for things on my behalf that I would never have the guts to ask for, and who dealt with my debut-author neuroses with kindness, patience, and humor. Without you, this book would not be.

To my editor, Stacy Cantor Abrams, who saw something in Amy and in me and encouraged me at every step of the way to cultivate it. For loving Amy as much, if not more, than I do. Without you, this book would not be what it is.

To my husband, Tim, who has been with me on this writing roller coaster for a decade and never once told me to stop. Without you, I would not be. I love you.

To my sister, Marcy, who has been a steady cheerleader or a steady shoulder to cry on depending on the day and sometimes even the time of day.

To my parents, who always believed I had talent and never once told me to pick a new major.

To my professors, classmates, and amazing "Blue Spark Ladies" at the Inland Northwest Center for Writers, who taught me what it means to be a writer and who read versions of this book way, way before it was this book, and liked it even then.

Finally, to everyone at Entangled Publishing for making my dream come true.

HE'S SAVED HER.

HE'S LOVED HER.

HE'S KILLED FOR HER.

Eighteen-year-old Archer couldn't protect his best friend, Vivian, from what happened when they were kids, so he's never stopped trying to protect her from everything else. It doesn't matter that Vivian only uses him when hopping from one toxic relationship to another—Archer is always there, waiting to be noticed.

Then along comes Evan, the only person who's ever cared about Archer without a single string attached. The harder he falls for Evan, the more Archer sees Vivian for the manipulative hot-mess she really is.

But Viv has her hooks in deep, and when she finds out about the murders Archer's committed and his relationship with Evan, she threatens to turn him in if she doesn't get what she wants... And what she wants is Evan's death, and for Archer to forfeit his last chance at redemption.

HUSHED

AVAILABLE ONLINE AND IN STORES EVERYWHERE

WARD AGAINST DEATH
BY MELANIE CARD

Twenty-year-old Ward de'Ath expected this to be a simple job—bring a nobleman's daughter back from the dead for fifteen minutes, let her family say good-bye, and launch his fledgling career as a necromancer. Goddess knows he can't be a surgeon—the Quayestri already branded him a criminal for trying—so bringing people back from the dead it is.

But when Ward wakes the beautiful Celia Carlyle, he gets more than he bargained for. Insistent that she's been murdered, Celia begs Ward to keep her alive and help her find justice. By the time she drags him out her bedroom window and into the sewers, Ward can't bring himself to break his damned physician's Oath and desert her.

However, nothing is as it seems—including Celia. One second, she's treating Ward like sewage, the next she's kissing him. And for a nobleman's daughter, she sure has a lot of enemies. If he could just convince his heart to give up on the infuriating beauty, he might get out of this alive...

Available online and in stores everywhere...

A DENAZEN NOVEL

TOUCH

"Memorable characters, heart pounding action, sizzling hot romance – TOUCH has it all!"

- Jennifer L. Armentrout, author of HALF-BLOOD

JUS ACCARDO

TOUCH
Jus Accardo

When a strange boy tumbles down a river embankment and lands at her feet, seventeen-year-old adrenaline junkie Deznee Cross snatches the opportunity to piss off her father by bringing the mysterious hottie with ice blue eyes home.

Except there's something off with Kale. He wears her shoes in the shower, is overly fascinated with things like DVDs and vases, and acts like she'll turn to dust if he touches her. It's not until Dez's father shows up, wielding a gun and knowing more about Kale than he should, that Dez realizes there's more to this boy—and her father's "law firm"—than she realized.

Kale has been a prisoner of Denazen Corporation—an organization devoted to collecting "special" kids known as Sixes and using them as weapons—his entire life. And, oh yeah, his touch? It kills. The two team up with a group of rogue Sixes hellbent on taking down Denazen before they're caught and her father discovers the biggest secret of all. A secret Dez has spent her life keeping safe.

A secret Kale will kill to protect.